AWAKENING SIN

Touch of Evil - Book Three

Kennedy Layne

Kennedy Layne Publishing, Inc.

COPYRIGHT © 2022 BY Kennedy Layne

Cover Designer: Sweet 'N Spicy Designs

ALL RIGHTS RESERVED: The unauthorized reproduction or distribution of this copyrighted work is illegal. Criminal copyright infringement is investigated by the FBI and is punishable by up to 5 years in federal prison and a fine of $250,000.

All characters and events in this book are fictitious. Any resemblance to actual persons living or dead is strictly coincidental.

Jeffrey — I love that you make me breakfast every Sunday morning!

Cole — Always remember that it's the little things in life that mean the most. ! I love you to the moon and back!

About the Book

A new sin awakens in the next gripping psychological suspense novel by USA Today Bestselling Author Kennedy Layne...

When a body is found, displayed crudely in the middle of a deserted rural road, the world is captivated by the gruesome murder. Media descends on a small town in the middle of West Virginia, desperate to uncover the one question everyone wants to know: Who killed a mother of two, beloved wife and friend, and pillar of her community?

Former FBI consultant Brooklyn Sloane and her team have spent the first half of the year taking cold cases that were once shelved to collect dust. They have always left the active investigations for law enforcement to solve, but as the case morphs into a media frenzy, a disturbing phone call changes everything.

Drawn into the dark mind of a killer, Brook and her team arrive at the crime scene where the case takes a stunning turn. The one thing they are absolutely certain of is that a serial killer is emerging from the ashes of his victims, and he's finally come out to play.

Contents

1. Chapter One — 1
2. Chapter Two — 7
3. Chapter Three — 21
4. Chapter Four — 35
5. Chapter Five — 41
6. Chapter Six — 53
7. Chapter Seven — 61
8. Chapter Eight — 65
9. Chapter Nine — 75
10. Chapter Ten — 83
11. Chapter Eleven — 95
12. Chapter Twelve — 103
13. Chapter Thirteen — 115
14. Chapter Fourteen — 127
15. Chapter Fifteen — 139
16. Chapter Sixteen — 147
17. Chapter Seventeen — 151

18.	Chapter Eighteen	159
19.	Chapter Nineteen	167
20.	Chapter Twenty	173
21.	Chapter Twenty-One	181
22.	Chapter Twenty-Two	185
23.	Chapter Twenty-Three	197
24.	Chapter Twenty-Four	203
25.	Chapter Twenty-Five	207
26.	Chapter Twenty-Six	217
27.	Chapter Twenty-Seven	223
28.	Chapter Twenty-Eight	229
29.	Chapter Twenty-Nine	237
30.	Chapter Thirty	241
31.	Chapter Thirty-One	249
32.	Chapter Thirty-Two	257
33.	Chapter Thirty-Three	263
	Other Books By Kennedy Layne	267
	About the Author	272

Chapter One

Brooklyn Walsh
October 2001
Friday — 07:34am

THE DISTINCTIVE SMELL OF bacon hovered in the air. The crackling pops of grease and the occasional click of a thin, steel meat fork scraping the bottom of a hot skillet echoed throughout the kitchen. Besides the low hum of the refrigerator, those were the only sounds drifting through the quiet house. The tedious routine was how the Walsh family always began their day.

Brook glanced at her father, who was reading this morning's local newspaper.

Pamela Murray's school picture was front and center above the fold, though the police had found her body a week after she'd gone missing last year. Her family had upped the reward for anyone who could provide information about what had happened that fateful night. Her brutally mangled body had been discovered in a patch of trees behind the public library. It was all the kids could talk about for months, because the sheriff's daughter had spread rumors that Pam's face had all but been cut off.

Half the town believed that a bum out near the town's nearby railroad switchyard had killed her, while the other half thought it was an unregistered pedophile who'd moved into one of the older neighborhoods. Days after, he'd been found beaten unconscious in his front yard. Word had it that he'd moved to Peoria shortly thereafter.

Brook and her friends hadn't gone anywhere alone since Pamela's murder.

"Mom, don't forget that I'm going to the football game tonight with Sally. Her mom said that she'd give me a ride home." Brook glanced at the clock on the stove. She still had five minutes before she needed to leave for school. "Did you sign my field trip permission slip for Mrs. Stafford? It's due today."

"It's on the entryway table by the front door." Brook's mom reached over the frying pan and turned off the burner. "Your brother is taking you to school today, so don't forget to grab the form before you leave."

"Why?" Brook blurted out the question before she could stop herself. She pushed away her plate, no longer hungry. "What does he need the car for?"

"Watch your tone, young lady."

Brook sat back in her chair in frustration as she stared at her father, who had lowered the corner of the newspaper with one finger. He was frowning at her like she was the one with the problem. Couldn't her parents see that she was the normal one? She was the one who still hung out with her friends. She was the one who didn't sneak out of the house in the middle of the night.

"Your brother asked to borrow the car." Brook's mom set the last of the bacon on the table. "It just so happens that I don't need it today. Besides, I'm glad to see that he's doing things with his friends again. Getting his license this past summer seems to have brightened his spirits. That reminds me, I have to call Mrs. Murray later today. She needs help putting up some new flyers this weekend."

Brook didn't bother to say anything else. All she would do was get in trouble, and she didn't want to get grounded before tonight's football game. Sally had a crush on Nate, and there was a chance that she was going to tell him during halftime.

It all seemed so pointless, though.

Pamela wouldn't get to enjoy her high school years with her friends. She wouldn't get to have a boyfriend or go to prom. She wouldn't even experience falling in love and getting married. Brook couldn't imagine the grief that Pam's parents had gone through and were still going through.

For some reason, Brook's parents believed that Pamela Murray's death was justification for Jacob's withdrawal. He no longer hung out with his old friends, he really only spoke when spoken to, and he hadn't joined in on family movie night in forever. He'd changed, but their parents always seemed to have a ready excuse for his odd behavior. Why couldn't they accept that he'd been a hollow version of himself for years way before Pamela had been killed?

"Jacob, I was just telling Brook that you'll be driving her to school. She's attending the football game tonight with Sally, so you don't have to drive her home." Their mother took a sip of her coffee before reaching for the obituary section of the newspaper. She always checked to see if someone they knew had unexpectedly passed, just in case she needed to send flowers. "Be home by eleven."

"I might be a little later than that," Jacob said as he reached for a piece of bacon. He didn't carry a backpack, and he never brought any books home from school. Brook had always been jealous of his ability to ace a class without ever cracking open a textbook. He said it was because he was attentive in class, but she suspected that it wasn't quite that simple. "I'll be home by midnight, though."

"That's fine," their mother said distractedly as she became engrossed in the listed eulogies.

Jacob didn't bother to say anything else. He simply walked to the refrigerator so that he could grab the orange juice container. As he poured himself a glass, Brook pushed her chair back and picked up her pink backpack. Sally had a matching one, though they had hung different colored beads from the main zipper to tell them apart.

"I'll be in the car," Brook said as she swung her backpack over her shoulder. "Bye, Mom. Bye, Dad."

They both mumbled their goodbyes, both absorbed into their own little worlds as if nothing were more important than the next section of the morning newspaper.

Brook made sure to grab her field trip permission slip from the entryway table. She was looking forward to spending a day in Chicago next week.

Sometimes, she wished that she was anywhere else but home.

She waited in the car for about another five minutes before getting antsy. Jacob was going to make her late for school. At this point, she was already going to have to skip going to her locker. She finally breathed a sigh of relief when she saw the front door open.

It didn't take him long to get settled behind the steering wheel.

"Seat belt."

Brook fastened in as her brother started the engine. He'd only had his license for a few months, and he'd only ever driven her to school once before. The middle school was a couple of blocks from the high school, so she would technically only be in the car for maybe two minutes total. She'd handled the silence between them before, and she could do it again.

Surprisingly, Jacob turned on the radio.

By the time he'd pulled up to the school in the appropriate drop-off lane, one of the more popular songs that she liked was ending. She clicked the button to unfasten her seatbelt and picked up her backpack from the floor.

"Don't forget this."

Jacob was holding out her permission slip, as if they'd done this a million times. She already had the door open with one foot out, the cool crisp air of the morning no different than the interior of the vehicle. The engine hadn't warmed up enough to produce any heat through the vents.

"Thanks," Brook murmured as she folded the paper and slipped it into one of the side pockets of her backpack.

"No problem."

She couldn't help but stare at her older brother in suspicion. He was talking to her like he hadn't been ignoring her for months on end. Longer than that, really. She'd gotten used to his dismissive attitude, and she ignored it the best she could.

Brook led her life, and Jacob led his own solitary existence.

They were three years apart in age, anyway.

She hated that she thought he was capable of hurting someone. There were times that she was actually afraid of him, though he'd never done anything physical to warrant such an unreasonable fear.

There was just something...off about him.

The night that Pamela Murray had gone missing from the library was rooted in Brook's memory. She'd never said anything to her parents, but a part of her believed that her brother might have been responsible somehow.

Brook had tossed and turned at night for weeks.

Eventually, Pamela's body had been found, but the whispered stories about some drifter or an unregistered pedophile floating around the hallways of school had eventually put Brook at ease. Had Jacob done something to Pamela Murray, the sheriff would have found some evidence pointing toward her brother's guilt.

"See you later."

She got out of the car and shut the door before stepping up on the curb.

The first bell was about to ring.

Hardly anyone was still hanging out on the steps near the entrance, but she saw Sally waiting for her by the double doors.

As Jacob pulled away from the curb, Brook couldn't help but slow her steps as she monitored his progress down the street. Were her parents right? Had getting his license triggered some sort of normalcy to spring forth in him? It would be nice to stop having to walk on eggshells every time that he entered a room.

"Hurry up!" Sally called out, opening the left side of the double doors. "We're going to be late for class. You know how Mrs. Howard gets if we aren't in our seats when the bell rings."

"Coming," Brook called out, quickening her pace. Jacob's brake lights were on as came to a stop at the intersection. All he had to do was drive straight through it, and the road would take him to the high school parking lot. "Have you decided if you're going to tell Nate that—"

Brook broke off her question when she caught sight of Jacob turning right. He hadn't used a turn signal, and he wasn't going to school. He'd borrowed the car because he was going somewhere that he didn't want their parents to know about. The usual nausea that she experienced when it came to her brother settled in her stomach.

He was getting better and better at putting on a show for their parents and others. Everyone seemed to be falling for it, too.

Not her, though.

There was something critical missing inside of him. A part of his soul, maybe. Either that or his soul had been stained with something dark...something sinister. It was as if a virus had infected him and left nothing but wickedness in its wake.

As if agreeing with her, grey clouds began to cover the sky above. The cold, autumn breeze became harsh, lifting the dead leaves off the sidewalk and sending them swirling into the air.

A warning?

Brook tore her gaze away from the empty intersection, focusing on her best friend, who was still holding open the door. Sally had been looking in the same direction, but neither one of them said another word as they entered the school. Neither one of them talked openly about Jacob anymore.

Brook wasn't ready to say aloud that evil had somehow gotten ahold her brother.

Doing so would make it all too real.

Chapter Two

Brooklyn Sloane
May 2022
Thursday — 5:17pm

THE FAINT SOUND OF ticking could be heard coming from the modern-styled black clock hanging on the wall in the conference room. It wasn't all that different from one of those standard issue Lighthouse of the Blind models seen in every government office in the United States. This one cost considerably more than its cousin, yet it functioned just as deliberately. The monotonous clicking of the second hand wasn't too loud. It actually had a rather rhythmic resonance that was rather soothing, if one took time to recognize its zen-like quality.

Hypnotic, almost.

The offices of S&E Investigations, Inc. were located in the heart of Washington, D.C. There was nothing tranquil about the city, other than it allowed one to have the illusion of blending in more easily with one's surroundings. Too many buildings, vehicles, pollution, and people were jam-packed into the same space.

Yet Brook wouldn't want to be anywhere else.

It was hard to believe that she and her team had managed to solve four cold cases in the span of five short months. Granted, three of them had been cracked with relative ease. Simple textbook murders, although there had been nothing mundane about them to the families involved.

The homicide detectives assigned to the investigations would have eventually brought the killers to justice, but they were overworked, underpaid, burnt-out, and buried under an avalanche of unsolved cases. There hadn't been enough hours in the day to follow up all the leads, write the reports, and track down the suspects. A couple of the investigations had been several years old, while the others had taken place ten years prior.

Brook never would have imagined the private sector being so gratifying if she hadn't summarily been forced into leaving the FBI last year. Starting a consulting firm that specialized in solving cold cases had turned out to be one of the best decisions in her life. The additional bonus was that she was still able to utilize her skills for profiling that she'd spent years perfecting alongside those inside the Bureau's renowned criminal forensics analysis branch.

She was also proud of the team that she'd assembled for S&E Investigations, eclectic as they might be.

It was time to pick another case for them to dive into, but she was inclined to wait until Monday. She might even give them the day off tomorrow. They certainly deserved a break.

Running the day-to-day ins and outs of a new business had taken up more time than she'd originally allotted for, which meant less time for the one case that really mattered the most. She leaned back in what was supposed to be an ergonomically designed chair, but it wasn't as comfortable as the leather executive one in her office. Did the scientists who studied ergonomics really believe that there was a difference in the backs of the working class?

She shifted a bit more until her left shoulder blade wasn't aching while staring at the white board that contained numerous photographs of her older brother and the women who he'd murdered over the course of twenty-two years.

CHAPTER TWO

Jacob Matthew Walsh.

A high-functioning, psychopathic serial killer who had evaded law enforcement for over two decades.

"Ms. Sloane?"

"Yes, Kate?" Brook used her black high heel to turn her chair. In the doorway stood their new receptionist, though she did a lot more than simply answer phones. To call her by such title was truly a disservice to her and everything she did for those in the office. "I didn't realize that you were still here."

Kate Lin was in her early twenties and of mixed Asian descent. Her father was a renowned scientist working at a division of the CDC in a BSL Level-4 containment lab at the Commonwealth of Virginia University. While the federal government no longer advertised the location of such laboratory, that didn't mean Takashi Lin wasn't directly subordinate to the supervisors in their employment. As for Kate's mother, she'd passed away when Kate was a young girl. Amy Lin had been brutally murdered during a meaningless home invasion, both of her killers serving life sentences for robbing the Lin household to feed their drug habits.

It didn't take a psychologist to understand why Kate wanted to be in law enforcement. S&E Investigations, Inc. was most likely a steppingstone for a much bigger career down the road.

"I know you said that you didn't want to be disturbed, but I thought you should know that the same man has been calling the main line every fifteen minutes for the last hour." Kate had her purse thrown over her shoulder. It was obvious that she wanted to leave for the evening, but she had been hoping to catch Brook leaving the conference room. "I explained to him that you weren't available at the moment. Each time, I transferred him to your voicemail."

"I'll check my messages before I leave the office tonight." Brook figured she might as well make herself some coffee for the long evening ahead. She stood up from her chair, leaving her cell phone and electronic tablet on the table. "I'll see you in the morning, Kate."

Brook had made the sudden decision against giving the team a day off tomorrow. She'd let them review the three requests that had come through recently and evaluate the merits of each case. They could decide as a group which case would be best to pursue, especially since all three were in the Midwest. It would mean a lot of travel expenses, as well as time spent away from home. They all had their own personal lives, and she had to remind herself of that fact quite often.

Kate appeared to want to say something else, but she simply nodded and closed the door behind her.

The young woman hadn't been Brook's first choice to fill the role of receptionist, executive assistant, and basically all-around jack-of-all-trades. She hadn't even been the second. It wasn't that her background hadn't come back clean, but it had more to do with the fact of how timid she'd come across during the initial interview process.

Truthfully, Kate still came across as rather meek and quiet.

Given who Brook was and the fact that her brother continued to pose a danger to those in her life, she'd wanted someone more assertive, direct, and essentially experienced in self-defense. Unfortunately, her team had pointed out her unrealistic expectations.

"Would it kill you to give Kate a compliment now and then?"

Brook hadn't even made it to the break room when Theo Neville gave his two cents.

"And have Kate think that I like her or something?" Brook replied wryly, not bothering to pause in the long hallway. She'd called out over her shoulder to make sure that her words had reached his office. "Not a snowball's chance in hell. Goodnight, Theo."

Brook chose a K-cup from the variety of coffee selections, sticking with her favorite medium roast. There were numerous flavors available, but she didn't need anything fancy this evening...just effective. She reserved going for a more flavorful coffee drink for her morning stop at a local cafe located between her condo and her office building. Nothing beat an extra-large caramel macchiato first thing in the morning.

"Don't you think that Jacob would have tried something by now if he was still in the city?"

CHAPTER TWO

Brook had just closed the lid on the coffee machine when Theo had joined her in the break room. She pressed the brew button with a little more force than necessary. He wasn't naive, and that kind of assumption led to mistakes.

Theo had once worked as a field agent for the FBI. He'd been injured in the line of duty, resulting in the loss of his right eye. The black patch he wore was a staple of his everyday attire. He'd opted not to get a glass eye, much to his mother's ire. As far as Brook was concerned, it was a personal choice that only he could make, just as she made her own choices when it came to her life.

"Brook, you haven't heard from your brother since last November. That was six months ago."

She technically hadn't *heard* from Jacob since the age of eighteen.

In reality, her brother much preferred to leave calling cards in her condo. A first edition copy of a leatherbound Harry Potter book, to be precise. It had become an inside secret that only they shared and knew the meaning of when it came to the popular series. Leaving one of the books on her nightstand was his way of letting her know that he'd been in town checking up on her. Of course, it hadn't been necessary for him to go to such trouble after he'd murdered her next-door neighbor in cold blood, leaving his signature method of butchery on display for everyone to see.

Jacob was all about his routine.

"I've got a lot of paperwork to finish up," Brook replied evenly, wishing the coffee would brew a little bit faster. She decided to keep herself busy by getting the creamer out of the refrigerator. Coffee was coffee. She didn't mind how it came into being, as long as it had the caffeine necessary to keep her functioning. "If this is your way of inviting me out for drinks with the rest of the team, I'm going to have to pass. Maybe next week."

Theo might have good intentions, but he had no idea the destruction that Jacob could cause should he decide that the people in her life were merely a means to an end. Almost every Thursday without fail the team went out to one of the local restaurants. She had encouraged them to get to know one another better, and she was pleased that they all got along so well.

Still, she would do what was necessary to keep herself at a professional distance.

Brook could sense that Theo was still standing in the doorway of the break room, so she turned and found that he was leaning against the doorframe. The dark blue dress shirt complemented his dark skin. His father was African American, his mother was Caucasian. Both had dedicated their lives to law enforcement. They'd raised an honorable man. He wasn't obtuse, and he understood more than most the damage that could be done at the hands of a determined killer. Maybe it was due to his parents' healthy marriage, but he also had idealistic tendencies when it came to friendships. Relationships of any kind, actually.

"Have you seen the news today?"

Theo's off-topic question took her by surprise. She'd thought for sure that he wouldn't leave well enough alone. The tension in her shoulders eased, and she turned back around to add the creamer to her coffee now that the machine had done its job.

"No." Brook twisted the cap back onto the carton once her coffee had lightened in color. "Why? Are we at war?"

"The body of that missing woman in West Virginia was discovered this morning."

Brook had become somewhat numb to the media spinning every story out of control. There was an odd obsession they had when it came to particularly gruesome murders or mysterious abductions. The latter was the case in this instance, but mostly due to the woman being a loving wife, dedicated mother, and a pillar of her community. The husband had been interviewed several times over the last week, clips of his pleas for help from anyone who might have seen her recently dominating the news coverage.

"Have they arrested the husband yet?" Brook made sure the carton of creamer was properly back in its designated place before closing the door on the fridge. She then picked up her coffee, deciding that she'd order Chinese food for dinner. She'd have it delivered to the office and make herself comfortable in the conference room. She did some of her best thinking over

CHAPTER TWO

takeout. "The sheriff made it sound as if he already had a cold dark cell waiting for the man."

While it was true that spouses were usually the first suspects in either a missing person case or a murder investigation, the sheriff should have used a bit more discretion in his briefings to the press. Small towns such as Stillwater, West Virginia didn't like to have attention drawn to them or their town. The citizens were close-knit, and they preferred keeping their personal business to themselves...even when it came to murder.

"No." Theo moved from the doorway when Brook began to close the distance between them. "Not yet, anyway. Apparently, the sheriff is handing the entire investigation off to the state police. One news report even had him reaching out to the FBI."

Theo's last statement gave Brook pause, and she ran through the details of what she knew of the case through her mind for any recognition. Serial killers had signatures, their personal mark on the victim or the scene. While there were a few active serial killers who abducted and toyed with their victims, those that she knew off the top of her head tended to take women who wouldn't cause such an obvious stir in the media. The sheriff could be right about the husband, or possibly even a consumed lover from a sordid affair who wanted the victim all to himself.

"Odd." Brook didn't want to come across as callous, but Theo had worked enough investigations to understand her next sentiment. "At least the family doesn't have to wonder anymore."

"It's been nice choosing investigations that are clean cut, hasn't it?" Theo asked as he fell into step next to her. She stopped at the entrance of the conference room while he continued toward his office. "I'll take murder regarding greed, love, or betrayal any day of the week."

"I'll see what I can do to meet your requirements for the next case then," Brook replied wryly, not taking offense to his attitude. The last thing she wanted was for her team or anyone around her to walk on eggshells because of her situation. "Clean, cut, everyday murder."

"You do that," Theo called out. "See you tomorrow."

Brook walked into the conference room and set her coffee down next to her cell phone. While her electronic tablet was synced to her laptop and desktop computer, there were times when she preferred pen to paper. She'd lost her favorite pen months ago, but she'd managed to replace it with one similar. She retraced her steps and walked back into the hallway.

"Incoming."

Brook glanced up to find that Theo must have already grabbed his car keys and was headed out to join the other team members. The only time that Theo used that particular warning was for one man—General Graham Elliott.

Usually, she was able to observe who was coming and going due to the location of her office. She'd chosen the first one off the reception and waiting area, where the panes of glass allowed her to not only view those locations, but also the main area right outside the elevator banks. The modern style offices basically consisted of glass windows with black furniture to complement the contemporary design.

She could hear the men exchange their greetings as she neared the reception area.

Graham Elliott was her silent business partner, although he didn't seem to comprehend the definition of the word *silent*. Granted, he'd stayed out of her way as promised. He'd kept his word that he would have no say in how the day-to-day operations of S&E Investigations was run outside of the financials.

Still, that didn't seem to prevent him from stopping by the offices a couple of times a week like clockwork. Whether it be from his time serving as a Commanding General Marine Forces Special Operations Command (MARSOC) in the military or just his obsessive-compulsive nature was up for debate.

"Enjoy your evening, Theo." Graham's rich voice traveled through the doorway to her office. She was already at her desk, picking up what she needed to take with her in order to spend the evening in the conference room. "I take it that you aren't joining them for their customary Thursday night outing?"

"I've got some work to do," Brook replied as she noticed the blinking light on her desk phone. Kate's reminder that a man had called numerous times today came to the forefront. "I thought you weren't due back until sometime this weekend."

CHAPTER TWO

After retiring from the Marine Corps, Graham had been highly sought-after by several government contractors. She'd never asked, and he'd never disclosed, the terms of those classified contracts. He also generalized his locations when he left the city, and this particular trip had been somewhere in Africa.

"I took an earlier flight home."

Graham was dressed in his usual business attire. The Italian cut suit had been impeccably tailored to fit him, and the fabric was flawless. He must have continued his workout regimen from his time in the Corps, because one would never know that the man was in his mid-fifties. He still maintained the close-cropped haircut, the polished leather dress shoes, and the perfect posture.

"You should know that I turned over the security footage of your home office to Special Agent Houser. I spoke to him this morning. Needless to say, he wasn't happy that I took my time in doing so." Brook monitored Graham's movement to get a feel for his mood. He was agitated, though he was hiding it well. "There are no new leads on Jacob's whereabouts."

While Brook was conducting her own search for her brother, she'd come to the conclusion that pressure from the feds wasn't such a bad idea. Jacob loved the challenge. It was the reason that he'd waltzed right inside Graham's residence without a care in the world, posing as a technician who'd merely been there to fix the chimney flue. He'd grown facial hair and worn a hat pulled low over his forehead to gain entrance.

Again, Jacob did so love the challenge of getting the best of others who pursued him.

In a reverse play of psychology, she was hoping that such adversity from more than one law enforcement agency would keep him in the city. She was confident that he loathed this new avenue that she'd pursued in her professional life.

It was only a matter of time before he made another move.

"Have you chosen another case yet?"

Brook's interest was piqued now, not that she would let Graham know of her interest.

Ever since she and her team had pieced together his daughter's murder and brought the young woman's case to a close, he'd never once asked Brook about their caseload. Their brief exchange of intimacy after his daughter's killer had taken his own life not fifteen feet from where she was standing had been nothing more than a heightened moment in time. Brook had put it out of her mind, and she'd made sure that all their subsequent discussions revolved around the financials of S&E Investigations.

"Not yet," Brook replied guardedly as she remained behind her desk. She wanted to listen to her voicemail messages before spending the evening perusing Jacob's latest invasion into her life. There was always a chance that she'd missed something, and it never hurt to double or triple-check her profile. "I've picked a few assignments out for the team that I find interesting. I was going to go over the merits of each of them tomorrow, maybe allow them to choose the next case that we work on. Any particular reason that you're asking?"

Graham reached into the interior pocket of his suit jacket and pulled out his cell phone. He must have had the device on silent, and the interruption had prevented him from answering her, though she could see from his frown that he wasn't pleased with the disturbance of their conversation. He read whatever message had been displayed before reverting his attention back to her.

"A meeting that I had scheduled has been moved up." Graham returned his cell phone to its rightful place. It took him a moment to formulate his next words. "Do me a favor. Take a case out of the city."

Graham had never asked her for a personal favor, if one discounted his request that she solve his daughter's murder. She'd not only been well-compensated for doing so, but she'd gotten her own consulting firm in the process.

They each had benefited, and the playing field was even.

Why would he want her out of D.C.?

Brook wasn't aware of any immediate threats to Washington, D.C., let alone the rest of the country. Just what had he discovered during his meetings in Africa?

They continued to hold one another's stare, but she didn't get the sense that he was challenging her. If anything, there was

CHAPTER TWO 17

concern within those dark eyes of his. He knew her well enough that she didn't have the type of personality to run at the slightest hint of danger. She certainly hadn't turned tail and run because of her brother.

Regrettably, she wasn't so sure his request was due to Jacob, and that put her in a quandary.

"I can't promise you anything, but I will keep you apprised of our plans," Brook assured him, not surprised when he gave a mere nod of respect at her decision.

"Goodnight, Brook."

With those parting words, Graham took his leave. It was his shortest visit to date, which told her that something serious was occurring in the shadows. She monitored his progress through the reception area and out the double glass doors.

Come to think of it, she wasn't sure that she'd ever seen him so distracted, either.

Brook tapped her pen against the palm of her hand as she observed him disappear into one of the elevators. Various and farfetched possibilities ran through her mind as to what could have him wanting her to leave the city. Few incidents could elevate such a dire threat level. She figured if it was serious enough, he'd know how to get the information across if it had to do with something classified.

In the meantime, she had her own work to focus on.

She picked up the receiver to her office phone and pressed the button that would retrieve her voicemails. The first one was from a reporter wanting a statement regarding their last case involving a high-profile murder of a real estate mogul. She forwarded the message back to Kate, who would type up something generic for the article. The second voicemail was simply static, as if the person on the other end of the line hadn't expected to receive a recording. The third was much of the same, though it came with a frustrated sigh from presumably the man who had been attempting to get ahold of her this afternoon.

Brook waited for the fourth message to commence, hoping to be able to delete it so that she could order some Chinese takeout and get on with her evening plans.

"Are you ready to play?"

The question had been asked in a harsh whisper, practically scratching her eardrum.

She had been taken aback by the rage contained within the inquiry. Unable to help herself, she replayed the fourth message again. She wouldn't deny hoping that the person on the other end of the line was her brother. She desired that more than she needed to breathe air into her body. It was the reason she quickly pressed the receiver closer to her ear, just in case she was able to pick up her brother's Midwest accent.

"Are you ready to play?"

Brook sighed with regret.

Her brother didn't have a hitch in his voice like the man who'd left the menacing message.

Still, the ominous voicemail set her on edge.

It had become public knowledge that she was related to Jacob Matthew Walsh, and her interview at the beginning of the year had no doubt attracted national attention. She'd gone into depth about their childhoods, although there were certain aspects of their lives that she'd kept private. It had been her choice to give the interview, knowing full well that Jacob would take it as a challenge.

This message, though...this message was something else entirely.

It was almost as if the male subject was challenging her.

Had she or the firm attracted the attention of someone not fully in control of their faculties? Worse yet, had the male on the other end of the line known exactly what he'd been doing when he'd left the voicemail?

Only time would tell, because there were no other messages left on her phone.

Brook carefully set the receiver back into its holder as she contemplated the situation. Had Graham received a call similar to this? Was that the reason he wanted her out of the city? She couldn't imagine that being the case, but there was nothing that she could do about it now. Her team had left for the day, Graham had gone to his meeting, and she had a date with the vast materials in the conference room and a few Chinese takeout containers.

CHAPTER TWO

Jacob wasn't about to turn himself in, which meant that she needed to think of another way to lure him out of hiding. She lifted the corner of her lips, twisting the message that she'd just received to suit her own set of circumstances.

"Are you ready to play, Jacob?"

CHAPTER THREE

Brooklyn Sloane
May 2022
Friday — 7:28am

"DO YOU HAVE A minute?"

Brook threw her to-go cup from the local cafe into the small garbage can underneath her desk. She'd finished her extra-large caramel macchiato seconds before Sylvie Deering had wrapped up her conversation with Kate at the reception desk. It was nice to see the ease in which the team had meshed together.

"I do," Brook replied, polishing off her last-minute notes on the three cases that she would present to the team in their daily meeting at eight o'clock. "If this is about your expense report, Kate should be signing for a packet from the firm's accountant later today with everyone's checks enclosed."

Sylvie Deering had been an analyst for the FBI for several years before agreeing to take a job with S&E Investigations. She'd had it rough in the past year, though. Her top-secret SCI clearance had been suspended due to her father's involvement in a fraud case.

Nigel Deering had purposefully used his daughter's name and social security number to open some numbered accounts into which he transferred his ill-gotten gains across several overseas accounts without her knowledge. Despite her being his unwitting accomplice, the federal government had to take the necessary steps to ensure the safety of classified information.

The government had removed her access immediately, and she would have spent the rest of her career in some dark basement. Even with Graham's considerable contacts, the revocation of her clearance hadn't been easy to remove. Ultimately, a congressional finding was entered into record, and Sylvie had eventually been cleared of any wrongdoing. Her clearance had been restored.

People had a tendency to underestimate her, though.

She was petite, blonde, and wore black-rimmed glasses that gave her an intellectual appearance. Not only was she highly intelligent, but she was extremely detailed and had the ability to compartmentalize and analyze complex information in a way that few people could in their field. She had close to complete recall of anything and everything that she had read or seen. Once read in on a case file, she was cognizant of every detail down to the lab results in the reports. Forensic analysis of accounting fraud had suddenly become child's play in her hands. Odd or noncompliant details simply became obvious to her upon a casual glance.

"Kate mentioned that you've been receiving calls from someone...odd." Sylvie had entered Brook's office, but she didn't take a seat. Instead, she slipped her hands into the white dress pants that somehow didn't have a stain on them. "Did he really leave a voicemail asking if you wanted to play?"

Brook cast an irritating sideways glance toward the reception area, but Kate was no longer at her desk. The young woman was technically everyone's assistant, helping wherever needed, but Brook didn't like her personal business being broadcasted unless she intended to do so herself.

"Don't be upset with her. I overheard you talking to Kate in the break room. I asked her about it, and she only commented that the man practically whispered everything he said."

Sylvie shifted awkwardly as she mulled over what Kate had shared, as if something didn't fit right with the call. Brook

CHAPTER THREE 23

agreed, but it wasn't like they could do anything unless the man called back again. It was obvious that curiosity had gotten the best of her, which was the reason she'd broached the subject with Kate in the first place.

Brook had requested that Kate personally seek her out, no matter where she was in the office in case the male subject reached out to her again. She should have made such a suggestion in private if she'd wanted confidentiality, and not in the break room where someone had clearly been listening in on their conversation.

Kate was not to blame.

"I'm sure it's nothing to be concerned with," Brook replied dismissively as she pushed her chair back. She collected her tablet and cell phone, wanting to get the larger of the two conference rooms ready for their meeting. "We had a lot of press with that last case. Truthfully, I'm surprised that we aren't getting more calls of that nature."

"I wish it was that simple."

Sylvie took her hands from her pockets and leaned over Brook's desk for the remote control. Last month, she'd had a fifty-five inch, flatscreen television installed in the left-hand corner of her office, opposite the door. She liked to keep abreast of the national and local news at specific times of the day, and she'd never had the luxury of doing so when she'd been employed with the Bureau.

"You're going to want to see this."

As Sylvie turned on the television and began to go through the various channels, Theo made an appearance. Shortly thereafter, Bit came waltzing in with an energy drink in his hand.

Bobby "Bit" Nowacki was the eccentric one on the team, but his knowledge of technology knew no bounds. His oval face and extended nose seemed even more defined by his long, blond hair. He usually had the greasy strands covered with a knit cap, even in the summer. Today was no exception. He was currently sporting a yellow one that matched his t-shirt, which contained the caption *Bazinga* with a lightning bolt underneath it.

"Morning, Boss."

"Good morning, Bit." Brook figured that she might as well take a seat until they all shed light on what had caught their interest. "Do I want to know what is in the large box that was delivered a few minutes ago?"

"You're going to love it," Bit replied enthusiastically, taking a seat in one of the two chairs that offset a black leather couch against the far wall. The chair gave him a pretty good view of the television set in the corner, thanks to the glass window overlooking the city being slightly tinted. "Isn't she, Big T?"

"I'm staying out of it," Theo muttered as he then took a seat in one of the two more formal guest chairs in front of her desk. "You know how she is about any kind of change."

"The benefits far outweigh the—"

"Found it," Sylvie called out in victory, still aiming the remote control toward the TV. She turned up the volume. "Shhhh."

Brook leaned back in her chair, wishing she hadn't finished off what had been left of her caramel macchiato. Movement out of her peripheral vision showed that Kate had decided to join them, though she remained just inside the doorway. She was holding an electronic tablet close to her chest with the stylus gripped tight in her hand. The way she was bracing herself for whatever was about to be revealed on national news indicated that Brook had successfully put the pieces together.

The phone call that she received last night had something to do with the murder in West Virginia.

How or why was another matter altogether.

"...tell us anything new?"

"No comment," Sheriff Kennard replied with irritation as he attempted to walk from his car to the crime scene maybe a hundred feet away from where the camera crews were stationed. The station had his name displayed underneath the taped footage. "Move."

"Sheriff, can you—"

"I already told you that I don't have a comment." Sheriff Kennard pulled his large hat a little farther down on his forehead. "The case is being turned over to the state police. I refer you all to their Public Information Office. You can address any future questions to Detective Stan Turner through their PIO.

CHAPTER THREE 25

He's their lead homicide detective who will be assigned to the case."

"Is there any truth to a message being left near the body?" The woman reporter was bold enough to have blocked the sheriff's path. "Did the note really have "Are you ready to play?" printed on it, and do you believe it was addressed to the victim or to law enforcement?"

Sheriff Kennard's stunned reaction and the way he brought himself up short gave the reporter and the viewers his answer. The other journalists pounced on the brief silence, and it turned into complete chaos until the sheriff practically shoved them all aside and quickly made his escape.

While Sylvie began to turn down the volume, Brook studied the scene in the background. The station had tagged the footage as having been recorded yesterday afternoon. In the distance, a state police forensics team could be seen canvassing the area.

It was easy to tell the difference between the various agencies by their uniforms.

Of course, their presence on a scene all depended on the crime. They would be collecting anything out of the ordinary, as well as using markers to indicate any tire marks, sole imprints, cigarette butts, candy wrappers, and anything else that stood out in the rough terrain. The narrow dirt road didn't seem to lead anywhere, but that most certainly wasn't the case.

All roads led somewhere.

A middle-aged man wearing a slightly oversized suit could be seen speaking to a female officer in the distance, and Brook assumed that he was Detective Stan Turner. The large cut of his suit jacket was to accommodate his full frame firearm in his shoulder holster, making it less obvious to the casual observer that he was armed. He wouldn't be pleased that there had already been a leak of information regarding evidence, and he would want it plugged right away. Unfortunately, having such an intel leak would be a distraction for him until he determined which of the local sheriff's deputies had been bought off.

"It's not a coincidence."

"No, it isn't." Brook didn't remove her gaze off the television as she replied to Theo. The camera had swung back to a male reporter, which told her that the woman who had asked the previous questions was not employed by his station. Such a morsel of information could come in handy should they ever need it. "You all know that I am not a big believer in coincidences. With that said, it isn't our case. For all we know, someone saw this footage last night and decided to have a little fun. Our firm's name is getting out there in the news, and it's bound to stir up some interest by certain parties. We tossed a lot of lines in the water during our previous investigations. Some game fish were larger than others. Our bait may have simply attracted some interest from someone with an ego. I'm sure there are still some hard feelings by those that we subsequently threw back."

"So, that's it?" Bit replied as he leaned forward on his seat. He rested his elbows on his ripped jeans. She'd allowed the team the choice of dress, and Bit rarely interacted with the public in a professional capacity. She didn't mind that he'd chosen the casual route. The more comfortable he was in his environment, the better his performance. "We're not taking the case?"

"We don't take active cases." Brook stood and collected the items that she would need for this morning's meeting. Her statement wasn't technically true. If a cold case involved a serial killer who was still hunting and active, then that was another matter altogether. "We are a consulting firm, and one that takes on clients of cold cases to keep the lights on. We don't even know if the man who called yesterday is even involved with what is happening in West Virginia. He could be a crank. Besides, he hasn't called back."

Bit looked over his shoulder at Kate, who nodded her head in agreement.

"I can't tell you the number of times that we had similar calls when I worked active investigations at the Bureau. We had to run down every one of those leads, and it took a lot of manpower to do so." Brook didn't have to abide by the agency's guidelines anymore. "Should the male subject contact me or the firm again, I'll reach out to Detective Turner and inform him of such contact. Bit, you can even supply him with a recording. In the meantime, we have work to do. Kate, please make sure that the messages on my answering machine are archived just in case."

"Answering machine?" Bit murmured to Theo as they both stood from their respective seats. "Is she serious? Answering machines haven't existed since..."

Brook fought back a grin as everyone vacated her office.

As she rounded her desk to follow them out and join them in the conference room, the itch to observe the scene in West Virginia was too strong to ignore. Though the volume had been turned down completely, she didn't need the sound to observe something of interest—there was a state arson investigator at the scene. She'd made such a determination from the logo sewn into his black polo shirt.

There was no denying that the specifics of the case had intrigued her. Even so, she had her own team to lead and several cases to choose from so that a family could finally get the answers they so richly deserved.

The rest of the morning and afternoon had been spent combing through three possible cold cases, though one of them had been discarded quickly based on DNA evidence that had been reexamined recently. The family wouldn't accept that one of their own had murdered a relative, but even Brook couldn't deny the concrete findings of the detective in charge. That left two possibilities, but neither one would have required her to travel. Theo and Sylvie could handle the groundwork, allowing the rest of the team to remain at their headquarters here in the city.

Graham's somewhat ominous request had continued to be in the forefront of her mind, but had he meant only her? Or was there a bigger picture being painted that involved the entire firm?

Bit and Kate had never left the office for an investigation, and Graham was well aware of that detail. His appeal had her believing it was more personal, but he should have been able to go into more detail had his reasoning involved Jacob.

Once four-thirty rolled around and Graham hadn't reached out to verify if she'd followed through with his request, Brook figured whatever issue had prompted him to seek her out last night had long since passed. She was comfortable with staying in the city unless Theo and Sylvie required her help doing some of the legwork sometime in the near future.

"Ms. Sloane?"

"Yes, Kate?" Brook had been studying the large white rectangular box that had been stored in the larger conference room. Her two whiteboards had been moved off to the side in order to make room for it, and Bit seemed to be waiting for just the right moment to unveil whatever was inside. "Do you know what is inside this box?"

Brook would never have sought out Bit to ask, because he was like a kid in a candy store when it came to anything remotely related to technology. It had taken her a while to get used to the electronic tablets they now all carried around in order to easily share information. She wasn't opposed to change, but she did like her routine. The way she mapped out her whiteboards was paramount to connecting leads in a case as they presented themselves.

As for Kate continuing to refer to Brook by the surname that she'd taken on her eighteenth birthday, she'd requested numerous times that the young woman be less formal. Brook had mentioned it at least four or five times over the last couple of months, but she couldn't hold Kate's hand forever. She'd either jump in with both feet or use those feet to walk out the double glass doors. Her hesitation thus far was the reason that Brook only permitted her to know surface details regarding Jacob's case.

Trust had to be earned over time.

"I do, but that man is on the phone again," Kate replied with urgency as she gestured toward the desk phone positioned on the side table. "Line one."

Brook made a mental note that the call had been made relatively the same time as yesterday, possibly indicating that the male subject hadn't been able to reach out earlier.

A hectic work schedule, maybe?

It just might be that his time wasn't his own to control.

"Would you please let Bit know that I need him?"

CHAPTER THREE

By this time, Theo had materialized from his office, shortly followed by Sylvie. Her pink purse was slung over her shoulder, evidence that she'd been about to head home for the weekend.

Brook left her spot in front of the large white box so that she could be close to the phone. She didn't bother to pick up the receiver, because she would be pressing the speaker button so that the conversation could be overheard by the others.

"Yeah, Boss?"

"I need this call traced," Brook explained, figuring that Kate had already filled Bit in on the situation. "Line one."

"On it."

She waited another brief moment until Bit called out that she was good to go as far as answering the call. In her opinion, waiting the additional time was actually a benefit. The male subject's patience would be thinning, and he might just say something that would tip his hand.

Brook pressed the button next to the blinking line, initiating the speakerphone function.

"This is Brooklyn Sloane."

Brook had done her best to sound as if she were just another bored professional answering the phone for the millionth time in any given day.

"Are you ready to play?"

It was definitely the same man who had left the voicemail yesterday. The way he whispered into the phone was identical, and she could still catch the slight southern accent in his tone. Subtle, but it was there all the same.

"I don't have time to play games, Mr..."

The fact that there was silence on the other end of the line suggested that he hadn't been expecting her direct response. Brook met Theo's dark gaze as he joined her near the thin black table against the wall.

"If you aren't going to give your name or expand on why you're calling me, I'm not going to waste my time inflating your ego."

Theo winced when Brook pushed the envelope, because a certain amount of time was needed for the trace to go through. It wasn't as long as the general population believed, but it still required more time to locate mobile signals than landlines.

"It's your turn," the man whispered angrily. "Make your move."

The line suddenly went dead.

"Doesn't sound like a prank call to me," Theo muttered, shifting his stance so that Sylvie could join in on the conversation.

"Me, either." Sylvie had already set her purse on the table. "He sounded determined...measured in his response. It was as if he wanted to get your attention."

Kate had been standing in the doorway, but she backed up when Bit came rushing into the conference room.

"Got it! He's using a burner mobile, though. The signal is bouncing off two towers in southern West Virginia. One hundred percent. No doubt." Bit waited for someone to fill him in, but Sylvie remained silent as she took a seat at the table. Theo was staring at the phone as if it would give him answers, and Kate fidgeted with the pen in her hand. "Is someone going to fill me in? What did he say? He's obviously the one who killed that woman, right? I mean, why call back?"

Brook had been certain before Bit had even come into the room that the man on the other end of the line was Detective Stan Turner's unsub. The unknown subject must have seen the recent press coverage of S&E Investigations. For whatever reason, he wanted to make this a cat and mouse game, only she'd been completely honest with him.

She didn't play games.

She hunted predators.

He simply wasn't aware how much of a disadvantage he would have if she ever got him in her crosshairs.

"Kate, would you please track down Detective Stan Turner? He works for the West Virginia State Police, so he'll be out of the closest barracks to Stillwater. Let me know once when you're able to get him on the line." Brook joined Sylvie at the table, who was busy filling Bit in on the short phone conversation. Theo had turned around to face them, but he opted to lean against the thin credenza. "There is no reason for the rest of you to stay. Go. Enjoy your weekend, and please give some thought to the two cases. We'll make our decision first thing Monday morning."

CHAPTER THREE

"That's it?" Theo asked as he crossed his arms. He clearly wasn't happy with her decision, but it wasn't like she had any other option. "We're just handing this case off as if we aren't involved?"

"It's not our case to hand off," Brook stated matter-of-factly. "We have no client."

Her statement brought everyone up short.

"We aren't law enforcement. We aren't obligated to take every case that crosses our desk," she reminded them. "We have paying clients who keep the lights on. General Elliott was able to get us operational and running, but it's up to us to continually bring in suitable funds to sustain operations."

The ease of which they had been able to do so had been surprising, but Brook attributed their success to each of their skillset blending together as a unit. Bit's unique and sometimes questionable approach for obtaining information balanced precipitously on the line between legal and illegal. She trusted that he was able to back up everything that he discovered and entered into their reports for use in a court of law.

The reporting system that Brook had chosen was quite the challenge for someone like Bit, who didn't appreciate having to voluntarily give a detailed account of his digital footprint. He'd proven to be a quick learner, especially when it came to wording things just right so as not to cause undue attention from outside agencies. Considering that he'd never had any real training in law enforcement and had basically once been under the thumb of a Russian racketeer, he'd come pretty damned far at the age of twenty-four. Sylvie had mentioned that his birthday was coming up, but Brook trusted that Kate had a handle on those types of things.

"I'll explain what has occurred to Detective Turner, and then I'll follow his lead on how he would like me to interact with the unsub should he choose to call again." Brook wasn't about to ruin their weekend, and they technically weren't involved in an official capacity. "In the meantime, we're going to keep things status quo."

Bit took her lead right away, which was predictable. He turned on his white running shoes, not that he probably ever ran a mile in his life. Fortunately, he'd been a very good shot at the firing range, and he'd quickly acquired his personal defense carry permit. Given his slight frame, it hadn't been a shock when he'd chosen to carry a Smith & Wesson M&P22 semi-auto pistol. He claimed it was a better fit to his hand.

Bit paused by the door, turning around to eye up the other two. He appeared a bit confused as to why they weren't right behind him. Theo still had his arms crossed, and Sylvie remained seated in her chair. Neither one seemed inclined to leave until they had some sort of further clarification.

"Am I missing something?" Bit asked, his gaze landing on Sylvie. "Little T?"

Bit had basically given nicknames to everyone in the office. It had taken Brook a while to figure out that his moniker for Sylvie had to do with her love for tea—black tea, green tea, herbal tea. She was as addicted to the stuff as Brook was coffee.

The only one who hadn't received a nickname yet was Kate, but Bit said he would have to feel her out for a while. That had been two months ago, and he still had not come up with a suitable moniker.

"The unsub reached out to you, Brook," Sylvie pointed out, not addressing Bit directly. "Doesn't that give us an edge?"

"He wants to build a rapport with you."

Theo was theorizing, but he wasn't too far off base. Still, there was a protocol in this situation.

One, they had no client to bill, as she had already stipulated.

Two, the detective involved had not requested their assistance.

Even if Detective Turner desired to do so, he would have to obtain permission from the state in order to pay the substantial fee that S&E Investigations, Inc. would charge for such aid. Unless, of course, it was feasible under a pro-bono type of arrangement, thus providing S&E Investigations with a tax break for services rendered. Brook didn't know the rules involved, and nothing would be decided until she had all the facts.

"This could be an easy open-and-shut case, should this Detective Turner decide to use you."

CHAPTER THREE

Bit mumbled something underneath his breath about Theo not being too smart, and Brook had to maintain a straight face. She hadn't had a lot to smile about in her life, but working with Bit made it possible for her to see that life sometimes needed a little bit of humor.

"No one uses me, Theo. You should know that by now. With that said, should we decide as a team to—" Brook broke off when both Theo and Sylvie raised their hands to mimic a vote. Sylvie then leveled Bit with a glare, but he was more intimidated by Brook than the others. He ended up raising his hand halfway to scratch his chin, causing Theo to rub his own jawline in frustration. "We'll discuss this after I've had a chance to speak with Detective Turner. Again, go home. Enjoy your weekend."

"You'll call us should anything change?" Sylvie asked, as if she didn't trust Brook to follow through with her promise to speak with the detective in charge.

"Absolutely."

It took a few more moments, but Brook had eventually been left alone in the conference room. She remained seated while she churned over the brief phone call with Detective Turner's unsub. She had to stretch to reach for her electronic tablet on the far side of the table, but once she had it in hand, she accessed the new software that Bit had installed on it last week.

Having been a consultant for the FBI, she'd been able to hone her abilities to the point where she'd had the best closure rate in the Bureau. Nothing had really changed in the use of her skillset to capture those responsible for various heinous crimes. Every case that S&E Investigations had taken the first half of the year had been aided by her profile. Such a tool weeded out potential suspects that had a tendency to steer the police in the wrong direction.

In today's information age, it wasn't the lack of information that stymied investigations. It was the overwhelming flow of information that slowed down the detectives. The trick had become parsing information effectively to determine what was and wasn't truly substantial to the investigation.

It was habit for her to outline a skeleton of a profile, using what she'd already learned about the unsub. He was impatient, competitive, and harbored a rage that would only build up over time. Brook got lost in her musings and she vaguely recalled Kate saying she'd left multiple messages for Detective Turner. There was nothing for any of them to do until he returned her call.

In the meantime, other cases were waiting to be dusted off and reopened, only to be closed when the family received their own ultimately decisive closure...closure which Brook was still seeking in her own life.

CHAPTER FOUR

Brooklyn Sloane
May 2022
Sunday — 5:16am

THE INCOMING RINGTONE OF Brook's cell phone had her stopping the treadmill just after completing an uphill portion of her workout. She waited for the rubber mat underneath her to slow enough so that she could step off without hurting herself, ensuring that she grabbed the small towel at the same time so that she could wipe the sweat from her brow. The new reduced-impact treadmill that she'd purchased had been worth every penny. Her knees had needed a break from her daily exercise routine.

Considering that her condo was an open layout, with the exception of her bedroom and the main bath, she'd purposefully positioned the treadmill to face the floor-to-ceiling windowpane. She didn't have to put much thought into why she'd chosen offices with the same accessory for S&E Investigations. She needed to see what was around her to have some semblance of security...a field of view, of sorts.

Not knowing what was hiding on the other side of a wall set her on edge.

The added bonus was that she got to witness a waking city.

"Sloane."

Brook had wiped enough of the sweat from the side of her face in order to press the phone to her ear. She'd been working at her dining room table, the far side wall basically a murder board that she'd spent years creating in the search for her brother. Her gaze was immediately drawn to the red, blue, and green strings that had been carefully tacked to the cluttered wall, floor-to-ceiling. Inside the maze of photographs, maps, and articles lay hidden the answers to Jacob's whereabouts.

Currently, she was almost certain that her brother was still moving around inside the Washington D.C. area. Her previous interview with an established journalist had been her throwing down a challenge that he wouldn't be able to ignore.

"Ms. Sloane? This is Detective Stan Turner, West Virginia State Police, returning your call." The detective had a very raspy voice, and she pegged him for a smoker. At least a pack day. "I'm sorry that it took me so long to get back to you. As you can imagine, I've been busy."

His reply hadn't been filled with sarcasm, and she appreciated that he was treating her with respect, especially given that she worked the private sector. It most likely had to do with her past association with the Bureau that had garnered a call back, but she wasn't above using those previous credentials to establish a rapport.

"I'm sure you are, so I won't take up too much of your time." Brook retraced her steps to the treadmill that was approximately fifteen feet from her couch. The living room furniture barely got used, so the off-white fabric still looked brand new. "I thought you should know that your unsub reached out to me last week. Both Thursday and Friday, to be precise."

Brook went into detail regarding the voice messages, as well as the actual call itself. She then explained that the call had been traced to a cell phone tower on the east end of their small town. After having researched the area, she'd come to find that there were two cell phone towers that serviced the small area.

"Why you?" Detective Turner asked warily, his exhaustion coming across the line loud and clear. She doubted that he'd

CHAPTER FOUR

gotten more than three hour stretches of sleep at a time. "Do you have ties to the town of Stillwater?"

"None." Brook had to wonder if this man had been living under a rock for the past year. Her name and face had practically been splashed across the news on a national level once it had been revealed that the FBI had once employed the sister of a serial killer. "I'm going to assume that your unsub saw some articles involving my firm, and he wants to believe that he's smarter than those who we've already brought to justice. I suspect it is a game to him."

"If you traced the call, that means you have a number. I take it you have a name, as well?"

"Unfortunately, no." Brook paused to drink a healthy amount of water. She hadn't been out of breath when she'd been interrupted by his call, but she'd been in the process of working up a sweat. Once she'd snapped the cap back into place, she continued. "It was a burner. If you'll give me an email address, I can have the information forwarded to you, along with the voice recording. It will make things easier for you when it comes to the paperwork."

Detective Turner remained silent, though she could hear the ringing of multiple phone and various conversations in the background. She had to assume that he was at the state police barracks instead of the small sheriff's station in Stillwater. There was too much commotion for it to be the other way around. She wasn't sure what else he wanted for her to contribute to the conversation, but she went against her better judgement and gave her opinion anyway.

"If I'm out of line, you can simply ignore the rest of what I have to say," Brook replied as she set her water bottle back into its holder on the treadmill. She then tossed the white hand towel over her shoulder as she made her way into the kitchen. "Your unsub is Caucasian, mid-to-late thirties, and knew his victim personally. He's impatient, competitive, and has developed an underlying rage against a certain type of female—a good friend, a doting mother, and a faithful wife. Depending on new information discovered during the course of your investigation, the initial findings can change, of course. I do believe this is the first time that he's allowed his anger to get the best of him, which places you in a very unique position, Detective Turner."

"And how do you figure that, Ms. Sloane?"

Brook had a lot on her plate, and she hadn't planned to use the weekend working up a draft profile for Detective Turner. Something about the persistent manner in which the unsub had wanted to connect with her had struck a nerve. Hell, it might have been Theo's suggestion regarding the unsub wanting to establish a personal connection with someone. Whatever the reason, she'd come to one conclusion, and this homicide detective was most likely going to regret his question to her.

"Your unsub is a serial killer in the formative stages." Brook let her words sink in as she opened the refrigerator and pulled out one of her preferred smoothies that she always made sure to have on hand. The sixteen-ounce bottle was the perfect size for an after-workout pick-me-up. She was certainly going to need it after this phone call. "This was most likely his first kill. There are mistakes that have been made, and you're going to need to capitalize on them as soon as possible."

"Do you know how many open investigations that I have on my desk? Eleven. Twenty-two, if you count the other detectives' cases in this barracks," Detective Turner replied with irritation. Not at her, but at his situation. "I'm due in court on Monday and then again on Tuesday, possibly. I don't have the luxury to give the hours needed to solve a case as big as this, Ms. Sloane."

"I feel your pain," Brook replied, though she might have been stretching the truth.

Even when she'd been with the Bureau, she'd taken her cases one by one per her consulting contract. She'd had that leeway, and she'd been grateful to see her official cases through to the end. Granted, there were some that had never been solved, and chances were they never would be.

Life wasn't perfect, and they all had to live with their individual limitations.

"I was simply giving you my opinion as a profiler. Use the information as you see fit. Again, if you'll provide me with an email, I'll have the information regarding the phone calls and

CHAPTER FOUR 39

the High Fidelity 24-bit MPP3 soundtracks of the messages forwarded to you today. They should be adequate to developing an initial voice print analysis."

Brook had to retreat from the kitchen into the dining room, where she had a pad of paper and a pen. She jotted down his email address, writing his name underneath and underlining it twice.

"Ignore my previous rant," Detective Turner instructed, expressing regret at his prior outburst. "I'm running on two hours of sleep, and it doesn't look as if I'll see my bed for another twenty hours. I'll be driving back to Stillwater today. I appreciate the call, Ms. Sloane. I assume you'll contact me should the perp try to contact you again?"

"You have my word, Detective Turner." Brook set her pen on top of the paper, leaving her bottled smoothie alone for the time being. She took a seat, folding one of her legs underneath her while lifting the lid of her laptop. "Good luck with your case."

Detective Turner ended the call, though she was relatively sure she'd heard him say something along the lines that he was going to need all the luck that he could get. She spent the next three or so minutes composing an email with the detailed information and files that she'd retrieved from the server's Dropbox before pressing the send button. There were often reports, files, and recordings which email services and normal file transfer protocols kicked back due to the size of the shear amount of data involved. For these types of massive files, Bit had established an online encrypted data service box.

She didn't envy Detective Turner's position, yet a part of her understood just how important this particular murder was in the grand scheme of things.

Brook planned to take a shower, dress, and then head over to her favorite cafe before walking to the office. The building that housed S&E Investigations was merely two blocks away, and she rarely drove unless the weather warranted it. Given that the temperature was supposed to be in the mid-seventies today, she wouldn't need her car.

The USB that she'd brought home, given to her by Graham months ago, contained the footage of Jacob entering his private office. She must have viewed the recording three to five times a week for the past four months, and each time she picked up on some small, overlooked detail in regard to why her brother had taken such a gamble.

She had to believe that today would be no different.

CHAPTER FIVE

Brooklyn Sloane
May 2022
Monday — 10:51am

"You haven't left town."

Brook leaned back in her desk chair, more curious than annoyed at the phone call. Graham's impatience was coming through loud and clear. Until he gave her a valid reason why she should leave the city, she wasn't going anywhere anytime soon.

"I wasn't planning on it, either," Brook responded as she reached for her coffee mug. Graham had called her office line. He'd done so with purpose, because he wouldn't have known her location had he reached out to her on her cell phone. He'd been deliberate with his choice, and now he had her curiouser than before. "The team and I decided to take a case that is based in Kentucky. We'll spend the rest of the week putting in the appropriate requests for the case files, setting up some preliminary interviews, and so on before Theo flies into Louisville sometime next week. There's no reason for me or Sylvie to join him this early in the investigation. At least, not until we develop some concrete leads that need to be run to ground."

The case they had undertaken could take months to investigate, if not longer. There was also no guarantee that they would be able to solve a twenty-year-old double murder of a middle-aged couple who had been discovered on their family farm. They had both been fatally shot with their own antique Sharps .45-70 rifle and left to bleed out in the barn. The local police had no suspects back then, their only son had been two thousand miles away at college, and any leads had long ago gone cold.

The son was now the mayor of the small rural town, and he wanted closure.

"If this is about Jacob, just tell me."

"My request has nothing to do with Jacob."

Brook waited for Graham to continue, but he fell silent. She could practically feel the tension on the line, and she was clueless as to what could have prompted such a reaction.

"Is this about the press? I know we stirred up a bit of a political dust storm with our last case. Is it blowing back on you?"

She broke off when Sylvie came rushing through the door, once again reaching for the remote when she was close enough to the desk. Déjà vu hit Brook as Graham responded to her inquiry, unaware that their call was about to be interrupted.

"No. The press and their partisan politics are the least of my worries. What if I were to ask you outright to leave town for a week? Maybe two. Call it a personal favor. I was thinking maybe you could host a team building retreat in Colorado Springs. I—"

"Graham, I need to call you back." Brook slammed down the phone after she got a good look at the news coverage on the television. She'd have to apologize to him later. While they often went toe-to-toe with one another, it hadn't been her intention to be rude. "What the hell is that?"

That was a reporter telling the world how Lisa Gervase's killer had called the sister of a serial killer—Brooklyn Walsh.

At least, that was the headline on the bottom of the screen.

The reporter was also the same woman who had questioned the sheriff on the earlier broadcast about the note left at the crime scene. Brook stood and walked around her desk as she studied the reporter.

CHAPTER FIVE

"The only way that reporter could have known that you received a call from the unsub was if she got the information from Detective Turner or the killer himself," Sylvie said as she pulled one of the guest chairs around so that she could watch the events unfold. Brook had given the team an update on her phone conversation with Detective Turner earlier this morning, so they were aware that there was nothing else to be done. "What are you going to do?"

"I'm going to reach out to Detective Turner." Brook made no effort to reach for her phone, though. Instead, she leaned back against her desk, wanting to hear more of the press coverage. "Turn it up, please."

"...where her body was left with a message. "Are you ready to play?" While the police still have no comment when it comes to the note, my sources have also told me that the killer called Brooklyn Walsh. She is the sister of a notorious serial killer. That's right, the infamous Jacob Walsh." The reporter tucked her hair behind her ear with ease, most likely having practiced such a move in the mirror countless of times. *"That leaves the Stillwater residents with one question—was Lisa Gervase simply another victim in this public cat and mouse game that Brooklyn Walsh has going on with her brother? Back to you, Brian."*

"Thank you, Sarah." The news anchor lifted his gaze to the camera. "That was Sarah Evanston, reporting from our sister network out in..."

"Oh, fuck," Bit murmured as he walked into her office, his gaze glued to the television. He'd caught the tail end of the news report, and Theo had been right behind him. They both sat on the couch. "Do you want me to take a look at her email accounts, instant messaging apps, and phone records? See who she's been communicating with?"

"Bit," Sylvie exclaimed with disapproval. "We have no warrant. We aren't even a part of their case, either."

"Oh, I wouldn't be doing it in an official capacity. You know, just a curiosity kind of thing." Bit began to bounce his leg up and down the way he did when he was tense. "We can't just let that reporter smear your good name, Boss. This has nothing to do with your brother, and everything to do with your professional reputation. On the streets, we wouldn't allow that to—"

"I appreciate your concern, Bit." Brook wouldn't do anything to jeopardize Detective Turner's case. "We stay above board. No peeking into her accounts. And Sylvie, despite my earlier denial, we *are* technically involved. The unsub clearly wants our participation, and he might be the one who is making sure that happens by calling us out publicly."

"You believe the unsub is feeding this reporter her information," Theo said, still reading the headlines rotating across the bottom of the screen.

"That's the thing. I don't." Brook had run through numerous angles, and it didn't fit the unsub's profile. Admittedly, it was all but a skeleton of a profile, but she'd prepared enough of an outline to send to Detective Turner in an email yesterday. "The unsub would view using a third party as cheating, and he wouldn't do that in this game that he's created in his head. The thing is...I'm not even sure that he considers this a game, so much as a challenge. He might consider this a litmus test, of sorts. I need—"

Brook firmly pressed her lips together before she finished her statement. Graham, Theo, Sylvie, and even Bit all seemed to want to take on a case that had no client, and all for different reasons. Theo and Sylvie itched to solve a brutal murder, Bit seemed to feel as if streets creds were being tested, and Graham had some undisclosed reason for wanting her out of the city. She appeared to be the only level-headed one in this situation.

"Ms. Sloane, Detective Turner is on the phone for you," Kate called out from the reception area. She normally would have used the intercom feature on the desk unit, but there wasn't much need for protocol since everyone had gathered in Brook's office. "Line one."

"It appears as if the detective has come to the same deductions as us," Brook said wryly.

It was unlikely that the team would allow her to take this call in private.

She reached behind her, picked up the receiver, and pressed the button correlating to the appropriate line with the blinking

CHAPTER FIVE

red light. It was time to set a tone, because she'd already dealt with enough damaging publicity to last a few lifetimes.

"Detective Turner, I wasn't aware that you had a personal relationship with Sarah Evanston," Brook greeted, not bothering to disguise the derision in her tone. She hoped that she was wrong in her assumption, just as she was aware that he would set her straight if that was the case. "I don't appreciate being placed front and center of an investigation that has nothing to do with Jacob Walsh."

"I've never personally met the woman, and I certainly don't have any desire to now." Detective Turner was no longer in his office, if the birds chirping in the background were any indication. "There's a leak in the county sheriff's department."

"Just how many deputies does this sheriff's department employ?"

"Four, not including the sheriff himself. And a civilian dispatcher."

"Then it shouldn't be too hard for you to figure out who is sharing pertinent details of your investigation with the press." Brook could sense the heavy stares directed her way. She was focused on the oil painting above the couch. It helped her brings things into perspective. "I would appreciate a public statement of some sort, giving more clarification to my lack of involvement. Or more importantly, complete non-involvement. Trust me, the last thing you want to do is grab the attention of someone like Jacob Walsh. The population of that small town would be negatively impacted by such a colossal mistake."

"You and I both know that this case has nothing to do with Jacob Walsh. I wish to keep it that way, too."

Brook figured that Detective Turner would have done an extensive search regarding her after their phone call yesterday. In all likelihood, he'd done his research before he returned her call in the first place. It was good to know that the case had fallen to someone who did his homework.

"I realize that this Sarah Evanston put a spin on the story to gain more viewers, but it's up to you to reassure the public that someone of Jacob Walsh's caliber hasn't invaded their small town. Your unsub isn't going to appreciate the so-called comparison that has been inadvertently put into play. There's no telling what he'll do now that this idiot reporter has thrown down the gauntlet."

"I scheduled a press conference for noon. I finished up at the courthouse earlier than planned. I give you my word that I'll put a stop to the rumors that Evanston's irresponsible morning broadcast has stirred up."

Brook decided there was no valid reason to reply, and she waited for the detective to continue. He'd called her for a reason, and it wasn't simply to inform her that a reporter was attempting to put a sensational spin on her morning segment.

"Your profile suggested that the perp is local."

"Yes."

Detective Turner was slowly easing his way into asking her what he truly wanted to know from their conversation yesterday. She'd mentioned to him on the phone that his unsub was a serial killer in the initial stages of development. She hadn't exaggerated her view, and nothing was going to prevent this case from turning into a shitshow for the media to blow up.

"Do you truly believe that this is the first of many?"

"Yes."

Brook didn't need to add anything else to her response. Detective Turner had desired a definitive answer, and she'd given it to him.

"I'll be in touch."

She slowly returned the receiver to its cradle. Something in his tone told her that he would be calling sooner rather than later.

"When did Lisa Gervase go missing?" Brook asked to no one in particular, not wanting to go blindly into the next conversation with the detective. She had no doubt that they had already looked into the details. "What is the timeline?"

"Two weeks ago," Theo replied, shifting his right leg so that his ankle rested on his other knee. "All I know is that the sheriff initially believed Gervase left town of her own free will. Something about a fight with her husband. The state police didn't get involved until Friday, after her body was discovered in the middle of a rural, secondary road."

CHAPTER FIVE 47

"I did a bit of digging myself over the weekend," Sylvie said without a hint of shame. "Lisa Gervase was thirty-one, the mother of a six-year-old boy and a ten-year-old daughter, and the wife of a prominent commercial real estate agent. John Gervase even owns his fair share of commercial buildings in the heart of town. Anyway, there seems to be no love lost between Mr. Gervase and the sitting sheriff. After a week of the husband talking to anyone who would listen, he finally took his concern to a local news station, even going so far as to say that the sheriff wasn't doing the job that he'd been elected to do. I believe the word *incompetent* was bandied about."

"That explains why the sheriff changed tactics and began hinting that the husband could be responsible for his wife's abduction a few days before her body was discovered," Theo surmised, resting his hand on his knee. "Sheriff Kennard was looking for a way out for his competence being tested publicly. Making inaccurate assumptions about a missing person who ended up the victim of a homicide is not the best way to get reelected."

Bit's knee was rising and falling at a rapid pace by this point.

"Would you like to share anything, Bit?"

He pulled a face and shook his head.

He was easier to read than the Chinese takeout menu that was on her desk.

"If you came across something when you were doing some digging yourself, please share it with the team. It seems that everyone was somewhat bored this weekend." Brook noticed that Theo didn't bother to hide his amusement. "Well?"

"I might have inadvertently stumbled across Lisa Gervase's autopsy report yesterday."

Sylvie stifled a groan, but it wasn't surprising to Brook at all that Bit had poked around online where he shouldn't have been. It was in his nature, and there was no changing the stripes on a tiger. While most everyone underestimated him due to his docile demeanor, his level of talent when it came to anything online was without measure. No matter how many times she'd requested that he keep things above board, he always dipped below the water line.

"And?" Brook ignored Sylvie's incredulous gaze. "It's not like we can put the genie back in that particular bottle."

"I couldn't finish it."

Bit's reply even got Theo to do a double take.

"What do you mean?"

"I mean, I made it halfway through the report and then had to stop reading." Bit visibly swallowed in disgust. "It was all I could to keep down my taco supreme lunch special. Plus, I had another two still in the bag that I didn't want to go to waste."

Brook had gotten used to Bit's unique way of talking and handling things over the course of the last five months.

Still, he had a way of trying one's patience.

"Can you share any details that might help? Was the victim stabbed? Strangled? Shot?" Those types of details made a difference in the profile of the unsub. Should Brook be pulled deeper into the investigation, which she would do her best to make certain that didn't happen, she wanted to be prepared. "One of the first things listed is the cause of death."

"It wasn't exactly that clean cut, but I think the root cause was shock."

Sylvie was gripping the remote control as she leaned forward with interest.

"Shock?"

"The unsub tortured her, and in places that should be off limits to such intentions, if you get my drift." Bit rested a hand over his stomach as he grimaced. "I stopped reading once I got to the part where he ignited her—"

"We get the general idea," Sylvie replied, holding up her hand to stop Bit from going into too much detail. "Brook, does this mean that we're going to offer our assistance to Detective Turner?"

"It's not that simple. Go on, Bit," Brook instructed him, bracing herself for an appalling description. Unfortunately, it was part of the job. She couldn't construct a profile without having all the facts, and she believed in being prepared for all situations. "Are you talking about the victim's breasts? Did the unsub use some type of acid?"

"Breasts weren't the only targets," Bit muttered, pointing lower on his body. Sylvie inhaled sharply, and Theo winced with unease. "Oh, and her left ring finger, too. No to the acid part, but I stopped reading halfway through."

Brook met Theo's startled gaze. He'd come to the same conclusion that she had, because the areas on the victim's body that the killer had focused on were of utmost importance.

"The unsub is burning the very things that define the victim," Theo said as Sylvie shot him a glare. He then backpedaled. "No. I'm not saying that her b...I'm not saying her feminine attributes defined her."

Theo began to hold up each finger for every characteristic of the victim.

"Her ring finger signifies the vows that she took with her husband, her private region indicates her womb, and her breasts could suggest her gender and that of her many friendships with other females." Theo looked toward Brook for confirmation. "You said yourself that Lisa Gervase was a good friend, faithful wife, and doting mother. That is the same description the press has been using for the past two weeks."

"Exactly," Brook murmured, pushing off her desk and walking around to take a seat. She touched the display of her tablet, turning it on so that she could add a couple of more elements to her profile. "The unsub believes that she desecrated those parts of herself."

"I'm going to need another cup of tea. Bit, I'll bring you back some. Anyone else?"

Both Brook and Theo opted for coffee.

"When are you going to tell her that you actually hate tea?" Theo asked when he and Bit remained seated on the couch after Sylvie left the room.

"I have no idea what you're talking about," Bit scoffed as he sat forward. "I say we order lunch in today. Who's in the mood for some Italian? I heard that a new pizza place opened a few blocks from here. I'll go see if Kate can find us a menu online."

Brook continued to add details to the profile using her stylus, becoming more accustomed to the manner in which the application aided in piecing together her profiling document.

Bit had outdone himself yet again.

"Are we really not going to address the elephant in the room?"

Brook saved her progress before glancing toward the television. Her name was no longer splashed across the bottom of the screen. Neither was Jacob's name, for that matter.

"No. I trust that Detective Turner's press conference will nip it in the bud."

"What if Jacob saw the news coverage?" Theo asked in a rather guarded manner. "Is there any real possibility that he would intervene with the case?"

It hadn't been easy for Brook to share information and pertinent details with the team regarding her brother. There hadn't been a lot of downtime between cases, but they utilized the smaller conference room to keep track of their hunt for Jacob. Brook fully believed that her brother was nearby, monitoring her daily life until he was reassured that she wouldn't give into the fallacy that her life was perfect.

A woman believing that she led a charmed existence was what motivated him to kill.

"Right now, our focus should be on our new case." Brook leaned back in her chair, the stylus still in her hand. "Nothing has changed, and we'll keep things on course for the time being. As the case files start coming in from the local police department and county sheriff's office in Kentucky, I'll start to draft up a profile."

Theo slowly nodded, accepting that she wasn't willing to waste another second of their morning on something that would be pure speculation. A part of her was always concerned that Jacob would seek to capitalize on a situation when her attention was diverted elsewhere. It was a constant fear that she lived with every single day of her life.

She wasn't afraid for herself, so much as she was for those who surrounded her.

There was no denying that Jacob wouldn't be pleased that she'd encircled herself with a team of professional investigators who would literally sacrifice themselves for her if the situation warranted it. She would do the same for them.

That was the problem, because as much as the team had strength in numbers...they were also her weakness.

CHAPTER SIX

Brooklyn Sloane
May 2022
Wednesday — 3:41pm

"WAS THIS YOUR DOING?" Brook asked, not bothering to hide her anger. She stood in front of the floor-to-ceiling window in her office. Not even the breathtaking view of the city could ease her level of frustration. "Wasn't it you who said that you wouldn't interfere with the day-to-day operations of S&E Investigations?"

The phone call that she'd received from Detective Turner an hour ago had changed the course of her trajectory. Two days' worth of work now virtually useless, and a client who in the short term was not going to be pleased to hear from her about delays.

"I have no idea what you're referring to," Graham replied from the other end of the line. She was gripping her cell phone a little too tight, but that was to prevent her from throwing it across the room into the wall. It was rare that someone could work her up to the point that she allowed her emotions to rule her head, but he'd gone and done the one thing he'd given his word that he wouldn't...and that was something she couldn't abide by in any professional relationship. "I haven't been by the office since last week. What seems to be the problem?"

Brook pulled her cell phone away from her ear to prevent herself from saying something that she'd regret. Her reaction to hearing from Detective Turner that the West Virginia governor had suggested bringing on S&E Investigations as a consultant in such a high-profile case told her everything that she'd already known—she'd let her guard down an inch too far when it came to Graham.

She'd begun to trust him, and that had been her first mistake in dealing with him.

"There is no problem, General Elliott," Brook replied without a single shred of emotion in her voice. "My team and I will be in West Virginia for the foreseeable future. Kate will remain here in the city should you need anything from the office."

Brook once again pulled the phone away from her ear, but this time she did so with the purpose of ending the call. He'd gotten what he wanted, and that was to get her out of the city. She didn't believe for one moment that the governor of West Virginia had decided five days was adequate enough time for Detective Turner to solve a murder. Add in that he could have also pressed for the FBI to assist the state police detective, and she would have said that a private consulting firm wouldn't have been anywhere on the man's radar with a well-timed push in the right direction.

Regardless that she'd been contacted by who she believed was their unsub, such an action wouldn't have warranted a high political figure bringing in outside resources.

Her cell phone vibrated in her hand, but she ignored it.

Graham should have thought twice before going behind her back to arrange her involvement. As it stood, she had a team to prep, travel arrangements to determine, and a phone call to place to a client who wasn't going to be too pleased with the delay in his case. Not necessarily in that particular order, either. Bottom line was that this last-minute change of course was bad for her firm's reputation.

At the end of the day, the blame was placed at her feet.

CHAPTER SIX

She was the face of the firm to anyone who cared to look their way. It was hard enough living down her relationship with Jacob Walsh. The firm didn't need any other smears across their name.

She retreated to her desk, picking up the receiver and requesting that Kate gather everyone in the conference room. It took Brook longer than she'd anticipated to speak with the client who'd just paid his retainer. Astonishingly, he'd been more understanding than she would have thought had she been in his shoes.

They'd reached an understanding regarding the initial legwork needed for his parents' murders, and she'd given her word that one of her team members would continue to gather the pertinent case files and any other relevant information needed so that as soon as the case in West Virginia was wrapped up, Brook and the team would then be able to pick up where they'd left off without too much difficulty.

Grabbing her water bottle, phone, and electronic tablet, Brook stood from her desk and began to make her way to her office door. She'd closed it earlier to obtain some privacy for her call with Graham, not that their conversation had lasted all that long. As she pulled on the handle, she caught sight of someone waiting for one of the elevators out in the main foyer.

Kyle Paulson worked for the hedge fund that occupied the other half of their floor. He was currently distracted by the biometric scanner that Bit had initially recommended as a security measure. No one could enter the front entrance of their offices without first having their left iris scanned into Bit's database for comparison with authorized personnel. As for guests, Kate had the authority to buzz them inside the foyer of S&E Investigations.

Kyle must have seen her in his peripheral vision, because he abruptly looked up at the red numbers above one of the elevators. She could understand his hesitation when it came to having S&E Investigations on the same floor as the hedge fund that employed him. Add in that it was common knowledge that she was the sister of an active serial killer, and such realization had a tendency to make people uncomfortable.

"It looks as if we're going to be taking a trip to West Virginia," Brook declared once she'd entered the conference room. There was no time to ease into it, and she didn't doubt that they were all secretly pleased with the last-minute nature of the announcement. Theo and Sylvie had made their feelings known since last week that they believed their firm should be involved after the unsub's first contact. Neither one of them were comfortable with the fact that he'd fallen silent since Brook had decided not to play his so-called game. "Kate, I'll need you to remain here. Would you please contact Jordan Miles? Ask if he would mind us using his G6 first thing tomorrow morning."

"Wait," Theo said, leaning forward in his seat with interest. He rested his forearms on the table as if to steady himself. "You know Jordan Miles?"

"You're not talking about the CEO of Miles Therapeutics, are you?" Sylvie asked in astonishment. She shared disbelieving glances with Bit. "Brook, he just made the rich list in Forbes magazine. I'm not talking about the *M for Millionaire* list, either."

"We're professional acquaintances," Brook replied nonchalantly, not wanting to get into specifics with the connection she had with Jordan. He owed her quite a few favors that she'd cultivated while with the FBI, and she had a very good reason for calling in a chip today. "We'll have too much equipment and weapons to get through TSA without proper paperwork and federal firearm permits. It will be easier for us to fly on a private jet."

"You will?" Bit asked with a frown. "What are you taking with you? I can get started on—"

"You."

"Who?" Bit asked, looking at the others as if she weren't addressing him directly.

"Bit, you're coming with us. We've been able to do the majority of our caseload from here in the past, while Theo and Sylvie have been out in the field. With this case, it's all hands-on deck. This is an active case where no one works alone, and we're going to need immediate results from you while we're in the field."

CHAPTER SIX 57

Brook began to run through the pertinent details so that everyone could head home and pack for an extended trip.

"Kate, you'll not only be covering our absences, but I'm going to need you to start the legwork for our client in Kentucky. Case files have already been sent over, but you'll need to comb through them and request lab reports and supporting information. Separate the suspects listed in the reports, accumulate lists of names and locations of family members, friends, and acquaintances, and then initiate our own background checks on all of them. Anything you read in those reports that feels even slightly off to you, make a note of it. Also, feel free to start putting together the basics of a murder board, similar to how you've seen us do in the past."

"Yes, ma'am."

Brook could hear the anticipation in Kate's tone. Her adrenaline had spiked upon being given her first major task at the firm. The results she provided would decide whether or not Brook would keep her aboard the team. She'd seen the young woman reading through the profiles that Brook had put together for the Bureau.

She'd been studying them.

Dissecting them.

It was time for her to put her knowledge to the test.

"Uh, Boss?" Bit had raised his hand, clearly still processing that he was traveling with the team to West Virginia. "You *were* kidding about me going with you, right? I mean, there are programs that I can't just—"

"Figure it out, Bit. Dedicated satellite data uplink. Whatever it takes."

Brook continued to debrief them on what had occurred over the last hour, leaving out that Graham had imposed his executive authority upon their choices of cases.

"The governor of West Virginia has requested our help. I've spoken to our client in Kentucky, and he was understanding concerning the delay in his case. I assured him that someone in our office would still be researching his parents' case files, and that someone is Kate. In the meantime, I'd like to be on our way before six o'clock tomorrow morning. Sylvie, I've already informed Detective Turner that you would be reaching out to him. Have him email his case files to you. I also want to know everything about the victim, arranged in our usual format—every detail from her marriage, her friendships, and her day-to-day life. Everyone has secrets, and we need to find out hers. Theo, I'd like background checks on the sheriff, all four deputies, and every single reporter who has been covering the case so far—specifically Sarah Evanston. I want to know the identity of her source. Any questions?"

Bit had begun muttering to himself about a list of mobile-mounted tech equipment outfitted in Hardigg rack-mounted equipment cases that would need to be source-packed and embarked by only him.

She decided to give him a little incentive.

"Bit, if you can create a remote working site, I'll let you keep whatever is in that white box." Brook had his full attention now. "I told you during our second case that there was a possibility of needing portable hardened laptops in the future. That future is now."

"It came sooner than expected," Bit replied as he pushed himself back from the table. "You had me won over with your deal, though. Road trip it is! I've already collected most of what I need. I just need to build a generic client, mirror it, prepare, and mount the individual components of the remote server suite and select a comms uplink package based on whatever last minute SatCom provider that I can arrange. Purchasing dedicated, unrestricted satellite access time for the period in question may be a challenge. Telecommunications satellite channels don't grow on trees. Maybe the governor can punch up our access priority, so I won't have to hack their feeds. All we need is energy on channel. I can take it from there."

Everyone simply nodded when he glanced at each of them. It was better to have him believe they'd understood a third of what he'd just said or otherwise they would still be sitting at the conference room table come sunrise.

Brook shared a knowing glance with Kate before the young woman turned and walked out of the conference room. Having knowledge of what was inside the box had lessened her stress, but the upgraded system was something that she could work with and adapt to, given that it would benefit the team.

Instead of a whiteboard, Bit had purchased a ninety-eight inch, 4K, LED display touch monitor that would replace the main whiteboard they currently used as a murder board. She had no doubt that he would incorporate the software program that she utilized for her profiles, meaning that anything added from their tablets would automatically integrate with the information displayed on the board. Bit referred to it as his own multiple source correlation system, displaying its own self-generated status update quality and relevant cross-decked source information on demand at the main display.

It was a far more efficient way of handling their cases, allowing everyone instant updates and secure access twenty-four-seven.

Sylvie followed Bit out the door, both of them wanting to get a jumpstart on their assigned tasks.

Theo remained behind, as was his usual response. He preferred to be thorough, wanting more information before he began his own quest for information.

"Are we setting up shop at the state police barracks, the local police station, or somewhere else?"

"The local police station, if possible," Brook replied as she took a seat. She used her tablet to pull up a map of their destination. "Stillwater is a small town, but I want our presence known. Our flag being displayed front and center will give the unsub some sense of satisfaction. At least, at first."

"What are you looking for?" Theo asked as he stood and walked around the table to join her. He rested a hand on the table as he leaned in over her shoulder. "A motel?"

"There." Brook pointed to the map with her stylus. She'd chosen to use Google maps, since it displayed accommodations. "A B&B. Whoever owns the place will know the residents and their histories. We can use that to our advantage. I'll see if Kate can secure four rooms. We know the press is in town, but most of them are likely staying in a nearby chain motel. They always want their people to seek out a corporate discount if they can get a rate."

Theo claimed a seat next to her as they continued to speak at length for a good fifteen minutes before Kate interrupted with news that Jordan Miles had given them permission to use his private jet. That was one problem solved, leaving them only a few more to go before they were able to set up a remote worksite. Brook had then given Kate instructions regarding their accommodations while in Stillwater.

"I can't help but wonder why the governor acted so quickly." Theo pushed his chair back underneath the table as he studied her. "Is there something else that I should know?"

Theo had always been quick on the uptake.

"Nothing that I can't handle on my own," Brook advised him, not wanting to draw him into whatever contention had built between her and Graham. "Go ahead and get started on those background investigations. Once you get those initiated, go home and pack. It's not every day that we get to stop a serial killer in the making."

Chapter Seven

Graham Elliott
May 2022
Wednesday — 6:09pm

"Is there anything that I can help you with, sir?"

Graham had been seen several times checking his phone during the meeting while he waited for his contact to call, but his introspective angst wasn't due to the current situation. He was half-expecting an incoming call, hoping that Brook would reach out to him.

"No, thank you. Has anything been recovered from the RPV?"

RPV stood for remotely piloted vehicle.

"We're still waiting to receive word on that, but the damage to the aircraft was quite extensive. It wouldn't surprise me if there was nothing salvageable in the wreckage. Readings are still within the normal spectrum. Nothing to report." It had been the task force commander's adjutant who had replied to Graham's question. He shifted his weight amid the tension. "Of course, that isn't an official finding, sir. The wreckage is twelve hundred feet down and the weather is turning quickly out there. They may need to start recovery of the RPV within the hour."

"Duly noted. I would appreciate an update as soon as the Admiral has a report on his desk."

"If and when I'm able to speak with him. I'll let him know of your request."

Graham headed across the courtyard in the opposite direction of his source.

He'd heard from multiple colleagues that there was a potential WMD threat to the city. Chatter had been picked up last week by the NSA, who in turn were now collaborating with multiple agencies, including the NRO.

Unfortunately, nothing more had been deciphered, although the FBI had located the small cell local to D.C. that had been loosely associated with the threat. It didn't sound as if there was much left for them to find. Considering the incident had taken place off the coast of the Atlantic where a tropical storm was disrupting recovery operations, it could be days.

Graham just hoped like hell that they had answers before it was too late.

He had no regrets with how he'd handled the situation with Brook. There were security protocols that needed to be adhered to in situations like these. If everyone sounded the alarm over every threat to their homeland, every citizen would be living in bunkers twenty-four-seven for years to come.

Life couldn't be led by fear, but he'd be damned if he wouldn't protect Brook when there was a clear and present danger of a credible threat being carried out right here in D.C.

Graham and Brook were nothing more than colleagues in her eyes, and that was as it should be. She only had one goal in her life, and that was to bring an end to her brother's sick and twisted hold that he had over her existence. Jacob's obsession with her would forever be a stumbling block to anything more, and Graham could only sit back and be a spectator waiting for her story to play itself out.

He wasn't used to that role, and he sure as hell didn't like waiting in the wings.

Still, something had grown between them during the chaotic course of his daughter's case. He hadn't experienced a connection with someone like that since the day he'd first met his wife. Olivia had been his rock over the years, the mother of his child, and he'd thought that he'd die long before she ever left this earth behind. Unfortunately, she'd taken that decision away from fate and had ended her own life.

He hadn't realized that he'd come to terms with her decision until he met Brook. It wasn't that his love for Olivia had faded in any way or that he'd allowed his anger over her selfish decision to eliminate the beautiful memories they'd made together, but it had more to do with accepting that he was still alive. His wife and daughter could now rest in peace knowing that the person who'd ruined their lives was currently burning in one of the darkest pits in hell.

Graham had simply been left behind in the aftermath.

It was time to pick up some of the pieces of his shattered life and look toward the future.

Unfortunately, his most recent decision to interfere with Brook's caseload had caused the professional rift between them to widen. It would be worth the distance if something did take place in the city that would otherwise have cost Brook her life.

He would stop by the offices tomorrow to see if Bit or Kate had remained behind, which would most likely be the case. Evacuation plans would have to be made, but only if Graham received prior notification of a planned attack. He would do what he could to get them to safety if the immediate threat materialized further.

In the meantime, there was nothing he could do but wait...

Chapter Eight

Brooklyn Sloane
May 2022
Thursday — 8:34am

The warm sunshine seemed to only enhance the pleasant scent of fresh cut grass. Brook could even make out the sweet, delicate scent of lilacs as she stepped out of the vehicle. The lovely fragrance reminded her of her childhood in suburban America, long before Jacob had turned into evil incarnate.

The Gulfstream G650 that Jordan Miles had allowed them to use was just as lavish as she'd expected, though it had more to do with the convenience of such travel over luxury. Kate had rented them two vehicles, both of which had been waiting for them near the private landing strip. Theo had remained behind with Bit to pack the second vehicle with the equipment brought with them, which had been quite extensive. He'd sworn that he couldn't leave behind any of the hardware that he'd loaded into ten ruggedized Hardigg cases, which had prompted them to be delayed taking off at six o'clock.

Bit shouldn't have any issues fitting all his equipment in the huge, black Lincoln navigator, but he refused to drive it because he referred to it as being the size of a semi. Thus, Theo would have to do the honors.

Considering that it was still before nine o'clock in the morning, Brook took that as a win.

"I wasn't expecting the town to be quite so charming," Sylvie said as she stood on the other side of the Lincoln MKZ four-door. "Did you see the ice cream parlor? I think it doubled as a malt shop, once upon a time. Maybe it still does. The fact that they have a teashop is surprising...and an added bonus."

"It's like we stepped back into the 1960s, isn't it?" Brook scanned her surroundings, noticing that the two-story dwelling had to be at least ten thousand square feet. The online pictures hadn't done the large home operating as a B&B justice. Built near the edge of town, the house was within walking distance of the quaint mom-and-pop shops. "The Gervase family must have sunk a boat load of money into this town."

"Motive, I guess. It's worth considering, anyway," Sylvie murmured, stretching her back slightly, even though they had only been in the vehicle for less than an hour. She took a deep breath. "My lungs aren't going to know what to do with this unsoiled air."

Money was the most popular motive for murder, but Brook didn't think that was the case this time around. As picturesque as this town may be, there had been an underlying foreboding in the faces of those observing their passage through town. From those townsfolk at the gas station to the two young men in front of the tavern. It was a bit early to be drinking, but the neon sign indicated that the establishment had been open to the public.

"It could be due to the time of day, but there wasn't a lot of people window shopping, was there?" Sylvie contemplated with a scrunch of her nose. She finally leaned down into the car and grabbed her purse from the floorboard of the passenger seat. "I take it that we're checking in first before walking down to the station? It's only a block from here."

"Let me pop the trunk."

Brook kept her gaze on the light blue church across the street. While those guests of the B&B had to park on the street alongside the curb, the church had a large gravel parking lot.

CHAPTER EIGHT

There were maybe six vehicles parked in it, all of them empty. There could be a meeting of some sort, or it could be that was how many had decided to go to the morning service.

It didn't take long for Brook and Sylvie to collect their suitcases. Brook had also brought along her leather bag that contained her laptop, tablet, and miscellaneous files that she'd printed before leaving the office last night. One was of the autopsy performed on Lisa Gervase, and the other was the criminal report that Detective Turner had emailed to Sylvie right after her request. She didn't want to leave anything of value inside the car while they were otherwise occupied.

"Whoever owns this place has a green thumb," Sylvie observed as they made their way up the porch steps. There were numerous hanging flower baskets full of trailing petunias that were vibrant in color, from pink to purple. There were also some bright white flowers thrown in the mix. "This town is so far out of the way, though. It's a wonder they can remain in business. Tourism certainly isn't going to draw them in."

"I have a feeling this is more of a home than anything else."

Sylvie had been the one to open the screened door, so Brook crossed the threshold first. She caught the scent of lemon and cinnamon wafting in the air. The lemon fragrance had a disinfectant odor to it, whereas the cinnamon was from its natural origin.

Someone was baking an apple pie.

She'd recognize that scent, anywhere.

"The woodwork in this place is downright stunning."

Sylvie's comment as she came to stand beside Brook was an understatement. The first level of the B&B was decorated beautifully. Antique furniture was sprinkled throughout the first floor in two strategic sitting areas parallel to the large dining room table on the other side of two rather large rustic beams. A counter made of the same cherrywood was positioned to the left.

"I'd say it is much better than the motel underneath the Interstate."

Brook wheeled her luggage over to the counter, not seeing anyone around. It didn't surprise her that there weren't any guests coming and going from their rooms. According to Kate, only two of the ten rooms were occupied, and both of those were with the media...one of them being Sarah Evanston.

The other individual happened to be her cameraman.

It wasn't ideal to be in such close proximity as them, but information was a two-way street. With any luck, they would soon know exactly who her source was that had been leaking information regarding the case. Brook had struck bargains with the press before, and she could imagine herself doing so again in the foreseeable future.

"You must be with S&E Investigations." A woman in her mid-sixties came out of the swinging door on the other side of the dining room table. She wore a white apron and was wiping her hands on a matching dish towel. "Your assistant called yesterday. I have four rooms all made up for you, and I'm in the process of making tonight's dessert. I'm Audrey Stiner, by the way."

"It's nice to meet you, Audrey. I'm Brook Sloane, and this is my associate—Sylvie Deering."

While Audrey was going above and beyond with her greeting, her smile didn't quite meet the corner of her eyes. She wasn't wearing a wedding ring, yet there was something maternal about her approach. It always benefited Brook to size up an individual who she would be dealing with on a daily basis. The fact that the woman's gaze kept shifting to Brook's holstered weapon told her that Audrey wasn't comfortable around firearms. Considering that she lived where hunting was a favorite pastime, Brook was confident in her assumption that Audrey wasn't married.

Brook had worn a holster that attached to the belt at the waistband of her dark jeans. She'd chosen to dress comfortably, yet professionally. Her black blazer usually covered her weapon, but the leather bag over her shoulder had shifted the material. She moved it back in place so that she could have Audrey's undivided attention.

"Our colleagues will be driving in shortly, but I'll be able to take their keys, as well," Brook replied, not bothering to reach into her purse for her wallet. "I'm not sure what our hours are

CHAPTER EIGHT 69

going to be, and they'll be joining me at the police station. It's my understanding that our assistant has taken care of the payment?"

"Yes, she was very efficient," Audrey praised as she reached behind her for four separate keys. They weren't keycards, either. They were old-fashioned keys, each looped onto hand-carved wooden leaves that had numbers burned into the surface. "If you'll just sign for the rooms right here, please. You'll only need the one key to get into your room. The front door is always unlocked."

Brook picked up the black stylus that was next to a signature block. Not everything was out-of-date, and it seemed that the town had embraced modern technology. Considering the upkeep of the older buildings, such a discovery wasn't too hard to believe.

Sylvie had released the handle of her large suitcase to browse the vast number of small figurines in a display case maybe twenty feet from the counter. With her attention elsewhere, she hadn't caught sight of the long shadow that had slowly begun moving toward them. Brook purposefully monitored Audrey's face for any sign that the individual approaching was a threat. Whereas the woman didn't come across as fearful, there did seem to be some tension in the lines around her eyes.

"Jake, I thought you were working today."

"I took the day off. You said you had a busy morning with new guests arriving, and I thought you might want some help."

Once Brook had finished signing her name, she placed the stylus back into its holder. She had attempted to compare the voice on the phone with the man standing behind her, but it was a futile task. While the accent was similar, it was too difficult to make a correlation between the two. The unsub had kept his voice low in a hoarse whisper.

"And Cyrus was okay with that?"

"I went over there a little bit ago. He only had a couple of oil changes lined up. After that, he was going to spend time working on Mrs. Freier's Cadillac." Jake stepped even closer, and Brook detected the smell of used motor oil. While he might have said he'd simply stopped by the garage, he must have done something there to warrant such a strong odor. "What room are they in, Aunt Audrey? I'll take up their luggage."

"I gave them the four bedrooms that we had remodeled last summer."

There was a tightness in Audrey's tone that Brook couldn't quite put her finger on.

Brook wouldn't allow a moment of opportunity to pass, though.

"Thank you so much for your help," Brook said as she finally turned to get a better look at Jake. He wasn't as tall as she'd been expecting, though he was rather wide through the shoulders. She pegged him to be in his mid-to-late twenties. He was dressed in jeans, a t-shirt that had a stain near the waist, and bunch of keys hooked to one of his belt loops. "Mr.?"

"Hudson." He nodded before picking up the two suitcases. He hadn't bothered with the wheels. "Jake Hudson, ma'am."

Sylvie had immediately spun around when Audrey had addressed Jake. She'd closed the distance and was now standing next to Brook.

"When you're done showing them to their rooms, would you please go out back and see if you can't fix the pushbutton on the fire-pit?" Audrey asked in a way that signified it wasn't necessarily a question. "I couldn't get it to light last night."

"I'll get right on it." Jake had answered, but his focus was on Sylvie. "Follow me, please."

Jake turned, the bags apparently weighing nothing to him, and led the way toward the wide staircase. The dark wood of the railing appeared to have been polished recently, giving it a freshly waxed sheen. There was a paisley runner that had been installed with precision. Brook had to wonder how Audrey felt about her nephew wearing dusty boots throughout the B&B. While the dirty soles were dry, it would still leave tracks across the pristine carpet.

"I take it you two are with the private firm that the governor brought in to help with Lisa's case?"

Brook hadn't pegged Jake as the talkative type. She nodded toward Sylvie, giving her the go ahead to respond. Jake had directed his question to her, anyway.

CHAPTER EIGHT

"Yes, we're with S&E Investigations, Inc. We're a private consulting firm out of D.C." By this time, they were halfway up the staircase. The wooden railing wrapped around and lined a long hallway that eventually veered to the left. The second story rooms could be seen from the lower level through the wooden spindles. Each of the doors had a gold number attached to the hard surface. "Did you know Lisa Gervase?"

"Everyone in town knew Lisa." Jake had stepped on the landing and continued following the railing. "There is a memorial planned for her tomorrow night at the high school. A lot of the kids are pretty torn up over her death."

This was the first that Brook was hearing about a memorial service.

"Lisa's daughter is ten years old, correct?" Sylvie asked, having also caught the oddity of such a memorial. The church or a community center having one would have made much more sense, but the high school? "Did Lisa have something to do with the public school system? I wasn't aware that she had a job."

"Lisa tutored quite a few seniors in calculus. She was close to her students, even attending a lot of the football games to show her support for the players who needed her help." Jake motioned toward the last four rooms that overlooked the main entrance of the house. "Here you go. Aunt Audrey had these rooms redone last summer. I'll be around today, so let me know if there's anything you need brought up to your rooms."

Brook glanced down to the main area, noticing that Audrey was still behind the counter. She quickly directed her focus to the hand towel that she'd thrown over her shoulder, but she hadn't been quick enough to avert her attention.

For some reason, she'd been monitoring her nephew.

"We appreciate your hospitality," Sylvie replied with a smile.

"Oh, dinner is buffet style. Aunt Audrey always has the meal set up by seven o'clock in the evening. She takes things down around nine o'clock." Jack had also snuck a brief glimpse toward the main level. He then shook his head when Brook would have reached into her purse for a tip. "We're not one of those fancy places in the city, ma'am. I appreciate the offer, though."

Brook nodded her understanding, all the while suspecting that Jake would have taken the proffered money if his aunt hadn't been keeping an eye on him.

Brook looked down at the wooden leaf attached to her key. She was in room three, whereas Sylvie was in room four. They each used their respective keys to open their designated rooms. Neither one of them made a move to unlock their doors until Jake was a good twenty feet away.

Once inside, the first thing to hit Brook was the sweet fragrance of wildflowers that had been put into a vase next to the mirror. It wasn't an artificial aroma, either. The ambrosial scent had been building up in the room from the vase full of fresh cut wildflowers positioned on top of the triple dresser. The room was just as beautiful as the rest of the house, accommodating a four-poster bed made from oak with matching furniture.

Brook deposited her suitcase next to the large armoire.

She would unpack later this evening, but right now, she wanted to be at the station when Theo and Bit arrived with all of their equipment. Before meeting Sylvie out in the hallway, she took a moment to pull out the electronic tablet from her leather bag. It took her mere seconds to power it on, access the software that would give her immediate search results on an individual, and type in Jake's name. While the results produced were merely surface details, she would then request a more in-depth background on the young man, including NCIC and a federal records check.

Jake Earl Hudson.

Twenty-seven-year-old male, single, no children, and on parole for third degree burglary.

He'd served three of the five-year jail term, being released for good behavior and some time served while awaiting his sentence.

No wonder his aunt kept a close eye on him around her guests.

"Ready?"

"Yes," Brook murmured as she went ahead and put in her request for a full background check of Hudson. It could take a day or two, but she would be emailed the results. The service they used collected information from many sources, and it would give her a better insight into Jake Hudson. "Let's go to the station."

Brook had slid her tablet back into her bag before latching the front. She usually didn't go around running background checks on every single individual who she ran into during an investigation, but males in their late thirties or early forties were the exception to the rule on this case.

Granted, Jake was in his late twenties, but there was always the slightest chance that she was off by five years or so. Rare when it came to her profiles. Actually, she'd never been wrong on the approximate age, but there was always a first for everything.

She truly believed that the unsub had never killed anyone before last week.

Lisa Gervase had been the unsub's first foray into living out his sick fantasies, and he'd finally gotten to get a small taste of what would surely be more to come if he wasn't stopped dead in his tracks.

Chapter Nine

Theo Neville
May 2022
Thursday — 10:08am

While the town of Stillwater, West Virginia had an endearing aspect to it, the close-knit ambiance brought back unpleasant memories for Theo. He could sense the hostility from the two deputies who probably should have been out patrolling the community of around twelve thousand people by now. He figured their shifts had begun around eight o'clock or so, and it was already two hours 'til noon. Neither one of them looked to be going anywhere soon.

"You don't like small towns, Big T?" Bit asked, plugging in some of the components that he'd brought in with him. Theo didn't question all the equipment that their tech genius had to have on this trip, and yet a part of him thought that maybe Bit had gone a little bit overboard. "My sister always wanted to move to a place like this, far away from the hustle and bustle. I couldn't do it, though. Not a chance. The only reason that I have survived to this point is food delivery, and the last fast-food restaurant that I saw on the way here was at least twenty-some miles away near the highway. Do you know how fast fries go cold? Minutes. And what do these people do at three o'clock in the morning when the want a pizza delivered?"

"I don't have anything against small towns," Theo replied, sipping a cup of coffee that he'd gotten from the small break room. It tasted like mud, but it would do until he could hit the diner across the street. Small town diners always had great coffee. Unfortunately, the bitter liquid in his cup wasn't the only thing leaving a bad taste in his mouth. "Bad memories, I guess."

The sheriff had permitted them to set up in his office, which just so happened to be the largest room in the station. Bit had been all excited that there was a window on the south-facing wall. He'd mentioned something about the angle of takeoff for the SatCom rig that he'd hooked up immediately after he'd plugged in his uninterruptible power supply system. It had been as heavy to carry as a box full of bricks. It also had rows of power outlets to distribute monitored power to the two six-foot-tall racks of equipment that he'd erected in the corner of the room, opposite the sheriff's desk. Since the sheriff had already been given a heads up that they were coming at the request of the governor, he'd cleared his stuff out yesterday, emptied his desk, and pulled in some extra chairs and a smaller desk from the bullpen. While the sheriff might be accommodating, his deputies were anything but.

At least the south-facing window was looking out over Main Street, giving Theo a chance to monitor the behavior of the residents. Bit had opened the window and strung out a black cable to a weird antenna that he'd fastened to the nearest upright post. He'd done a half-dozen equations, punched in their GPS coordinates, and determined exactly how he'd wanted to point the black angular contraption at the sky. Afterwards, he'd announced with some amount of self-congratulatory satisfaction that he'd had energy on the channel.

Bit had then started to hook up one box to the other, connecting a series of completely unmarked cables to various connections in what appeared to be a completely random order.

CHAPTER NINE

Theo had stayed out of his way, although he had been able to take up a position looking out over the street. Those sitting inside the window of the diner had been staring his way for the past five minutes. Bit's odd black satellite antenna must have looked like aliens had landed and taken over the sheriff's office. There were also two teens who probably should have been in school hanging out in the alley a block down, leaning up against the side of an antique store.

"Ah, fuck, man." Bit finally straightened, almost losing his knit cap in the process. Theo had asked about them once. Turned out Bit's sister had learned to knit while she'd been going through chemotherapy. His hats were the first items that she'd completed, followed shortly by a pair of matching gloves to each color. Theo had no choice but to stop giving Bit crap about them. Family was family. Cancer was heinous. "This was the kind of small town that you...ah...you know."

Bit had pointed to his own eye, but his meaning had been clear.

"Yeah, something like that." Theo shrugged, having turned away from the window after deciding to take a walk. "The last place was more like a ghost town. This town, well, they are clearly thriving here."

"Did you see the large ice cream factory on the way in?" Bit asked, shifting some equipment around on the second table beside him that he'd confiscated from the bullpen. "I'm sure that place employs over seventy percent of the population here. Did you see how many vehicles were in the parking lot? Chances are they have two shifts and a maintenance shift, so that means—"

"All set?" Brook had been out in the main bullpen, talking to the sheriff about escorting some of the team to the crime scene. It was no longer roped off, and chances were that everyone and their mother had tromped through the area by now looking for clues, but Brook still wanted to get a feel for the place. Bit and Sylvie would remain behind, while Theo joined Brook. She had also wanted to discuss Lisa Gervase's tutoring sessions with some of the high school students. Brook wanted a list of names so that they could interview the students to see if there was a possibility that Lisa had inadvertently mentioned something that could help move the investigation forward. "Theo, we leave in five."

"That gives me time to do something," Theo replied as he set his cup of coffee down on the windowsill. "I'll be back."

Brook didn't even bother to ask where he was going, and he appreciated her trust.

Hell, if it hadn't been for her quick reactions last year, he would have lost more than his right eye.

After everything that went down, the FBI had required that he pass a psychiatric evaluation to return to desk duty. Desk duty, as if his mental wellbeing needed to be tiptop shape to shuffle some damned paperwork around. He hadn't joined the FBI to be in data entry. It wasn't that he had anything against therapy. Quite the opposite, because he'd taken away some valuable advice during those few brief sessions that he'd been mandated to attend. It was simply unfortunate that he'd all but been forced to leave behind a career that he'd pursued since childhood.

This case, this town...well, it all took him back to the time when he'd been at his lowest. It was all much too familiar and far too soon after finally settling in at S&E Investigations.

He'd accepted the tragic events that had led up to this moment, and this investigation was his chance to prove to himself that he'd emotionally healed from the entirely random circumstance that he'd fallen victim to and the damage inflicted upon him. S&E Investigations had come through for him when he'd believed that there was no path forward. Brook had delivered. He no longer needed to hide in the background, and he certainly wouldn't allow a psychological barrier to define him.

The warmth hit him as he opened the door, giving Sylvie a wave to indicate that he'd be back soon. She flashed him a smile as she made her way back to their temporary office space. Bit had asked that she obtain the station's modem and router information so that he could deconflict his settings from theirs.

Theo waited for two vehicles to drive past before he crossed the road. He sported a pair of khakis and a dark green dress shirt. He'd already unbuttoned the cuffs and rolled up his

CHAPTER NINE

sleeves. Warmer weather was called for today, which meant storms on the horizon. The humidity was already rising by the minute. Right now, the sky was clear of any clouds. For such a beautiful day, it was hard to believe that someone who had severely tortured and brutally murdered a woman was walking around without a care in the world.

Theo felt the weight of the stares from those inside the diner.

Without glancing in their direction, he continued down the sidewalk with one goal in mind.

"Hey," Theo greeted the two teenage boys. Upon a closer inspection, they were younger than he'd originally guessed, both maybe sixteen. "I'm Theo."

Neither of them said a word.

One even backhanded the other's arm, signaling it was time for them to leave.

"You both knew Mrs. Gervase, right?" Theo asked, garnering the taller of the two boys to hesitate. "I'm with the team that the governor brought in to help solve her murder. I was hoping that you two would want to make a bit of money on the side."

His offer brought both boys up short, but Theo had known he would need something lucrative to get them talking and sharing information. While there might be major differences between a small town like this one and a bustling city where everyone minded their own business, high schools were all the same. These kids wouldn't want to openly rat on someone for fear of retaliation, and they were also leery of law enforcement leaning on their friends and family.

"Twenty bucks a day for each of you while I'm here if you let me know what you hear around town. Who is doing what, who might be saying things, all because we're here." Theo reached into his back pocket, noticing that both of their gazes fell to his weapon. Neither one of them had said a word, but he figured that would change soon enough. He pulled out two twenties, making a mental note to hit the ATM at the gas station sometime today. "First impressions?"

Theo held out the money, waiting patiently for them to take it.

"What do you want to know?"

"Anything out of the ordinary," Theo replied, folding his wallet and tucking it into the back pocket of his khakis. "I trust that you'll know the difference between useless and useful information."

"You don't know us," the older boy replied skeptically. His cynicism didn't stop him from pocketing the twenty-dollar bill. "How do you know that we won't just take your money?"

Theo might have regretted how his career as a field agent had come to an end, but there had been priceless tradeoffs. Working side by side with Brook for the past six months had given him experience that he never would have had the privilege to learn otherwise. She'd had no choice but to keep her cards close to her chest due to her past, but her talent of reading others was beyond the pale. Her ability to do so was the reason she was so good at profiling people.

He'd watched, learned, and picked up a few new tricks himself.

"You care about finding justice for Mrs. Gervase," Theo pointed out, slipping his hands into his pockets. He kept his posture relaxed so that they wouldn't be as tense. "Otherwise, you wouldn't risk being seen in an alleyway near the diner when the two of you should be in class. How well did you know her?"

"She's my aunt," the older boy responded cautiously. He narrowed his eyes at Theo. "You already knew that."

"Your red hair gave you away."

"Here. Take back your money."

"Keep it. I'm serious about my offer." Theo could respect the kid's choice. "You are close to the situation, and you have a personal stake in the matter. We're also going to need all the help we can get if we want to catch the bastard who killed your aunt. I can't learn in five days what has taken you sixteen years to understand. You know the locals, and who is doing what. I need to know what you know."

The younger boy had remained silent this entire time, but he was nodding his approval so that his friend would take Theo up on his offer.

"I'm Devin. This is Brody."

"Well, Devin, I'm truly sorry for your loss." Theo held out his hand. "I never promise an outcome on a case, but I can give my word that we will do everything possible to find who—"

"My uncle did it," Devin replied fiercely, dropping his arm back to his side. His cheeks had become almost as red as his hair. "I know he did, and I can help prove it."

Chapter Ten

Brooklyn Sloane
May 2022
Thursday — 10:31am

"He's a sixteen-year-old boy, and he's looking for someone to blame," Brook replied after Theo had finished explaining the details of what had transpired before they'd left the station. "He's angry. He's watching his mother grieve over her sister, and he's feeling helpless. He's basically targeting someone who he feels threatened by."

They were in one of the SUVs, following close behind the sheriff's car. Bit had placed a ruggedized laptop in each rental vehicle. They both had cellular and SatCom access back to the local server that he'd set up in the sheriff's office. Each would act as a Wi-Fi hotspot for all the team's digital devices.

The sheriff had been astonishingly helpful throughout the morning. It was more than evident that he wanted no part of this investigation now that he'd been proven wrong about the victim simply desiring some space from her husband and family. Sheriff Kennard also made his thoughts clear on Mr. Gervase's guilt, just as Devin had with Theo.

John Gervase owned the only real estate company in town. He and his family had planted their roots three generations ago. According to the list of property owners in the area that Bit had provided the team this morning, the Gervases owned a minimum of fifty percent of the buildings along Main Street. One piece of land that they did not own was the property the ice cream factory had set up business on back in the 1970s.

"That's odd. The sheriff is pulling off the main road already," Theo pointed out, pressing the handle to activate his turn signal. "We can't be even a half mile away from Main Street."

Brook reached into her purse and pulled out her sunglasses. She unfolded the frame while surveying their surroundings. The dirt road seemed to lead to nowhere, but it might be an important factor to discover what was beyond their destination, which was the primary crime scene.

"What else did Devin say about his uncle?" Brook asked, hoping to get more insight into the Gervase family. "I had Sylvie stay back at the station to set up some interviews with the family. It will be good to have some insight into their dynamics before we speak with them."

"Apparently, Devin said the reason his aunt tutored students in calculus was due to her husband not giving her discretionary funds. For all intents and purposes, John Gervase is one overtly controlling son of a bitch. He couldn't give a damn who knew it, either."

"Bit was pulling their financials when we left the station, not that I believe that the husband is our guilty party. If her murder had been about money, he would have taken her hiking and pushed her off one of the local cliffs."

Her statement had Theo doing a double take, turning his head far enough to stare at her with his left eye. Brook shrugged, having read about such a case in the paper. She'd gotten into the habit of searching any and all murders committed throughout the country. It was how she'd tracked Jacob before, and she was hoping to do so again.

While she still believed that her brother was staying locally in the city and keeping tabs on her, he would eventually either make a move or get bored that she traveled so often out of the

CHAPTER TEN

area. He wouldn't be able to go too long with getting his fix. He'd reach out for some unfortunate soul.

"I know you haven't finished your profile, but can you provide me with a couple bulletin points before we walk the crime scene?"

"Caucasian male, late thirties. Competitive. He has a severe inferiority complex, which he hides extremely well. It manifests as him becoming an overachiever. He's been able to smother his urges to kill his entire life. I believe he went through the motions...school, college, job, marriage, and possibly even children. Something made him snap."

Brook and the team had combed through the autopsy report on the flight in this morning. The unsub had piled little mounds of thermite compound on specific parts of the victim's body. He then used some type of torch—probably a culinary butane torch—to ignite those areas.

"The unsub wasn't only making a statement when he seared away the victim's flesh. He might have started with her left ring finger, but he almost certainly experienced a sexual high upon hearing her screams. As he moved onto her breasts, she probably passed out from the shock."

"It's why he had her for so long," Theo murmured in disgust. "Sick bastard."

"I'm thinking he also had her for so long due to his schedule. Each call placed to me was roughly after four o'clock in the afternoon. He has a job that requires him to work during the day. Maybe even some type of family obligation in the evening. He took his time when burning the victim's skin to basically ash." Brook had gone over the timeline multiple times since the governor had called, courtesy of Graham. She pushed her resentment aside. "Like I said, there's a good chance that the unsub is married or was at one time."

"I was hoping that I'd heard wrong. Married? How could—"

"We're here," Brook said moments before the sheriff pressed on his brakes. She motioned up ahead at the trees. The area was remote, giving the unsub all the time in the world to pose his victim. "Those pine trees were in the footage with Sarah Evanston. Speaking of which, I'd like you to question her. Bit couldn't find one email or text to or from her accounts that contained any information regarding the case or me. He said that he was turning his focus to those apps that make messages harder to trace."

"How did Bit access—never mind," Theo muttered, shaking his head in disbelief. "He's the reason we're all going to be behind bars one of these days."

Brook hadn't had the urge to smile so much in the past fifteen or so years as she had in the past six months. A part of her longed to laugh with the team as if she didn't have a care in the world, but that would be a lie. As Theo pulled somewhat off the dirt path behind the sheriff's patrol car, it still didn't leave much room for another vehicle to pass.

"Looks like someone has been waiting for our arrival," Brook stated as she placed her hand on the door handle. Detective Turner hadn't even bothered to pull off to the side of the dirt road. As a matter of fact, he'd done a half U-turn, allowing him to lean up against the back door of his car while facing their direction. "Is that..."

The detective had the driver's side door of his unmarked patrol car opened, revealing a large male subject sitting in the passenger seat of the vehicle.

"Detective," Sheriff Kennard replied as he stepped out of his patrol car. There didn't seem to be any animosity between the two men. "I see you got my text."

"Am I missing something?" Brook asked tersely, unable to walk the crime scene the way she'd wanted to upon arrival. "I'll be completely honest, gentlemen. I don't like surprises."

She had thought it odd that Detective Turner hadn't been at the station upon the team's arrival, but he'd stated numerous times that he had other cases, court appearances, and several interviews lined up. He was a busy man, and she respected his ability to juggle such a schedule.

"Let's just say that after my interrogation of John Gervase this past Monday, I probably wouldn't receive a favorable welcome in town right now." Detective Turner held a cigarette in his left hand as held out his right. While his hair was charcoal black,

CHAPTER TEN

his five o'clock shadow had a hint of silver. "Call me Stan. You must be the infamous Brooklyn Sloane."

Brook sized him up, coming to the conclusion that he wanted people to underestimate him. He tried to come across that he didn't care too much about his cases, but it was quite the opposite. She'd heard the frustration in his voice when they'd spoken on the phone last weekend. She was still curious about who the male subject was in the passenger seat.

"I would be disappointed in your investigative skills if you didn't know that I was Brooklyn Sloane, especially since you looked me up online." Brook shook his hand before introducing Theo. "This is my colleague, Theo Neville. What's the real reason that you didn't make an appearance at the station? I'm assuming it has to do with the individual sitting in your car?"

Sheriff Kennard coughed in unease before walking a few steps away.

"Nathan," Detective Turner called out, waiting to continue until a somewhat nefarious individual opened the passenger side door and unfolded his large frame. He was fair-skinned, had long brown hair, and his beard could have used a trim. He also sported numerous tattoos and a hoop through his right eyebrow. "Nathan Klein runs our narcotics division."

Everything was screaming inside of Brook that this murder had nothing to do with drugs.

"Give us five minutes before you fill us in with your theory," Brook requested as she began to walk around the trunk of Turner's vehicle. He sure as hell didn't look like a Stan. "Theo?"

"Wait." Nathan had taken steps to meet her halfway from his side of the unmarked patrol car. "It's not what you think. No one involved in this case has anything to do with any of my ongoing investigations. I happened to be tailing someone to a drop site around three weeks ago. Let's just say that he took the scenic route, which happened to pass through Stillwater."

Brook studied Nathan before stepping back and returning to her previous spot in front of Turner. She'd always been very focused and detailed in her profiles, and she didn't have time for farfetched theories that only muddied the facts. After reading over the autopsy and comprehending just how much suffering Lisa Gervase had undergone in the last two weeks of her life, Brook would have staked her life on the fact that this investigation had nothing to do with drugs.

"Your target has a lover in the area."

"And?"

"I was in the parking lot of the bar, last row in the back." By this time, Nathan had walked all the way around the car. He then held out a file that he'd been carrying in his hand. "I was taking pictures of the subject as he entered the establishment. You'll be interested to see who was sitting inside an SUV one row in front of me."

Brook took the file and opened it.

Several photographs were inside of Lisa Gervase sitting in the passenger seat of a black SUV. The pictures had been blown up, but the driver's face couldn't be seen from the angle Nathan had in his car. Lisa had been leaning toward the male subject, which was why her side profile could be seen so clearly.

"Was this the night that she went missing?" Theo asked as he stood next to Brook. He must have seen that there was no date stamped in the corner of the photo. Brook slowly went through the rest of the pictures, stopping when one contained the back of the vehicle. "Shit."

There was no license plate.

"That was actually a couple of days before your victim went missing. I didn't realize right away that was even Turner's victim until Monday. Something about the victim stood out, but I couldn't place it until I had the photos processed. I didn't think anything of it at the time. A woman sitting in a vehicle with a man outside a bar? Pretty common. I figured they were either using or screwing, so I snapped a few shots and went back to my surveillance. She was inside the SUV for maybe fifteen or twenty minutes. She then got out, and the vehicle pulled away. I was keeping an eye on the front door of the bar, so I couldn't even tell you what direction she went, if she walked, or if she got into another vehicle. I'm not sure that these are going to help you, but it gives you some insight into her life. She was clearly doing something shady in the parking lot of that bar."

CHAPTER TEN

Nathan pulled out his cell phone and glanced at the display. He then addressed Turner.

"We need to go. You need to drop me off at my car before anyone notices that I'm gone."

Brook didn't ask where that location might be, but she appreciated that Nathan had been willing to meet with them. These photographs helped to have insight into the victim's life, as well as her behavior in the days leading up to her abduction.

"I'll meet you at the station later today?" Detective Turner had turned his statement into a question, prompting Brook to nod her agreement. "Sheriff."

Sheriff Kennard nodded from his place over by the road. He had been chewing on a toothpick, but he removed it from in between his lips.

"Ms. Sloane, I'll show you where the body was found. Follow me."

Theo indicated that he wanted a closer look at the pictures, so she handed him the file. They both then walked to the side of the road so that Turner could leave the way they'd driven in. Brook caught the way Nathan had slid down in his seat so as not to be spotted once they hit Main Street.

"How well do you know Detective Turner, Sheriff?"

"Met him for the first time last week in this very spot. Seems solid enough." The sheriff lifted the toothpick back up to his mouth. "I really thought the husband had something to do with it. While I'm not one of John's biggest fans, all signs pointed to him. John and Lisa even had a huge argument regarding her tutoring so late into the evenings, and it was overheard by numerous people the night before she went missing. Anyway, once I saw her body, I had a change of heart. No one I know would have ever been able to do...that. Anyway, we simply don't have the resources for a crime scene of that nature, which was why I called in the state police. To be honest, I'm relieved that you're here. The feds should be involved, too. What I saw was..."

The sheriff had swallowed hard, as if his mind would forever be stained with those images.

He'd be right.

Where he'd gone wrong was in his belief that he didn't know someone capable of such reprehensible acts.

"Who found the body?"

"Two young girls, picking leaves out for some biology project they were working on. Shame. To have their innocence ripped away like that is sickening. The governor filled me in on you and your team's former connections to the FBI. I also know who you are, Ms. Sloane. I get why you consulted with the FBI for so many years, and I understand your need to want to see monsters like the one we're dealing with get his due. I just want to say that I'm glad you're here. I wouldn't have the first idea on where to start."

Brook didn't bother to correct the sheriff's assumption that she'd consulted with the FBI on her brother's case. That had been the conjecture of the public ever since her relationship with Jacob had been ousted by the agent in charge of his case. She hadn't bothered to go on record to state the opposite, even during an interview that she'd given to a popular journalist at the beginning of the year.

"Did they immediately call their parents when they found the body?"

"Yes." The sheriff finally came to a stop where the ground had basically been trampled. Foot traffic had compressed and shifted the dirt and rocks along the path. He pointed ahead. "Little Morgan lives a little ways up from here, and the family uses this access road. This town lives and breathes due to the ice cream plant, but there are quite a few farms that are still operating in the outlying areas. The Solanos are farmers, and they own property on the opposite side of town, too. This path is basically for their tractors after some of the local folks complained that they were a traffic liability on the country-paved roads."

Brook stood where Lisa Gervase's body had been left behind. She doubted the girls were who the unsub had wanted to stumble across the victim's remains, so why leave her here?

What was so important about this area?

"I take it that tree line over there separates this area from one of the town's neighborhoods?"

CHAPTER TEN

"You could say that," Sheriff Kennard replied, once again removing his toothpick. He pointed with it toward the tall pine trees. "The developer back in the seventies thought that the ice cream factory was going to be built on this land. Never happened. The Boyles ended up purchasing the property a half mile out of town, much to irritation of the Gervases. Their bid was turned down by the previous owner."

"Are the Solanos the only ones who use this dirt road?" Theo asked, shading his eyes as he surveyed the area. His line of thinking correlated with hers. "Why leave the body for them to find?"

"The Solano family's tractors are what packed this ground down, but a few of the locals use it for shortcuts. The ice cream factory rotates three shifts, and the second shift coincides with when school lets out. I wouldn't say everyone uses it, but it's common practice to drive on this road, especially after a good rain. Let's just say that there are times that the locals get impatient."

"Can you provide us a list of those who might use it more than the others?" Theo inquired right as his cell phone rang. "Excuse me."

He took a few steps away to answer the call, leaving Brook alone with Sheriff Kennard.

"Which way was the body facing?"

"East."

"Clothed?"

"No." The sheriff cleared his throat, still holding onto his toothpick. "There really wasn't a need. There was nothing left of her private areas. I mean, her chest area was nearly burned in half. That stuff practically burned clear through her body."

"Eyes open or closed?"

"Open. Ms. Sloane, why are you asking me these questions when I know damn well that you've seen the crime scene photos?"

"Forensics didn't arrive for two hours and sixteen minutes from the time you reached out to the state police." Brook had seen enough, and she began to walk back toward their vehicles. "You stated that Morgan Solano and her friend called their parents while basically running for home. Mr. Solano called you immediately, and statements line up that you were then on scene shortly thereafter. I need to make sure that everything you saw upon first arriving was the same images in those photographs that were taken by the crime scene techs."

Sheriff Kennard nodded his understanding, following up with his plans for the rest of the day. She had assumed that he hadn't viewed the crime scene photos that had been provided to him by state forensics. He was too close to the families involved, and in his mind, he'd already seen enough. He'd handed off the responsibility of the investigation to Detective Turner.

"I'll head back to the station and look them over. You know the way back."

Sheriff Kennard would probably be found at the local bar after his shift today. She could have told him that no amount of alcohol could bleach the images out his mind, but he'd most likely still try. He continued walking until he reached the driver's side of his patrol car. The dull brown color of the paint job was the same as his uniform. He stuck the toothpick in between his lips, removed his large hat, and settled in behind the wheel.

She waved him off as she took one last look around the area.

Desolate.

Isolated.

Quiet.

Yet the unsub had chosen this particular spot for a very specific reason.

Brook had left her cell phone in the car. She might as well wait until she was at the station to have Bit look more into the Solanos and those other families that lived along the twisting track of this secondary country road.

"We should head back to the station."

Theo had slid his cell phone into his back pocket before handing the manilla folder off to her. She'd have Bit see what he could do about enhancing them, but she already knew it would be a futile effort. There just wasn't enough to work with.

"Why? I was hoping to stop by the Gervase's family home." Brook had mapped out her day and even scheduled through the

CHAPTER TEN

sheriff a time to address his deputies. There were four—three men, one woman. Two deputies worked a twelve-hour shift, one worked a night shift, and one more rotated to give the others time off. Each of the deputies worked three days on and one day off with the rotation. The sheriff was basically on call twenty-four-seven. "We technically don't need to be at the station until four o'clock."

"Oh, you'll want to be at the station for this," Theo replied wryly as he opened the driver's side door. He addressed her over the top of the car as he rested his forearm on the roof. "Sarah Evanston and her cameraman just parked out front of the station. They're about to go live for a noon segment, and our involvement is about to be her lead story."

Chapter Eleven

Brooklyn Sloane
May 2022
Thursday — 11:19am

Brook made sure that her sunglasses were secure on the bridge of her nose before she opened her car door. The sheriff's vehicle was parked in his reserved space, indicating that he'd made it back to the station without any issues. Two patrol cars that had been in the small lot next to the building were no longer in their allotted spots. That wasn't a bad thing. It simply meant less witnesses for the upcoming confrontation.

She slung her purse over her shoulder as she slammed the door closed, keeping ahold of the manilla envelope. This was one piece of information that Sarah Evanston wouldn't be getting her hands on anytime soon. Detective Turner had mentioned on the phone with Brook yesterday that he hadn't been able to figure out who had been feeding information to the reporter. Bit loved logic puzzles such as that, and he'd been working on it since yesterday. Most likely beforehand, but she didn't want to know the specifics.

As Brook and Theo rounded the corner of the station, Sarah Evanston had readied herself to pounce. Seeing as it probably wasn't time for a live segment, the cameraman was already recording a possible piece to add into the afternoon newscast. While Brook wasn't a big believer in fate, she was appreciative of when events began to go her way...such as another media van pulling up in front of the diner across the street.

"Ms. Evanston, unless you'd like to be the topic of your competitor's upcoming broadcast, I suggest you tell your cameraman to stop recording and follow me inside," Brook stated as she brushed past the woman. "Or not. I couldn't care less one way or another. I'll be happy to conduct my interview with you out here in the open."

Neither the reporter nor the cameraman had expected such a response from Brook, which gave her the initiative. Theo wasn't far behind, and he managed to reach out for the door handle to the station by the time Brook turned around for her answer. As if she'd orchestrated the arrival herself, the other news crew was doing everything they could to make it across the street before Brook gave any kind of formal statement to one of their rivals.

"The choice is yours."

"Dean." Sarah briefly shook her head, giving him permission to cut his feed. "I'll be right back."

Sarah had handed off her microphone before trailing after Brook. There wasn't a strand of her chestnut hair out of place, and her makeup had been applied perfectly. As a matter of fact, Brook would have sworn on her life that the reporter had used some type of airbrush for her foundation.

No one had such flawless skin.

"Wise decision, Ms. Evanston."

The station was relatively quiet with the exception of a dispatcher, who seemed to be on a personal call rather than a resident with a problem. The sheriff had explained this morning that most of their calls came through a 911 center thirty minutes away. Those within town knew that they could call the station's number for mundane matters, such as drunk and disorderly at the local pub or a cat up a tree.

Brook silently alerted Theo that she'd like him to question the cameraman before leading Sarah to a desk that wasn't in use. It wouldn't be wise for her to see the murder board that Sylvie had

CHAPTER ELEVEN 97

almost certainly begun assembling in the sheriff's office while they'd been gone.

"Have a seat, please. I'll be with you in a moment."

Brook noticed that the sheriff was using the corner desk, going through the photographs. He barely glanced her way. She assumed the pictures were of the crime scene, as she'd requested. She would know soon if anything had been touched from the time he'd arrived on scene until the moment the forensics team stepped foot in Stillwater.

"Bit, would you please try to enhance these and see if there is anything of use on them?" Brook asked quietly as she handed off the file. She took off her sunglasses and shoved them inside her purse before hanging the strap from one of the chairs, noticing that Sylvie had been reading something over, barely registering Brook's arrival. Whatever held the analyst's interest must have been fascinating. "Oh, and you know the stretch of land where the victim's body was found? The Solano family owns the majority of a farm that runs parallel to that area, but would you pull me the names of the other property owners?"

"Sure thing, Boss."

Brook made sure the door was closed as she retraced her steps.

Sarah had taken a seat, but her frown all but screamed of her displeasure at being put in such a position. Seeing as S&E Investigations wasn't law enforcement, the reporter had no obligation to answer any of Brook's questions. The key would be how she addressed the situation. She sure as hell wasn't going to apologize for Sarah's own ignorance.

"Ms. Evanston, I'm Brooklyn Sloane."

"I know who you are," Sarah replied as she narrowed her eyes in Brook's direction. "You're Jacob Walsh's sister."

"And you are playing a very dangerous game by interfering in a murder investigation," Brook warned, taking a seat in a chair that must have belonged to the female deputy. There was no need to adjust the setting. "Do you want to call the attention of a serial killer?"

Brook's question brought Sarah up short, but it was evident she didn't believe that she'd done such a thing.

"I was merely pointing out that there could be a connection," Sarah explained, her attention being pulled from Brook when the dispatcher radioed one of the deputies. When the call was for a family dispute over a car, Sarah then refocused her attention on Brook. "You have to admit that it's odd the killer would call you."

"I'd like to know who provided you with that specific piece of information. And before you go on about protecting your sources, you should be more concerned about protecting yourself." Brook leaned forward and clasped her hands together on the desk. "This isn't a game, Ms. Evanston. A woman was tortured for two weeks before her body gave up. You should ask yourself what kind of human being can torture someone for that long and somehow enjoy each and every scream that passes her lips, because that is the individual who you are antagonizing with your suppositions. The other journalists are reporting the facts as they know them, and yet you are purposefully instigating a killer. Do you have a death wish?"

"My viewers have the right to know if they are in danger," Sarah countered, as if she was doing them a personal service. "It was only a fair assumption that the killer reaching out to you was, in fact, your very own brother."

Brook loathed obtuse people, and Sarah was one of them.

Brook decided to try another tactic.

"Has Lisa Gervase's killer reached out to you?"

"What?" Sarah seemed taken aback by Brook's question. So much so, Brook was confident in her previous assumption that her source wasn't their unsub. "No. Look, I'm not telling you who my source is, and I don't appreciate the way you railroaded me into believing that—"

Bit chose that moment to open the office door. They'd closed the blinds, not wanting anyone from the public to inadvertently set eyes on anything related to the case. He closed the door before walking over to them and handing off a piece of paper to Brook. Oddly enough, he remained in place, as if waiting for an answer. Brook quickly read the information, comprehending the severity of what he'd uncovered so far.

CHAPTER ELEVEN

"Would you please inform Sheriff Kennard?" Brook asked, ensuring that her tone remained even. Bit had managed to figure out what application Sarah had been using to contact her source. "I'll speak with Detective Turner myself later this afternoon."

Sarah's interest in what was on the piece of paper was evident, and she monitored Bit's progression across the station. Brook sat back and allowed Sarah to take in the sheriff's response. It didn't take long before the reporter became a bit uneasy upon witnessing Sheriff Kennard's angry outburst.

"Gail, pull Rogers into the station. Now!"

"How long have you been seeing Lionel Rogers, Sarah?"

"I don't know what you're talking about," Sarah denied, straightening her shoulders.

She was wearing a light green blouse to match her eyes, which were now filled with concern. While she'd been diligent in her quest to keep her relationship with the deputy a secret, Lionel had been quite lax in keeping the app open on his cell phone. Although there had been the slightest chance that their unsub had contacted Sarah, it was a relief to know that Brook's profile was still on point.

Detective Turner had received a warrant to comb through the deputies' cell phones for evidence. The warrant must have been signed when Brook had been at the crime scene. It hadn't taken Bit long at all to find the connection.

"You care for him." Brook hadn't expected Sarah to react in such a manner, but it didn't change a thing. Lionel Rogers would likely lose his job, and Sarah would no longer be able to obstruct the investigation. "You should have thought of his employment prospects before entertaining that job offer in New York."

"Lionel didn't tell me anything," Sarah quickly denied, shifting in her seat as she put one hand on the desk. Brook had already pushed back her chair to signal that their talk was over. "I swear to you, Lionel had nothing to do with me receiving that information. An anonymous source called into the station. They left a voicemail."

"Do you still have it?" Brook asked, inclined to believe her. There was a desperation to her that couldn't be faked, but Sarah

Evanston was damn good at her job. Otherwise, she wouldn't have had offers for two major media outlets. "Do you still have the voicemail?"

Sarah hesitated with her reply, giving Brook her answer.

They both stood at the same time.

"I swear to you that Lionel had nothing to do with this," Sarah said as Brook walked around the desk. "You have to believe me. Don't let Lionel lose his job because of his connection to me."

"I'm here to solve Lisa Gervase's murder, Ms. Evanston. Anything that happens as a result of your irresponsible broadcasts rests on your shoulders."

Brook began to walk back to the office. Bit hadn't stuck around after putting the sheriff in a worse mood than before, and he was already holding the door open. She waited until they were both inside before making her request.

"Is there a way to retrieve deleted voicemails?" Brook asked, immediately regretting her question. Of course, there was a way to retrieve deleted voicemails. Bit always made it seem that there was a way around everything. "Sarah Evanston claims that Deputy Rogers wasn't the one who gave her the information. Did you see anything in their text messages to prove her wrong?"

"No, but they meet up at least three times a week," Bit shared as he took a seat in front of three monitors. Why he'd needed to bring three of them was beyond her, but she wouldn't haggle over something so tedious. "I'm sure that they talked before...you know."

Bit had glanced at Sylvie, who was still reading over whatever it was that had captured her interest.

"There was something about her denial that has me believing Lionel Rogers might not be her source. Ms. Evanston claims that someone called into the station and left her a voicemail message. Can you try to retrieve it? I'm sure that the warrant included her work line, as well. Let's see if she's telling the truth."

"On it, Boss."

"Sylvie?" Brook walked over to where Sylvie now had several papers strewn across a desk that had been set up near the far wall. It served as a double workstation for someone able to sit on the other side. "What did you find?"

CHAPTER ELEVEN

Sylvie finally sat back in her chair with a smile.

She'd found something of significance, and that meant they were about to make headway in their investigation.

"Lisa Gervase had cut back on the amount of money that she was depositing from her tutoring sessions into the joint account that she held with her husband," Sylvie shared with a sense of satisfaction. "Once a week for the past two years, she never missed making a deposit for around the same amount. The last six months? She only deposited around sixty percent of her usual revenue stream. She was hoarding cash, Brook."

Brook picked up one of the bank statements, scanning over the deposits. Sylvie had highlighted each one, making a note in the margin of the diminished amount. Granted, their victim could have had fewer students in her schedule. Seniors graduated, and sometimes students didn't need tutoring services after having grasped the subject. On the other hand, Lisa had been secretly meeting someone in the parking lot of the local pub.

To have an affair?

Or better yet, to leave town?

"Lisa Gervase was going to leave her husband."

Chapter Twelve

Brooklyn Sloane
May 2022
Thursday — 3:41pm

"Are there any questions on the profile?" Brook asked as she twisted the cap back onto her water bottle. She paused long enough for Sheriff Kennard, Detective Turner, and the other three deputies to inquire about the profile that she'd spent the past few hours polishing for the debriefing. Two state police officers who would be patrolling the area from this point forward had joined them, as well. "Moving onto new leads in the investigation, it has come to our attention that Lisa Gervase was possibly paying someone to provide her with fake identification documents. We have proof that she met someone in the parking lot of the local pub. Black SUV. No plates. It would seem that the victim was working up the courage to leave her husband."

"And you still believe that John didn't kill her?"

The question had come from one of the deputies. Jennifer Rhamon, mid-thirties, single mom, and very outspoken. Her expression alone told of her bias in the case.

"Detective Turner interviewed Mr. Gervase a few days ago." Brook wasn't stating anything that these deputies and officers didn't already know, but it always benefited to start from the beginning. "During that interview, Mr. Gervase provided a solid alibi for the date and time that the victim was abducted from Main Street."

Since the office that Brook and her team had basically confiscated was too small to host such a debriefing, they were all in the bullpen of the station. It was good to have Gail, the dispatcher, hear what was being said during the course of the meeting. While she only worked first shift, she had received calls from residents who had so-called tips.

In all likelihood, none of calls had or would pan out, but it was well-documented that other cases had been solved on less obvious leads.

"I understand that you're not from around here, but the Gervase family has money," Jennifer replied as she garnered nods of agreement from the other two deputies. Lionel wasn't in attendance. He'd been suspended upon further investigation into the potential leak of crucial information in an open case. "John could have paid someone to kill her."

Jennifer was showing her lack of insight and professionalism, but Brook wouldn't bite.

"A professional hired to murder a spouse would have handled the situation quickly and efficiently," Theo said from his position beside Brook.

He was using a desk as leverage, half sitting while Bit sat in a chair on the other side.

Sylvie was also in attendance, though she was quietly scrolling through social media accounts of the night that Lisa Gervase had been photographed in the parking lot of the pub. Brook didn't doubt that Sylvie heard every word that was being said.

"Lisa Gervase was abducted and tortured for two weeks before her body gave out. That was done by someone who enjoyed what he was doing, and he prolonged her torture for his own pleasure. Make no mistake that the unsub would have preferred to have more time with her."

Jennifer lost a bit of color in her face, but Theo's explanation had been enough to get his point across.

CHAPTER TWELVE

"I'm aware from speaking with Sheriff Kennard that John Gervase is controlling, manipulative, and cunning. While Mr. and Mrs. Gervase put a show on for the town, no one can completely hide that type of marriage from onlookers. She most likely told her sister, a friend, or even someone from her church that was contemplating such drastic measures. Unfortunately, those three traits don't mean that he killed his wife. We are still waiting on DNA from the lab. What we do know is that the area where the victim's body was discovered was not where she was tortured and killed."

Brook spent time giving a rundown on how S&E Investigations would proceed from this point forward.

"Theo will be speaking with Mr. Gervase and his children, I'll be conducting interviews with the victim's sister and her family, while Sylvie and Bit remain here at the station to go through the vast amount of evidence, reports, and statements provided to us by Detective Turner. He's done an outstanding job thus far, and he'll be essential in compiling the case and apprehending the unsub."

Brook had a chance over lunch to look over what he'd provided the team, and she hadn't been exaggerating her praise. Detective Turner might come across as indifferent every now and then, but he took his responsibilities seriously. He'd crossed every T and dotted every I, even going above and beyond with his highly detailed paperwork. Nothing had been missed that she could see at first glance, and his ability to read situations and think outside the box had her wanting him by her side during the upcoming interviews.

The insight of a local detective might prove key to breaking the case.

"What about the note that was found on the body?" Jennifer asked as she rested her hand on her utility belt. "Has anything come from that?"

"The unsub wore latex gloves," Detective Turner replied as he cracked his knuckles. "Our lab technician believes the killer used his non-dominant hand to write the note so that we wouldn't be able to compare it to other handwriting samples that we might obtain from any given suspect."

"Sheriff Kennard has reached out to the high school," Brook continued as she monitored each and every one of their reactions. Five of these individuals had personal ties to the community. "They provided us with a list of students who had been receiving tutoring sessions from the victim. The principal is reaching out to the parents to obtain their permission for me and Theo to speak with their children. We'll be driving over to the school first thing in the morning."

"We've given you a list of the students' names. If you notice that anyone is missing from the list, please let us know," Theo directed, holding up a sheet that Bit had printed out earlier. "While the Gervases are comparatively wealthy, the victim didn't want her husband to know that she was saving a sum of money on the side. It's most likely the reason she wanted to begin tutoring students to begin with, which means she had been planning to leave for some time. Bud, you said that your wife is a teacher at the high school. Would she be willing to meet with us before the first bell tomorrow? We need some background questions answered."

"Sure," Bud Wright replied, his eagerness to learn and help was in contrast to the other two deputies. He was the youngest of the three in attendance, and his desire to gain some experience was evident. "Anything to help out. Addy is six months pregnant. Needless to say, the news of what happened to Mrs. Gervase has my wife stressed out."

"Getting back to this black SUV, are you really suggesting that Lisa Gervase wanted to buy fake IDs for her and her children? If so, maybe something went wrong during the transaction." Fred Braun rubbed the side of his face in skepticism. "I mean, this whole talk of a serial killer in the making just seems a bit too farfetched. I grew up in this town. Trust me, I don't know one person who could have done something like that to anyone."

Brook wasn't going to waste time debating facts.

No one wanted to believe that someone they personally knew could carry out such horrific torment of another human being.

"I agree," Jennifer said, backing up her fellow deputy. "A culinary blowtorch? Thermite? And in those private areas? No. No, I don't believe it. If we're going with your theory, it's

CHAPTER TWELVE 107

someone from out of town. A drifter of some sort. He'd be long gone."

"Has anyone moved into town recently?" Brook inquired, already knowing the answer to her question. Bit had already pulled recent residential purchases and rental agreements, and the majority of the sales had been local residents moving into either larger or smaller houses. "Has anyone reported someone strange in the area? Any odd altercations of any sort?"

"Not that we know of, but the ice cream factory has interstate truck drivers coming and going at all hours of the day and night," Fred replied, attempting to solidify his theory. "Have you checked into them?"

"We are in contact with the Boyle family, as well as the management at the factory. They are using a non-union trucking company to handle their deliveries," Theo replied, having taken lead on that front, as well. He'd already given the long list to Sylvie, so that she could sort through the data and compartmentalize individuals against Brook's profile. "That goes for any delivery drivers to any of the local shops, though a lot of them use the standard services, such as UPS or FedEx. Most of those are regular route drivers, but we aren't ruling anyone out."

"Getting back to the black SUV, I'd like for all of you to keep an eye out for it during your patrols. Look for paper tags in the window or new plate registrations with brand new tags." Brook then gave details on the make and model, clarifying that the vehicle had no plates at the time that it was recorded. Whoever had been driving was either good at covering his tracks or the vehicle had been a recent purchase. Granted, whoever had been behind the wheel could have been the victim's lover, but all signs pointed to an illegal transaction. "It's doubtful that the male subject selling the victim fake IDs would make another appearance, especially given the coverage of the victim's murder. With that said, we can assume that he has done business in this part of the state before. The victim got her contact's name from someone, and it would be beneficial to the case if we had an opportunity to question him."

Brook paused, waiting to see if there were any more questions.

The two state patrol troopers had been quiet, but they were used to aiding their fellow officers in unique investigations such as this one. State police troopers also benefitted from a great deal more training. They understood interagency protocol, and they would keep their presence known to provide a sense of security to the locals, as well as report anything suspicious to dispatch.

"Detective Turner? Is there anything that you would like to add?"

"Yes." The detective had been leaning against the far wall near where Sheriff Kennard had set up his temporary workstation. He straightened his stance, slipping both of his hands into his light brown slacks. "This is one sick son of a bitch. In all my years working homicide, I've never seen anything like I witnessed last week. The same goes for Sheriff Kennard, which was why he'd originally reached out to the FBI. Unfortunately, they aren't going to take a single homicide, no matter the suggestive details or physical provocations that we're dealing with right now. Ms. Sloane and most of her team have the experience that we all lack, so I suggest you trust their opinions and follow their leads."

In that moment, Detective Turner had garnered Theo's respect. Brook could tell from the way he nodded his appreciation, and the same went for Sylvie. It was a nice change to have a camaraderie with law enforcement agencies instead of having to chip away at the institutional barrier that was usually in between them.

"Detective?" Brook caught his attention as she began to walk back toward the office. Bit had already beat her to it. He was already in his chair and checking the results of some of the national database searches that he'd submitted earlier in the day. He'd also been in contact with the news station to see if he could access their system to retrieve the so-called deleted voicemail that Sarah Evanston stated she'd received last week. "We all appreciate the support that you displayed to them."

CHAPTER TWELVE

"It's the truth." Detective Turner pulled out the chair next to Bit, who barely even registered the movement. "I'd really prefer it if you'd call me Stan, though."

"Fine. Stan it is." Brook figured it was the least she could do in return for his endorsement on S&E Investigations' credentials. "As I stated out there at the beginning of the debriefing, I believe that the unsub figured out the victim's plan. For some reason, he mentally had her on a pedestal of some sort. Until the evidence contradicts our theory, we'll stick to it for now. From what Deputy Rhamon shared out there, it was common knowledge that Mr. Gervase was—"

"A complete jackass." Stan smiled as he crossed his right ankle across his left knee. "Trust me, she's right as rain on that account. He's a condescending asshole to just about everyone in this town. Doesn't mean that I don't feel for him. I think in his own way, he loved his wife."

Sylvie had chosen that moment to walk into the office. Her arched brow at Stan's commentary had him holding up his hands in surrender.

"I'm not defending the man, by any means. I'm simply stating facts." Stan lowered his hands and linked his fingers together, resting them behind his head. "Something doesn't add up with the victim wanting to buy fake IDs, though. Her sister lives here, she had a solid group of friends, the support from her church...I don't know. Something feels off about it."

"I agree," Sylvie replied as she walked over to the desk. She moved aside some papers and sat on the hard surface, using the chair to prop up her feet. Her blonde hair was contained in a bun, as was her usual style. "If the victim was really going to leave her husband, she would have told someone. And why not simply divorce his ass?"

"That person would have most likely been her sister," Brook pointed out as she stared at the murder board that Sylvie had put together.

The victim's picture had been positioned on the left-hand side with a magnet. The right-hand portion of the whiteboard that they had brought with them contained one of the photographs that Nathan Klein had provided them. Toward the bottom were facts that had been learned during the case.

They were basically at ground zero, but that was how all investigations started out.

"Stan and I will drive over there a little before six o'clock, but I'm going to visit the family's church in a few minutes. I'd like to speak with the pastor."

"I'll join you," Stan announced before turning to look at the numerous monitors that Bit had strategically positioned on the table in front of him. "Hey, is there a way to go back and see the movements of the victim's cell phone a week leading up to her death? I got to thinking earlier this morning that she might have gone somewhere or met with someone else. If we had some locations, we could split up and see if anything comes of it. I put in a request for the information earlier this week, but I haven't received the results from—"

Bit silently reached in front of Stan to press a key on another keyboard. The display changed to show a map of cellphone towers, along with a list of incoming and outgoing numbers on the bottom of the screen.

"The victim didn't leave town, and there was nothing unusual about her call history." Bit continued to work on the monitor in front of him while tacking on more details. "She was abducted in front of the dry cleaners right around closing time, and her phone was found in her car, along with her purse."

Stan shifted his gaze from the display to Bit and then back again. He finally focused his attention of Brook. The printer started spitting out a hardcopy of the phone data for the detective.

"Well, shit." There was a spark of curiosity in his brown eyes. "No wonder you quit the feds and went into private practice."

"No," Brook responded to the objective that had just filtered through his mind.

She grabbed the printout and handed it to the detective.

"No, what?" Stan asked, the left side of his mouth upturned in a half grin. "I didn't ask anything yet."

"You didn't have to." Brook gathered her sunglasses and purse, making sure that her cell phone was tucked into the side pocket.

"You're as easy to read as the back of a cereal box. You're not using Bit to look into your other cases."

"Is she always like this?" Stan murmured underneath his breath, knowing full well that she could hear him.

"Trust me," Bit replied, never once tearing his gaze from the monitor in front of him. "You don't want to get on Boss' bad side."

"Duly noted." Stan took the piece of paper and folded it in half. He slid it into the interior pocket of his suit jacket before pulling out a pack of cigarettes. His addiction was going to be the death of him, but Brook wasn't the man's keeper. He would probably have one smoked and another lit before they even made it to the church, which was literally one block away. "Shall we?"

Stan waited for her to go ahead of him, but she hadn't made it to the door before it opened and revealed Theo.

"He's on the phone."

He meant their unsub.

Brook immediately sought out the black and white clock hanging on the wall behind her.

Sure enough, it was now after four o'clock.

The unsub was very regimented, confirming her original suspicion that he had to abide by a schedule. Was it because of a job? Was this the time when his wife left the house? Could she be picking up the children, leaving her husband alone in the house to make his call?

"Bit?"

"You're good to go."

"Gail, what line?" Theo asked over his shoulder.

"Four."

Brook set down her purse and sunglasses before walking over to where Bit had positioned the sheriff's desk phone on the edge of the table holding all three monitors. She cleared her throat, going through numerous scenarios on how she should handle the unsub. Now that she and her team were in close proximity to him, there was no telling what he would do if she upset him.

S&E Investigations' involvement changed the trajectory of her stance.

She pressed the designated button next to one of the flashing lights, leaving the receiver in its cradle. The speakerphone was now active.

"Sloane."

Brook wasn't going to answer the call as if this was her personal cell phone and he was a long-lost friend. She'd ensure that her replies were professional, concise, as well as do her best to keep him on the line. If history repeated itself, as it often did, he was using a burner phone that he could easily throw away. This call would only be beneficial if she could get the unsub to inadvertently reveal something about himself.

"You came to play."

"I've already told you that I don't play games," Brook replied before pressing her hands against the side of the table. "Why don't you make this easy on yourself? Turn yourself in at the station. You wouldn't have called me all the way in D.C. if you didn't want me to stop you. Isn't that what you want?"

The unsub's breathing became somewhat labored upon hearing her inquiry.

"You don't like what you've done to that poor woman, but you can't take it back." Brook noticed that Stan had reclaimed his seat as quietly as possible. His intense gaze was focused solely on the phone, as was Sheriff Kennard's scrutiny as he stood behind Theo. The others were observing her, waiting for anything that she might want or need in the heat of the moment. "You're torn, and that's okay. Come into the station, and—"

"Did you notice that the press gave me a name? Clever, too. They *see* me. And so will you."

Brook pressed her lips together in agitation, already knowing that he was going to disconnect their call.

The media was a double-edged sword. There were times that they could assist during investigations like these, and other times they were nothing more than a hindrance.

"The call pinged off the tower to the east of town, but I couldn't get an exact location from where the call originated from."

The cell phone tower east of town covered a lot of area.

CHAPTER TWELVE

"You said that the perp had an inferiority complex." Stan ran his fingers through his hair as he finally sat back in his chair. They'd all been on edge during the call, and his adrenaline was still pumping through his veins. "Damn, if you weren't right."

"Sheriff?" Brook pushed off the table so that she could focus on the one person who might have been able to recognize the unsub's voice. "Can you identify him? Was there anything familiar about his tone? Accent? The way he spoke?"

"No," Sheriff Kennard replied as he leaned against the doorframe. "Nothing. He spoke too low...too raspy."

"East of town is where the victim's body was found," Sylvie pointed out. She held up some papers that she'd grabbed from the station's printer that was positioned on the far desk. "I'll start combing through the property owners, see if anyone stands out who had a connection with the victim."

Sylvie was onto something, because there was a reason the unsub had chosen that particular area to leave the victim's body. Once they figured out the significance, maybe then everything else would fall into place.

Chapter Thirteen

Brooklyn Sloane
May 2022
Thursday — 4:57pm

"Is it always like this?"

Brook didn't bother to look over her shoulder at the two media crews that were filming them walk through the parking lot. They'd driven Stan's unmarked police cruiser instead of walking the two blocks for just that reason. The less anyone said to the reporters, the better.

The Culinary Killer?

It was lazy reporting, at best.

Such a moniker also fed into their unsub's ego, which wasn't the best thing to do at this stage in the investigation.

"Not on cold cases." Brook had made sure to learn the press' nickname for their unsub before leaving the station. The media had all but given him everything he'd ever wanted—recognition. "They'll soon see that we're simply doing legwork and leave. There are two rooms reserved at the inn for the local press, which are Sarah Evanston and her cameraman. The others are staying at the motel near the underpass of the highway. If nothing happens within the next twenty-four hours, most of them will be pulled away for other stories."

One thing Brook had noticed as they had pulled into the parking lot was Jake Hudson. He'd been clipping some of the bushes out front in the inn when he'd caught sight of the press. In turn, he'd noticed that Stan and Brook were in an unmarked vehicle. No doubt, he was also keeping close tabs on them as they walked up to the tall, wooden, church doors.

Stan's cell phone rang before they could walk inside.

They both paused, giving him a moment to see if the call was important enough to answer.

"I've got to take this. I'm sorry."

"I'll get started," Brook informed him, lifting her sunglasses up so that they pulled her hair away from her face. Stan wasn't the only one who needed a trim. Her own black strands hadn't seen scissors in at least four months. Her lack of commitment to any given hair stylist was the reason that she kept her hair long and layered, allowing her to go extended lengths of time without a scheduled appointment. "Join me when you can."

Brook pulled on the heavy door. As she crossed over the threshold, the first thing that hit her was the musky odor of wet, rotting timbers. The roof must have had a leak at one point in the past. She remained where she was while her eyes adjusted to the dim lighting of the interior foyer. She honestly couldn't remember the last time that she'd set foot in an old rural church like this one.

Fifteen years ago?

Maybe sixteen?

No, that wasn't quite right.

Brook had once attempted to seek solace in her college chapel in the months following her roommate's death.

Cara Jordan.

The young girl had been carefree, optimistic, and full of life. She had been enjoying every single moment of her senior year before Jacob had come to check on his baby sister.

The rest was history.

CHAPTER THIRTEEN

As much as Brook had wanted to find peace within the walls of her tiny college chapel, she'd left the university with nothing but pent-up anger and a burning need for retribution.

Nothing had changed since, no matter how much she had longed for peace.

As with anytime that Cara crossed through Brook's thoughts, her stomach tightened, and she became short of breath as her airway constricted. Now wasn't the time to get sidetracked.

The silence of the church was as stifling as the mildewed air. There was an elderly woman sitting in the front pew, a couple talking quietly with another woman near the altar, and someone up above in the loft area moving about. Brook could make out an old pipe organ through the wooden spindles.

She stayed in the back for a few moments, taking in her surroundings.

The church must have been nearly as old as the town. The stained-glass windows gave off a rather spiritual aura as they allowed streams of colored sunlight to blanket the dark wood of the oak pews. The canvasses on the wall had faded from the exposure to the warm rays, though the woodwork had been polished recently with Murphy's Oil Soap.

The unsub had done his best to fit into this town, which meant there was a chance that he'd attended sermons in this very church as he mimicked the understanding of the lessons that the pastor had been trying to impart upon his parishioners. The unsub had sought acceptance his entire life, displaying emotions that he most certainly didn't inhabit. What better place to receive such affirmation than from God and his disciples?

If only the unsub understood what it was to be repentant.

The couple who had been engaged in a private conversation with the second woman began to walk up the long aisle. Brook's presence had clearly caught them off-guard, and they stared at her with mild, awkward interest.

She sensed the exact moment when they recognized her.

Everyone knew that the sheriff had handed off Lisa Gervase's case to the state police, who in turn supposedly asked the governor to bring in an outside investigation firm. Little did they know that the state police hadn't requested any such thing, but the residents of Stillwater had been kept apprised of most everything else through Sarah Evanston.

Brook wasn't completely sure if the reporter would continue her coverage now that she'd managed to get a deputy suspended from his duties. If not, another journalist would be stepping into the woman's high-heeled shoes within a few days.

Whispers began to drift toward Brook, and she assumed that the man who had entered from a door to the right of the altar was the pastor. He'd stopped to speak with the other woman, who was currently glancing back in Brook's direction. There was no point in having him walk all the way to the back of the church when she was about to request of him that they take their conversation to a more appropriate and private setting.

It wouldn't do to have their discussion overheard by one of his parishioners.

Word would race through town like wildfire.

"Pastor Wilson?" Brook asked quietly as she came to a stop before the couple. They were of the same age, maybe late thirties or early forties. The way the woman's hand rested on his arm, along with their matching wedding rings, was a dead giveaway that they were married. "My name is Brook Sloane. My firm is in town at the request of the governor to help with the Lisa Gervase case, and I'd like to ask you a few questions concerning her, if you have a moment."

"Of course," Pastor Wilson replied, glancing toward the front pew at the elderly woman who wore a scarf overtop her grey hair. "We can speak privately in my office."

Pastor Wilson put his hand on his wife's lower back as he guided her toward the door that he'd previously passed through. Brook glanced over her shoulder, but there was no sign of Stan.

It appeared that she would be conducting this interview alone.

They were on a time limit due to their scheduled meeting with Lisa Gervase's sister, and Brook wanted to get as much accomplished today as possible.

"This is my wife, Julie." Pastor Wilson motioned toward one of the guest chairs in front of his desk. "Please, have a seat. We were devastated to hear about Lisa. She was an important part

CHAPTER THIRTEEN

of our parish. She sang with our church choir every Sunday, and she even volunteered with some of the other younger parishioners in our daycare about once a month."

"What can we do to help?" Julie asked as she took a seat in the second guest chair. She was who Brook would consider the perfect pastor's wife. She wore a powder blue suit with a white ruffled blouse. Her dark blonde hair was swept up in a clip, though she'd taken time to curl the tendrils that had been sprayed in place against her cheekbones. "We are so worried about Aiden and Madison."

Brook found it somewhat odd that they hadn't asked her if the police were close to catching the killer. It was usually one of the first questions asked in these types of interviews, but this couple also had a sterling reputation to uphold. That stature involved providing solace to those left behind and counseling faith to those who became lost. One could not do so if they were seen to be talking out of line or failing to keep the confidence of their congregation.

"Did Lisa ever come to either of you with concerns about her safety or that of her children?" Brook asked, getting right to the heart of the topic.

She had her answer the moment Julie's eyes flickered toward her husband.

"Lisa struggled with her marriage," Pastor Wilson replied, only sitting in his chair behind the desk after Brook had taken her own seat. She set her purse on the floor to the left of the chair before making herself comfortable and crossing her legs. The more relaxed she appeared, the greater the chance the Wilsons would take her cue. Placing a barrier between them wasn't in keeping with that objective, thus why she'd set her purse to the left. "We were merely a sounding board. We helped where we could, offered her solid guidance as determined by the church, and lent an ear when she needed someone to confide in. The key word being *confide*. We can't discuss specifics."

"And when she confided in you, did she tell you that she was planning on leaving her husband?"

"It was an option that she was considering," Pastor Wilson shared with a frown. "The last we spoke, she hadn't made a definitive decision one way or another. She was worried about maintaining custody of her children. We kept her confidence, of course."

Brook noticed the way Julie had clasped her hands together during her husband's responses.

"Did Lisa talk about her students?"

Brook had purposefully changed her line of questioning. She didn't want to focus too much on John Gervase. While he factored into the situation, she was fairly confident that he wasn't their unsub. His movements had almost certainly been scrutinized since the moment his wife had disappeared, which meant he wouldn't have had the required amount of unsupervised time to torture his wife for almost two weeks.

"I know Lisa tutored students in calculus. Was she close to any of them?"

"Lisa loved all her students. She was vested in them," Julie said, even though her knuckles were still white. "Most were juniors and seniors at the high school, but she also extended her tutoring services to those wanting to better their future."

"How so?"

"Jake Hudson, for one. After some poor decisions, he decided to turn his life around," Julie explained, garnering her husband's agreement.

"That's right. Jake dropped out of high school and then ran into some trouble with the wrong crowd. He recently made the decision to finish his GED, and Lisa agreed to help him study for the state test next month."

"Oscar sat in on those sessions, too," Julie shared, as if it was common knowledge.

Brook found it interesting that Julie was so open to sharing the names of those who might be involved, especially after the pastor had placed such an importance on being the town's confidants.

"Oscar?"

"Oscar Riviera. He's a custodian at the high school. He's going for his GED, also," Julie said with a genuine smile. "He's come so far, and we are so proud of him. The state sends a proctor on the second Saturday of every month if there are students signed up

CHAPTER THIRTEEN 121

to attend the session. Military recruiters arrange for the ASVAB to be given over at the same classroom at the high school on alternating Saturdays."

"We have several outreach programs here at the church," Pastor Wilson explained, motioning toward a bulletin board that Brook had already scanned before she'd taken her seat. There seemed to be a meeting scheduled every evening here at the church, from AA to grief counseling for lost loved ones. "Jake and Oscar both attend one of our outreach programs every Tuesday night."

"And Lisa offered her tutoring services to this group?" Brook inquired as she encouraged the direction this course of questioning had taken. "Was that her suggestion or yours?"

"Ours, of course."

"Would you mind if I took one of the brochures for that specific program? I'll also need a list of names of those who attend those Tuesday evening groups." Brook immediately sensed the pastor's reluctance to hand over such sensitive information. "Please. I can have Detective Turner obtain a warrant, if need be, but I'm hoping it won't come to that."

"These men...they are trying to turn their lives around," Pastor Wilson explained with reluctance. "They do not deserve to be harassed by the police simply because Lisa crossed their paths or they received help from her at some point."

"I'm not the police, Pastor Wilson," Brook reassured him. "I'll be discreet with my inquiries. It's not my intention to cause trouble for anyone seeking help. My goal is to bring justice for Mrs. Gervase and some semblance of peace to her family."

"Very well." Pastor Wilson opened the bottom drawer of his desk, searching through some files. "I keep the sign-up sheets for each group. Here is a month's worth of attendees."

Pastor Wilson handed Brook the papers across the desk while he searched his bulletin board. He frowned when he couldn't locate the brochure that advertised Jake and Oscar's outreach program.

"Julie, would you please—"

"Julie, what can you tell me about choir?" Brook asked, intentionally interrupting the pastor's request. His wife was withholding something, but her behavior indicated that she wasn't comfortable with her husband's presence while being questioned. "Do all the women get along?"

"You're not suggesting that a woman could have done those awful things to Lisa, are you?" Julie asked in disbelief.

"No, no," Brook reassured her, though she'd seen her fair of women commit horrendous crimes. "I was just wondering if Lisa was close to anyone in the choir. Someone who she might have confided in? As much as church can be a safe haven, some women will only disclose their most closely held secrets with those in similar situations. Let's face it. Everyone seemed to know how Mr. Gervase treated his wife, yet everyone looked the other direction. His influence over this town caused most people to turn their heads."

While Brook had been addressing Julie, Pastor Wilson had muttered underneath his breath that he would go and collect the brochure that she'd requested, leaving the two women alone.

"If Lisa confided in anyone, it would have been her sister," Julie divulged, appearing quite uncomfortable now that her husband had left his office.

"And do you believe that Lisa would tell her sister that you were the one to give her the name of an individual from who she could acquire fake IDs?" Brook asked, having put two and two together the moment Julie had brought up Jake and Oscar. "I have no reason to tell your husband, Julie, but I do need to know who you put her into contact with who had the ability to do something of that nature."

"I didn't—" Julie had raised her tone upon voicing her denial. She gripped the arm of the chair as she searched the doorway for her husband. "I didn't give any such information. I overheard her speaking with Oscar, that's all. He's a good man. I don't want him to get in trouble for trying to help someone, either."

"What did you overhear, Julie?" Brook asked quietly, wanting more details so that she could follow up with Oscar Riviera.

"Around a month ago, Lisa had come to the church to tutor Jake and Oscar. After their session, Jake returned to the group, but Oscar stayed out in the hallway with Lisa. I was coming

CHAPTER THIRTEEN

back with some cookies that we always put out for the group attendees. I overheard her ask if he knew of anyone who could give her four fake identifications." Julie glanced nervously toward the door. "If my husband thought for a second that anyone in the group was committing a crime or falling back into their old ways, he would put an end to the group. Those men need our help, Ms. Sloane."

"Four?"

"Yes," Julie responded, sitting back when she heard the sound of her husband returning down the hallway. "Please, don't—"

"It's good to know that Lisa was close to her sister," Brook replied smoothly as Pastor Wilson walked back into his office. "I'm meeting with her and her family this evening. I'm sure that they can help provide insight into Mrs. Gervase's life."

"Here is the brochure that we hand out to those who want to turn their lives around." Pastor Wilson didn't reclaim his seat. Instead, he remained standing to impress upon her that he'd like this meeting to end. Brook had mostly gotten what she'd come for, and she would be having Sylvie and Bit conduct a more intrusive background check into the pastor and his wife. "I simply ask for you to be discreet in your questioning of them. Most live in the trailer park on the outskirts of town. We're the closest church to host these types of group meetings. Of course, Jake lives with his aunt across the street."

"Who runs this particular group?" Brook asked as she picked up her purse and stood from the chair.

"I do, as a matter of fact," Pastor Wilson admitted, gesturing toward the papers in her hand. "As my wife said earlier, these men need guidance. I can offer them that."

"You and your wife keep referring to men. Are there no women in this particular outreach group?"

"No, but we did have a couple of women join last year. They had the support of their families, so they didn't need to be with the group for long. Both are doing well and maintain fulltime jobs, the last I heard."

"Well, I appreciate you taking time to speak with me." Brook shook both of their hands, not reacting when Julie squeezed tight in her appreciation for Brook's discretion. "Have a good evening."

Brook was already halfway down the aisle of the church when the front doors opened, revealing Stan. Upon catching sight of her, he halted his advancement near the last pew. There was no need for him to come any farther into the church when she'd already concluded her meeting.

"I'm sorry about that," Stan replied with disappointment. "The court hearing that I'm involved with is dragging on longer than the prosecution originally thought. I'm being recalled to the stand first thing tomorrow morning."

"I understand," Brook replied softly as they fell in step with one another. She didn't want her voice to carry even though the elderly woman was no longer sitting in the front pew. "I was able to find another lead that we should follow up on, not that I think we've found our unsub yet."

Brook went into more detail about the information that Julie had offered regarding Oscar Riviera. Brook then spread the papers that the pastor had given her onto the hood of Stan's car, taking pictures so that she could send them to Bit. She then handed the list of names over to Stan, shoving the group's brochure into her purse.

"These are the sign-up sheets for the past month or two. Can you ask around the station about those included, maybe see if anyone stands out? The support group is meant for ex-convicts attempting to turn their lives around. If anyone is to be questioned from those lists, you and I will be the ones to assign the interviews." Brook opened her car door as Stan walked around to his side, already folding the papers to store inside his vehicle. "Mr. Riviera is a custodian at the school, so I can't imagine his rap sheet being too serious. I'll wait until tomorrow to speak with him, though. I don't want him to have any advance warning that we know about his connection to Lisa."

Stan waited until he was settled in behind the wheel to finish their conversation.

"Do you think Riviera is our perp?"

CHAPTER THIRTEEN

"Doubtful, but we should give consideration to everyone on the board." Brook could sense the weight of Stan's gaze. She'd already discounted the husband. While that was true, she didn't want to box herself into a corner, either. "If Oscar Riviera was helping our victim, there might be a chance that she said something or that he noticed something unusual during their meetings. There was one thing that stuck out to me when talking with Julie Wilson, though."

"What's that?"

Brook rolled down the window after he'd started the engine. His cigarette habit had infiltrated the fabric of his suit. In close quarters, he reeked like a used ashtray.

"When Julie overheard the private conversation between our victim and Oscar Riviera, Lisa mentioned four identifications, not three. Lisa Gervase planned on taking someone else with her." Brook took a deep breath of the clean air, preferring the pleasant fragrance of lilac over stale ash. "Let's see what the victim's sister has to say."

Brook already had the phone pressed to her ear.

Bit picked up on the first ring.

"I have a few names that I want you to run through NCIC and our standard background checks," Brook said as she noticed Julie Wilson walk out the front doors of the church. She had a set of car keys in her hand. "Oscar Riviera, Pastor Kevin Wilson, and his wife—Julie. Something is off about them."

"Pastor Wilson? Hold on, Boss."

Brook could hear Bit discussing something with Sylvie, and it was not long before she took the phone from him.

"Brook? Pastor Wilson and his wife Julie are one of the eight owners of properties that run parallel to the dirt road where the victim's body was found. Bit has already initiated background checks on all eight property owners."

"Good work," Brook murmured, wondering if there really was a connection between the Wilsons and the victim. Small towns like this had connections everywhere, and it was easy to get led down the wrong proverbial path. "Call me if you find any other red flags."

CHAPTER FOURTEEN

Brooklyn Sloane
May 2022
Thursday — 6:01pm

THE MODEST HOME OF Ron and Patty Lincoln reminded Brook of her own childhood home.

The two-story house was nestled in a quiet neighborhood with full-grown trees, manicured lawns, and family porches that were no longer used the way they were in the old days. There was a pink bike with matching tassels hanging from the handlebars abandoned in the front yard, as if long forgotten by a young girl. A basketball hoop with part of the net unfastened from its rim was positioned above the garage door, which just so happened to be opened at the moment. Inside the two-car garage was a minivan and a midlevel sedan.

The entire scene could have been from Hollywood set of a family movie.

"Patty Lincoln is the older of the two sisters," Brook murmured as she walked side by side with Stan on their way to the front door. The wood had been painted a beautiful blue that complemented the exterior color of the house, framed by white accent shutters. The Lincolns took care of their property. "Patty works at the public library. Her husband, Ron, is an insurance agent with a local agency. They have two children—Devin and Lily."

"Devin is the one who Theo ran into this morning, right?"

"Yes," Brook replied as they stepped up onto the small porch. There was a glider swing in the corner that looked as if it hadn't been used in years. Families grew up, their daily lives became busy, and those fleeting moments that had once been enjoyed were put on the backburner until retirement. "Not that we're going to divulge that piece of information to his parents. I doubt that he'd want them to know he was skipping school today. Devin was pretty adamant that his uncle had something to do with his aunt's murder."

"And you're not," Stan said as he pressed the doorbell.

Brook didn't have the need to cover her reasoning again, so she remained silent as she waited for someone to answer the door. Besides, Stan was the one who had thoroughly vetted John Gervase's alibi.

Brook had removed her sunglasses that she'd been using to hold her hair back and placed them inside her purse before she'd gotten out of the car. The sun wouldn't set for another couple of hours, but some clouds had begun to move in recently.

There would be rain falling sometime tonight.

The familiar scent hung in the air.

"You must be Brook Sloane," a woman with red hair asked after she'd opened the door. There was no screen door, so Brook and Stan were able to walk right in without having to open a secondary barrier for pests. "I'm Patty Lincoln. Detective, I wish I could say it was good to see you again, but..."

Patty's voice caught in her throat. She was still emotional over losing her sister, which was completely understandable. There were bags of exhaustion underneath her eyes. Brook waited until Patty had closed the door behind them before shaking the woman's hand.

"Please, call me Brook," she said as Patty gestured ahead of them.

"Ron is in the kitchen making some coffee. Or tea. I'm not sure which."

CHAPTER FOURTEEN

Patty led the way through a small foyer entrance, once again reminding Brook of her own childhood home. The living room was directly to the right and a staircase was on the left in a short hallway, which led toward the back of the house.

Brook slowed her pace down to survey the heart of the Lincoln's home.

A Barbie doll, clothes, and a house were spread out on the carpet. The sound on the television was barely perceptible, and the furniture hadn't seen a dust rag in a few weeks. Most likely since the day Patty's sister had gone missing. Brook noticed that a couple of framed photographs had been removed from the entryway table. Patty had almost certainly used one of them to give to the various media outlets.

The kitchen was straight ahead, and Brook caught a glimpse of the Lincoln's family over the years. Devin as a baby, their children together after Lily had been born, and a lot of precious moments in between then and now.

Instead of a dining room being located in the front of the house, it was off of the kitchen in the rear just as Brook had predicted. The smell of coffee lingered in the air, and it wasn't the sludge that the deputies made at the station, either. This aroma was a delicious dark roast of some sort.

"Ron, you remember Detective Turner," Patty said once they came to a stop in between the kitchen and the dining room. "This is Brook Sloane."

"I'm sorry that we have to meet under these circumstances," Brook replied, having used that opening many times in the last six months. Not so much throughout her career though, given how rare it had been for her to meet the families of the victims. "Although I do appreciate the two of you taking time out to meet with me."

"Please, have a seat," Ron said as he came to stand by his wife. "I made coffee if either of you would like some."

"Yes, please."

Brook found that having something to do with their hands relaxed those being questioned, allowing them to recall details that they normally might have overlooked. Stan nodded his reply before Patty led them to the dining room table.

It took a few moments, but Ron finally joined them after doling out coffee to Brook and Stan, along with one for himself. He set a cup of hot tea down in front of Patty, though. His wife attempted to smile her appreciation, but she was too concerned about Brook's presence to give him her full attention. He was not like her younger sister's husband. Ron doted on his wife, and it was evident that she'd gotten used to his attention.

"Have you found anything?"

"My team and I just arrived this morning, Mrs. Lincoln. We're still running preliminary background searches and combing through the evidence that has been collected so far. Detective Turner has been helpful catching us up on the facts, as well as Sheriff Kennard and his deputies."

Ron shook his head as if he disagreed with the latter part of her praise. She might as well lead with that subject since he and his wife were sharing a look of agreement—or disagreement, as the case might be—upon their consensus.

"I take it that you aren't fond of Sheriff Kennard?" Brook asked, pleased that Stan allowed her to lead with the questions. Granted, he'd already interviewed them, but she appreciated his ease in which he'd handled her involvement. "I can understand your frustration with—"

"My sister was missing for two weeks," Patty stressed as she leaned forward, wrapping both of her hands around the teacup. "Two weeks wasted. It took the sheriff one week to admit that Lisa might not have run off because of some argument with John. What if we'd been able to find her? We could have—"

Ron rubbed his wife's forearm back and forth in support as she attempted to control her emotions. He appeared quite tired himself. He still had a dishtowel over his right shoulder, and Brook figured he'd been stepping up when it came to the family chores. Her father had done the same after Brook had given her statement to the police regarding Jacob. Wanting to hide away from the world after a tragedy was understandable...but it only worked for so long.

Patty had children who would look to her for guidance.

She needed to get clear of her grief before she allowed it to destroy her own family.

CHAPTER FOURTEEN

"Is it true that the killer reached out to you?" Ron asked, though Brook had a sense that the question had really come from Patty. "That reporter said—"

"I'm aware of what Sarah Evanston has been suggesting on the air, and the answer is yes." Brook didn't want the conversation to turn to her, so she'd answered as directly as possible before doing what she could to get back on topic. "I wouldn't put too much stock in Ms. Evanston's reporting, though. The most important thing we can do now is try to figure out what Lisa's state of mind was in the weeks leading up to her abduction."

Patty was still attempting to keep her emotions in check.

Brook and Stan both directed their gazes toward her husband.

"Lisa wasn't the type of mother who would leave her children behind." Ron reluctantly filled in the silence, confirming what they already knew of the victim. "We believed right away that John had done something horrible to Lisa. Those two could really get into it when they fought, but she loved him anyway. She would always go on and on about how hard he worked, and that it was her job to make sure that he didn't have any worries at home. Patty tried her best to get Lisa to file for divorce, but..."

Ron let his words trail off as Patty wiped away her tears.

"Do you still believe that he murdered Lisa?" Brook asked as she pulled her own coffee mug closer to the edge of the table.

She'd caught movement of a shadow cast from the hallway in her peripheral vision, and she assumed that it was one of the children listening in...maybe both. They were most likely hovering near the stairwell that led up to the second level of the house.

Patty had her back to the main area of the kitchen, and Ron had taken the chair next to her. Brook had taken a seat at the end of the table, leaving Stan to sit down opposite the Lincolns. Stan had a better view of the entrance from the hallway, but he didn't give any sign that he'd noticed anything unusual.

"I'm sure you already know that John had an alibi for the date and time that your sister was abducted. I'm aware that Detective Turner explained to you how she was discovered and the terrible things that were done to her body. Do you truly believe that your brother-in-law is capable of that type of behavior?"

Brook had been very careful with her words since Devin and his younger sister were eavesdropping in on their conversation.

"I don't know anymore," Patty murmured, looking down at her tea. "I just don't know."

"Patty, did Lisa say anything to you about leaving town?"

"Leaving town? What do you mean?" Patty appeared taken aback by Brook's question. "As Ron said, Lisa would never abandon her children."

"I'm talking about leaving town *with* her children."

"Of course not. She'd never do that to me. Our parents died when we were quite young. I was in my early twenties, and Lisa had just turned nineteen."

Brook was beginning to suspect that Lisa hadn't been completely honest with her sister, after all.

Patty had been genuinely taken aback by the question. If a woman didn't confide in her husband, her sister, or her friends...then all signs pointed to a confidant. Possibly a lover...and thus the need for a fourth fake ID.

Lisa Gervase *had* been having an affair, and the unsub must have discovered her dirty little secret.

"Why would you think that Lisa would leave everything behind?" Ron asked cautiously, having picked up that the question had more validity behind it than mere speculation. They weren't going to like Brook's thoughts on the subject, which was why she wasn't going to be completely honest with them. "My God, do you think that Lisa was having an affair?"

"No," Patty responded vehemently, her red curls hitting her cheeks as she shook her head with force. "No. Not my sister."

Pretty soon, the Lincolns were going to believe that Brook belonged in a snake pit beside Sheriff Kennard. Detective Turner wisely remained silent during her line of questioning. It was always beneficial for individuals involved in a case to believe that someone was on their side.

"I know this isn't pleasant, picking apart your sister's life, but know that I am only trying to figure out who could have done something so horrific," Brook explained, though she doubted

CHAPTER FOURTEEN

that her words made much progress. She attempted one more time to cover some ground. "Sisters have a special bond. I'm hoping that Lisa confided in you something that would give us a direction in her case. Had she met someone? Had her demeanor changed recently? Did she ever ask to borrow money?"

This time, it was Ron who seemed slightly uncomfortable. Patty had also caught the way his hand had tightened around the coffee mug. She stared intently at him, almost as if she was mentally begging him not to make this devastating situation worse.

"Ron?"

"I swear, I didn't think anything of it at the time. Lisa came to me about a month ago, asking if she could borrow five hundred dollars." Ron reached for his wife's hand, but she quickly pulled away from him. "Patty, I honestly didn't think anything of it."

Ron looked on helpless as Patty was still shaking her head in disbelief.

"Lisa said that she wanted to surprise John with a birthday present, and she didn't want him to see a charge on their bank statement or credit card before the date. She even asked that I not say anything to Patty, because she didn't want her sister to make a big deal of it. I mean, it made sense at the time. Patty isn't the biggest fan of John, and the two of them often got into arguments over him."

"That's because he treated her like shit," Patty defended herself as she glared at her husband. "Did you give her the money?"

Ron seemed even more distressed than before, because it was evident that he hadn't forked over the cash. Patty leaned back in her chair and crossed her arms in disappointment.

"No, but—"

"What the hell is wrong with you? And why didn't you tell me?" Patty asked accusingly, her eyes brimming with unshed tears. "I don't care that Lisa asked you not to say anything to me. You're my husband. Why didn't you give her the money?"

While Ron tried to explain that they hadn't had an extra five hundred dollars in their bank account to give Lisa, Brook didn't need someone to tell her that the money hadn't been going toward a present for John Gervase. Lisa had been saving and scraping every penny that she could in order to pay someone for four fake IDs. As for tight finances, it was typical of a middle-class family to sometimes live paycheck to paycheck.

"I would have found a way to help her," Patty muttered as she pushed her tea away in disgust. "I can't believe you."

"Wait a second." Ron might have been attempting to garner his wife's forgiveness, but he'd seen the look that Brook and Stan had shared over the revelation. "Do you think that Lisa needed the money for something else? That she was lying about getting a present for John?"

"Now you're calling my sister a liar?"

"Patty, I'm just trying to—"

"We're not sure," Brook replied smoothly, not wanting to further strain Patty's support system. It was obvious that Lisa hadn't wanted to hurt her sister, which was why the victim hadn't shared her plans with anyone. That wasn't technically true, because she *had* turned to someone for help—Oscar Riviera. Had the victim found someone else to give her the money that Ron couldn't? "Did Lisa ever talk about any of her students?"

"Not really," Patty responded with a furrowed brow after a time. She'd needed a few moments to compose herself. "She loved all her students. She supported them, went to their games, cheer squad, you name it."

"That's not true."

Ron and Patty had turned around immediately at the sound of their son's voice.

Devin had shown himself, along with his sister. She was maybe eight years old with freckles spread over the bridge of her nose and across her cheeks. She was holding onto her brother's hand as if he was her savior, and Brook's chest tightened at what could have been for her had things been different.

"What's not true?" Brook asked, clearing her throat and doing her best to concentrate on the present. "Was your aunt having trouble with a student of hers?"

CHAPTER FOURTEEN

"Aunt Lisa got into it with Reed Feltner during one of their sessions," Devin revealed, his narrowed eyes trained on Brook. "I still think my uncle killed Aunt Lisa, though."

"Devin?" Patty quickly pushed back her chair and gave her husband a glare when he would have joined her. Her emotions were running high, and she viewed his pervious silence as a betrayal. "What is this about Reed Feltner? And why didn't you mention this before now?"

"Because Reed didn't do anything wrong," Devin replied adamantly, tugging his sister closer to his side. "Uncle John did, and no one seems to care."

Brook wasn't going to push the issue. Theo had already established a trust with the teenager, so she would have Theo press a bit more on the high school student angle. Her interest was more in the daughter, who was staring at Brook with curiosity.

Technically, it was Brook's weapon that had caught the girl's attention.

"I do care, Devin." Brook adjusted her jacket so that it covered her holster as she shifted in her chair to face them. "That's why I'm here. While I can't promise you an outcome, I can give you my word that I will do everything I can to apprehend the person responsible. The thing in cases like these is that even the slightest piece of information could make a huge difference. Everyone speaks so highly of your aunt. It's clear that people adored her. We're thinking that someone noticed something out of place, like one of her students. She spent hours a day with them, so it's possible that they saw someone following her. The more we understand what happened in those last few days before your aunt was taken, the better chance we have of making an arrest."

Brook stood and walked over to where Patty was now hugging Devin, who didn't seem to want his mother's attention. He was focused on Brook, as was Lily. Stan had engaged Ron into a quiet conversation behind her.

There had not been a reason for Brook to be around a lot of children over the years, so she spoke the way she would have wanted someone to talk to her back when her life had all but been uprooted.

"Hi, Lily." Brook lowered herself until she was eye level with the young girl. "I'm really sorry about your aunt. I lost someone really close to me when I was young."

There was truth in her words.

It shouldn't matter that Brook had been eighteen when she'd discovered the body of her best friend.

A loss was a loss.

"Did you hang out with your aunt a lot?"

Lily slowly nodded her answer.

The thing about children was that adults never wanted to accept that everything they said and did was not only observed by the littles ones, but that those actions were stored away in their memories as if they were vaults.

Unfortunately, Patty was hovering over both her son and daughter.

They wouldn't speak as freely as if they would without such an audience.

Still, Brook had to try.

"May I?" Brook asked softly, hoping that Patty wasn't so overcome with grief that she couldn't see the value her daughter could add to the situation. "Please."

Patty's answer was to lead Devin over to the table where the men were still engaged in a deep conversation. Stan had picked up Brook's cue, and he hadn't hesitated to step in and give her the time she needed to carefully engage with an eight-year-old little girl. She even heard Stan inquire about Reed Feltner and what had happened during his tutoring session.

Brook motioned that she and Lily should sit down.

They moved to the far end of the kitchen, where Brook used the bottom cabinets as a back rest. She'd hoped that Lily would follow her lead. Sure enough, Lily sat cross-legged on the tile floor, subconsciously playing with her shoelaces.

"I bet your aunt was really cool."

Lily nodded once again.

"Was she the kind who would sneak you candy when your mom wasn't looking?"

Lily shrugged, still not talking the way Brook had hoped she would after a few questions.

"Wait." Brook made it seem that an idea had just come to her. "Your aunt wouldn't have been able to sneak you candy, because then your cousins would have wanted some, too."

"Aiden always tries to take my candy. Aunt Lisa would always wait for him to fall asleep before letting the rest of us have extra cookies."

"Aiden is younger than you, right?"

"He's only six." Lily made it seem that her being two years older was a huge age difference. To her, it was a monumental distinction. "He still goes to bed at eight o'clock."

"Did you spend a lot of nights over at your aunt's house?"

"Sometimes." Lily looked down at her shoelace. "Not anymore."

"When you had your sleepovers, did you ever overhear your aunt on the phone?"

Lily fell silent once again.

"Nothing you say to me will get you in trouble, Lily." Brook leaned forward and held up her pinky, hoping that such a promise was still a thing. She remembered doing the same with her brother, and she'd learned early on that pinky swears were worthless to him. She held out hope that Lily was different. "I pinky swear that I won't share what you tell me with anyone I shouldn't."

Right or wrong, Brook would do what was needed to bring Lisa Gervase justice. The only way that Brook would break such a promise was if Lily's life was in danger. Other than that, everything she said in this tight circle of theirs would remain between them.

The little girl glanced over her shoulder, and she discovered that everyone was sitting at the table and talking to her brother. Every now and then, Brook had caught Patty glancing their way, but Stan was doing an exceptional job at keeping the other family members occupied.

"Okay," Lily whispered, holding up her hand and hooking her small pinky around Brook's longer one. "Pinky swear."

Once they'd released each other, Lily leaned in to ensure that her words didn't carry into the dining room table.

Her red pigtails fell forward.

"We were all supposed to be asleep, but I was really thirsty. I found Aunt Lisa in the kitchen. She was crying."

Brook pictured in her mind the scene that Lily was describing, but without having been in the Gervase's house, she wasn't sure of the layout.

"Was your uncle with her?"

"He was asleep."

"Did you ask your aunt what was wrong?" Brook asked, leaning forward until she was able to rest her elbows on her knees. "Did you ask why she was crying?"

"No," Lily replied with a shake of her head. "Aunt Lisa was on the phone. She didn't see me, and I didn't want to get in trouble for eavesdropping. Devin says it's wrong to eavesdrop."

Lily glanced over her shoulder once more before she leaned in even closer to Brook.

"Aunt Lisa said that she didn't have a choice. She was going to leave town, with or without him."

"Without who, Lily?"

Brook tensed as she braced herself for the little girl's reply.

"Jake." Lily's eyes filled up with tears. "I didn't say anything, because I didn't think anyone would believe me."

"You mean Jake Hudson? The man who lives at the inn with his aunt?"

"See, I knew you wouldn't believe me."

"I *do* believe you, Lily." Brook had gone over the numerous ways this investigation could explode right out of the water, and Lily's secret had the potential to do just that. The ramifications of such an affair could ripple throughout a community such as this, but Brook had made a promise to a little girl that she wouldn't break. The sordid details would make themselves known in time by someone else's hand. No skeletons ever truly remained buried. "I do believe you, sweetheart."

Chapter Fifteen

Sylvie Deering
May 2022
Thursday — 10:09pm

THE LOWER LEVEL OF the B&B was quiet as Sylvie made her way back down the wide staircase. There had been so much information contained in the materials to sort through that Bit had been sending her throughout the day that she'd decided to work in the comfort of her room for a while. She'd even eaten from the buffet that Audrey had set out for the guests earlier, catching a late dinner right before the owner had begun to clean up for the evening.

Sarah Evanston and her cameraman were the other two guests. The reporter must have sprung for the additional cost to stay somewhere a little more comfortable than the motel near the underpass. Others in the media didn't have the luxury of living beyond their per diem lodging rate. Their presence was the main reason Sylvie had taken her plate up to her room.

Fortunately, Sylvie had been able to read, organize, and even discard data relevant and not relevant to the case. By tomorrow morning, she'd be able to decipher and concisely explain a more detailed look into those individuals connected to the case. She had done her best to distill information down to its most basic elements. She wasn't emotional nor conversely motivated to insert her opinion when facts were sparse. She would identify what information was on hand, ascertain shortcomings in the investigation, and offer possible avenues to pursue leads that would need further scrutiny.

Right now, what she really needed was some type of sugar rush to keep her going in order to finish at a decent enough time to grab maybe five or six hours of sleep. She usually strived for at least eight hours of solid rest, but that was all but impossible during a case such as this.

Not that she would change her role at S&E Investigations, Inc. for anything in the world.

Becoming part of a well-oiled machine...and even what someone could label a family...had most likely saved her from going down a rabbit hole after her abrupt departure from the FBI. Having her life blown apart by her father's money laundering scheme hadn't been part of her plans. While her life might have gone off the rails temporarily, she was finally on the right track in her professional life.

Her personal life was another matter altogether.

Dating apps were now completely out of the picture, for which she wasn't sorry for in the least.

"I can heat that up for you."

A piece of apple pie hadn't been the only reason that Sylvie had ventured down to the first level of the inn. Brook had phoned earlier, and it had turned out that there was a good chance Jake Hudson had been having an affair with the victim. While there had been one or two similarities between Jake Hudson and their profile, Sylvie wasn't convinced that he was their unsub.

Brook's ability to create a profile based on crime scenes was a talent unlike anything that Sylvie had ever seen in her career. Sure, she'd witnessed other profilers while at the Bureau, but never one as tuned in as Brook. Considering that Sylvie was an analyst, she also understood that there was never one hundred percent accuracy when one factored in human fallacy.

Brook came as close as anyone Sylvie had ever seen.

CHAPTER FIFTEEN

"I'd appreciate that," Sylvie replied without turning around. She'd been in the process of transferring the piece of apple pie onto a small plate. It wasn't until after she'd covered the remaining slices with the large glass cover that she turned around. "How are you holding up?"

Jake tensed at her question, but Sylvie had been monitoring the way Theo and Brook worked out in the field for the past six months. She reached back and picked up the plate as if her question hadn't contained a separate meaning.

"I can't imagine my hometown going through anything like this." Sylvie closed the distance between them, holding up her plate due to his previous offer. "Thirty seconds should be sufficient."

"Yeah, yeah," Jake said as he took her plate. She could sense that he hadn't really thought that she would take him up on his offer. There was a sign posted on the kitchen door that all guests were free to utilize the appliances, but having Jake be the one to keep busy meant that Sylvie could keep the conversation moving along. "I'll be right back."

Sylvie had every intention of following him.

It was obvious that he wanted to know if they had any leads in the case, and she could use that to her advantage.

"I mean, you *knew* Lisa." Sylvie stated, causing Jake to startle a bit. He hadn't heard her slip into the kitchen behind him. "I know the high school is hosting a memorial for her tomorrow. Will others in your support group be going?"

Jake faltered in his step as he walked over to the microwave, which had been installed above the stainless-steel stove. While he kept his back to her, she could sense that he was watching her closely through the reflection of the microwave door. She purposefully kept her posture relaxed as she leaned forward on the large butcher block. It served as an island for the kitchen, which was smaller than she would have thought given the size of the house. Still, the updated appliances ensured the kitchen was worthy of a good cook.

"Your partner was over at the church today." Jake's keys jingled as he shifted his weight. "Am I a suspect?"

"Everyone in this town is a suspect," Sylvie answered truthfully right as the microwave beeped that the time had come to an end. She wasn't ready for their conversation to be cut short, so she forged ahead in a direction that she hoped wouldn't be littered with potholes. "If you're thinking you're a suspect because of your criminal record, you would be wrong. What your support group is attempting to do is admirable. Not a lot of people get a second chance these days, and you're lucky to have a steppingstone in the right direction. Not only is everyone a suspect until we obtain more leads, everyone in this town could also be very beneficial in helping us apprehend the guilty party."

Jake remained silent as he collected her plate, closed the microwave door, and set her piece of pie down in front of her on the butcher block. He genuinely seemed to be listening to her versus just trying to leave the kitchen. She'd been holding a fork that she'd chosen from the utensil tray in the dining room, but she made no move to sink the prongs into the warm crust.

Instead, she met his gaze head on.

"I could sense earlier that you stayed home from work to see firsthand what we were like," Sylvie said softly, hoping that she was establishing a connection with him. "It's obvious that you cared for Lisa. How could you not? She was helping you study for your GED. She was helping you build a better life for yourself, and—"

"Lisa *was* my life."

It was as if the words had been torn from Jake's throat.

He turned back around so that he wasn't facing her, most likely because he didn't want her to witness his tears. He leaned the palms of his hands against the counter, hanging his head low as he grappled for composure. He might be in his late twenties, but he was still a young man who'd made a lot of bad choices. Just when he thought his life was turning around, he'd been dealt another blow.

"Were you having a sexual affair with her, Jake?"

Brook hadn't wanted to bring Jake into the station officially without first attempting to speak to him where he'd be his most comfortable. Being around a police presence while he was on parole would only put him on the defensive when what they

CHAPTER FIFTEEN 143

really needed was his cooperation. His affair with Lisa gave him insight into her true motivations which no one else had, and there was a good chance that he'd crossed paths with their unsub at some point.

"Yes." Jake wiped his nose with the back of his hand as he turned around. His dark gaze was filled with anguish. What he thought was his salvation had been brutally stripped from his life in the most heinous way imaginable. It caused Sylvie to suddenly question whether or not they should be focusing on the husband. What if this case was that one in a million where Brook got the profile completely wrong? "It wasn't just an affair, though. We loved each other deeply. Her husband is who you should be looking at, not any of us."

Us meant those in the support group.

"Jake, while I already stated that everyone is still a suspect, do you really think that I would be talking to you all alone over a piece of warm apple pie if I truly thought you murdered Lisa?"

Sylvie was grateful that there was a door between the kitchen and the dining room.

The last thing they needed was for Sarah Evanston or her cameraman overhearing a private conversation that they would no doubt splash across the front page of a newspaper. Such a headline would grab the attention of the nation, not that this case hadn't already done so in an awkward, quirky kind of fashion.

Lisa Gervase had already been labeled a doting mother of two, a faithful wife, and a pillar of her community. What would the world's opinion be of the victim once they discovered that she'd been having an affair with a younger man...and an ex-convict to boot?

Society certainly wouldn't view her as a doting mother and a faithful wife then.

Jake took a moment to mull over her question, giving Sylvie additional time to choose which direction she needed him to focus on in the short term.

"Did anyone else know about your relationship with Lisa?"

"Her husband, obviously."

"If that was the case, I highly doubt that you would be standing in this kitchen unharmed," Sylvie pointed out, needing him to refocus on someone other than John Gervase. "Right?"

Jake narrowed his eyes in contemplation of her challenge to his masculinity, and he seemed to be listening to common sense.

"If John Gervase thought that you were sleeping with his wife, he probably would have confronted you a long time ago." Sylvie set her fork down on the plate. "Did anyone else know? Someone from your group? Oscar Riviera, maybe?"

"I don't think so. I mean, Lisa wanted to know who could make us some fake IDs, and I told her that Oscar would probably be able to help. He knows some guys, and he hooked her up. She met with someone, but she didn't have enough money yet. She was going to meet up with someone last week, but..."

Jake didn't need to finish his sentence, but Sylvie needed to clear something up before she could ask him anymore questions. Plus, it was only a matter of time before someone walked into the kitchen looking for a late evening snack.

"And you don't think that Oscar got curious as to the reason she wanted the fake IDs or who she wanted them for? He never saw the two of you together outside of your tutoring sessions?"

"No." Jake crossed his arms in what she was sure he wanted to come across as confidence, but he appeared more like a lost little boy unsure of how to find his way. He had no idea the ramifications of such an affair. Sylvie had seen time and again affairs ruin marriages and destroy families. While she had no sympathy for the guilty parties, no one deserved to die a horrific death like Lisa Gervase. "I swear to you, Lisa and I both knew how dangerous and manipulative her husband was, and we didn't want him to try and take the kids from her before we had a chance to leave town. There was only one time that we came close to being busted, but we managed to keep our cover with the tutoring sessions. No one knew that we were together, not even Aunt Audrey."

"Where did the two of you meet then?"

Sylvie had a vague idea of their meeting place, but having it confirmed would go a long way to verifying her suspicions. The fact that Jake could no longer even look at her spoke volumes.

CHAPTER FIFTEEN

"That's why you were so convinced that Lisa's husband killed her," Sylvie said, her heart rate accelerating at finding a major missing piece of the puzzle. "You were meeting Lisa on the dirt road where her body was found, weren't you?"

"Yes."

A breakthrough like this could be monumental, but Sylvie also didn't want to ignore the other leads that could be just as important.

"Do you know the name of the individual who Oscar had—"

The door to the kitchen suddenly opened, revealing Sarah Evanston.

From the woman's startled expression, she hadn't been expecting to find anyone in the kitchen. For it being so late at night, it was odd that her makeup and hair were still applied and styled to perfection. She'd either just come back from doing a segment or she was about to go live for the nightly news.

"Sorry. I didn't realize anyone was in here. I was just going to grab one of my smoothies for the road." Sarah bounced her gaze off Jake to focus on Sylvie. It was clear that she hadn't overheard any parts of their conversation, which was a relief. "I'm surprised that you're still here."

Sylvie tensed at the implication that something major had happened. She'd left her cell phone upstairs in her room, only intending to be gone a short time.

"Why?"

"You two really don't know?" Sarah pulled a face, not that her skin showed any unwanted lines. Her foundation was flawless, and the Botox treatments that she must receive on a monthly basis had held up well. "Nancy Buckner is missing. Her husband came into the station about a half hour ago and filed a missing person's report."

The name meant nothing to Sylvie, but that didn't mean anything at this point in the investigation. Sarah waited for a response, but she was going to have to wait a long time for one. Sylvie wasn't going to be caught saying something inadvertently that would cause S&E Investigations to look bad in the press.

"You came into the kitchen for your smoothie."

Sylvie's reminder had the reporter walking around the butcher block to the fridge that was positioned on the other side of the kitchen. Jake remained silent, but there was something in his stance that had her wondering if something hadn't come to mind for him.

Was there some type of connection between Lisa Gervase and Nancy Buckner?

"Dean and I are driving to the Buckner's farmhouse. From my understanding, your team is heading over there now with Detective Turner." Sarah had already collected her health drink and then retraced her steps. When Sylvie and Jake remained silent, the reporter gave an agitated sigh. "Fine. I guess I'll be the one who goes and does her job."

Sylvie refused to be baited, but it took making a fist and digging her nails into the palms of her hands to be successful. Sarah was damn good at her job, and she had even waited a brief moment to see if she'd succeeded in garnering some type of comment. She eventually shrugged in minor annoyance and left the kitchen.

Once the door closed, Sylvie waited a good amount of time before checking the other room to make certain that Sarah and her cameraman had left the house.

"Jake, now isn't the time to be withholding information." Sylvie could only imagine that Bit or Theo had been trying to get ahold of her for the last twenty minutes or so. She needed to return to her room and collect her things before she headed back to the station. "Who is Nancy Buckner, and what connection does she have with Lisa Gervase?"

"Nancy Buckner works for John Gervase," Jake replied with disgust. He'd already made up his mind that Lisa's husband was guilty, and Sylvie could see that nothing anyone said could change his mind. "I told you that this all has to do with that son of a bitch. Nancy is John's personal assistant."

Chapter Sixteen

Unsub
May 2022
Thursday — 10:29pm

THE STORMFRONT THAT SHOULD have moved into the area had stalled just west of town. Instead of thunderstorms throughout the night, Stillwater had received a twenty-four-hour stay. The grace period afforded them didn't include humidity, which had steadily risen throughout the evening. This reprieve allowed the nocturnal predators to continue their hunt without the interference of the storm.

The screams of his victims would feed the beast tonight.

He used a white handkerchief to wipe the sweat from his forehead as he took in his surroundings. Crickets and frogs could be heard from the midst of the woods on either side of the cabin. There was only one approach to the structure, and that was behind him. Directly on the other side of the cabin was a large pond that his uncle used to fish in when he'd been alive.

The convenience of such a property hadn't gone unnoticed, but he'd done his best to resist the urge to teach others the value of life.

Hadn't his mother always stressed the importance of appreciating what one was given?

Lisa Gervase certainly hadn't appreciated the gift of the roles that she'd been given—a faithful wife, a good mother, and a pillar of her community. At least, that's how her husband had described her when he'd been pleading for any information regarding her abduction.

She hadn't deserved any of those reputations.

And he'd made sure that she'd paid dearly for her sins.

Everyone had always underestimated him. He'd never been good at sports, hunting, or anything that involved athleticism. Mentally, though? His mental acuity was on another level, and he'd never been given any credit. Every single person in his life had judged him as useless, but he was turning the tables now.

The truth was that he was sharp as a knife and just as deadly.

He slammed the trunk of the vehicle closed before reassuring himself that no one had seen him earlier tonight when he'd lured Nancy Buckner away from her car. She was no better than Lisa Gervase. Nancy had not technically cheated on her husband, but her thoughts had strayed in that direction. Plus, they had both paraded around town as if they'd had the morals of a saint. Their poor children shouldn't be kept in the dark concerning their sins.

The truth needed to be revealed.

He silently walked to where he'd left the door to the cabin open, using the headlights of the vehicle to illuminate his way. The cabin hadn't been used in many years. Sections of the wood had dry rot, but he didn't need the place to offer physical comfort. The rancid smell that had been left behind by Lisa Gervase had all but been wiped away by the bleach that he'd practically doused the floor with after he'd so proudly displayed his work to reveal how Lisa had violated her vows.

She'd told him all about it when he'd used the culinary torch to melt the wedding ring right off her finger.

His dick became hard just thinking about her painful screams echoing throughout the cabin.

"You're awake." He hadn't expected Nancy to come around after he'd used a hefty dose of chloroform to knock her out. She was heavier than Lisa, and it had been a struggle to carry her from the vehicle to the cabin with so much dead weight. "It's too bad that I have to leave you so soon. I guess some time alone will do you good, though. You can think about the reasons why you're here."

He'd used zip ties to keep her bound to the metal table that his uncle had used to clean his fish. The legs had certainly held up well given the previous struggle that Lisa had put up during her punishment. Word had spread like wildfire around town about what had been done to her, so it wasn't like Nancy didn't know what was waiting for her in the weeks ahead.

Such a destiny was certainly the reason that she was fighting against her fate at the moment.

"Even though no one can hear you this far out of town, I'm going to leave the gag in your mouth."

He began to pull his dress shirt and undershirt out of his pants to show her the mark of his manhood.

It was still hard to see inside the cabin, but the headlights were hitting the middle of the room just right for him to observe the fear on her tear-streaked face.

"Did you know that one of the most effective ways to teach a lesson is with the purifying touch of fire? Whenever I would act like anything other than a true gentleman, my mother always made sure I knew the consequences of my actions." He shifted slightly so that the beams of the headlights shined directly on his chest. Nancy had begun to sob in fear once more. "Now, now. Don't get shy on me now. I know that you were going to spread your legs for other men beside your husband. Look. Look at my scars!"

His booming voice bounced off the walls, causing Nancy to jerk against the zip ties. She had quickly lifted her drenched lashes, focusing on the scars that his mother had left behind in her bid to teach him right from wrong. He wasn't sure why he'd never thought to pass on his mother's wise lessons to others, but doing so with Lisa had been liberating in more ways than he'd ever imagined.

"I'm a true gentleman now, Nancy. I would never do anything to jeopardize my standing in this community." He used his fingertips to rub the rough scars the way his wife did every night in their bed. "Unlike you. Your filth was way too obvious."

He leisurely began to make himself presentable, enjoying the muffled whimpers coming from Nancy.

"I would so love to begin our sessions together right now. Do you want to know where I'll start?" he asked, adjusting his cock so that the material didn't constrict his blood flow. Once his shirts were tucked back into place, he reached for her left hand that was fastened to an eyebolt on the side of the table. "First, I'll dip your ring finger in thermite powder. I'll then ever so slowly melt the metal and then burn the flesh right off the bone with my culinary torch. You'll want to die from the pain, of course. But my method won't allow for you to expire, because your wound will basically be cauterized so that I can choose another area that you were so willingly going to stain with your vile choices."

He sighed in disappointment when an alarm went off on his phone, letting him know that his time with Nancy had come to a brief end. He supposed having an entire night alone to think over her mistakes would be beneficial.

Who knew that such pleading could be music to his ears?

"I must leave you for a while, Nancy." He patted the same hand that come tomorrow would be missing the unwarranted gift from her husband on their wedding day. "You might think that the people who have come to town might save you from such punishment, but I brought them here for me. What fun would it be to not have other participants in this game of ours? You see, these sessions of ours aren't only therapeutic for you. My mother never thought that I was any good at games, and this is my way of proving her wrong. It's a win-win, wouldn't you agree?"

He stepped away while pulling his phone out of his pocket. It didn't take him long to silence his alarm. Restraint had always been one of his biggest lessons to learn, but his ability to walk away from Nancy and go home to the loving arms of his wife proved just how far he'd come in life.

"Sweet dreams, Nancy."

Chapter Seventeen

Brooklyn Sloane
May 2022
Friday — 8:21 am

The high school students didn't even try to hide their curiosity as Brook and Theo entered through the main doors of the school. The huddled groups had all but stopped talking at once to monitor their progress. It was easy to see which groups had been tagged as socially significant and which ones weren't by their locations and body language. The unpopular students were near the walls, leaning up against it as they stayed far away from those walking down the hallway in large groups. Those particular clusters had stopped and stared at first. Now, they weren't even bothering to lower their voices as they expressed their curiosity.

"...federal agents."
"...sister of a serial killer."
"What do you think happened to his eye?"

"Do you ever wish you could do it all over again?" Theo asked wryly as he pointed toward a sign that indicated the office was down the hall to the right.

Brook shot him a sideways scowl that had nothing to do with their long night at the station. Another woman being taken hadn't come as a complete shock, but the short time in between the first killing and the second abduction was cause for some immediate concern. There were proper procedures to follow in cases like these, and Stan had no choice but to follow them and check the boxes. It was the reason that Brook had gotten everyone to agree that the state police should focus on the most recent abduction while S&E Investigations continued to follow the leads that they'd recently uncovered.

Of course, she'd offered Stan their assistance for the duration of his search. Should he need the help of Sylvie or Bit's expertise, they would step up to the plate. They were more than capable of pulling double duty for both sections of the investigation.

"Forget I asked that question," Theo muttered as he comprehended the scope of his question. Her childhood wasn't something that anyone would ever want to relive. "What is it with high schools and that smell, though?"

Brook would have responded had she not caught sight of a woman walking out of the principal's office.

"Theo, that's Julie Wilson."

Julie hadn't caught sight of them in the throng of students moving about inside the hallway. She had also turned to walk in the other direction, and Brook motioned for Theo to follow her.

Why was the pastor's wife at the high school this morning?

Brook paused by the door to the administration office as Theo continued down the hall to follow Julie.

The team had held their morning debriefing, as usual.

Theo had filled everyone in on his visit with John Gervase. Basically, the man had an inflated sense of self-importance that measured far above the norm. The man was a complete narcissist. A key component of narcissistic behavior was that he lacked empathy. He'd spent a full hour explaining his reasoning for utilizing the press during his wife's disappearance as to why he didn't trust Sheriff Kennard, which basically had stemmed

CHAPTER SEVENTEEN

from the sheriff not kissing the man's ass every time they ran into one another.

John Gervase hadn't managed to change Theo's initial opinion of the man.

There had been nothing to gain from the private interview. The husband hadn't believed for a second that his wife had been going to leave him, and he'd gone on and on about how he was going to sue everyone from the governor on down for defamation of his wife's character.

Unfortunately, John Gervase wouldn't allow Theo to question either Aiden or Madison. Though children were the most prone to lie in everyday life, during an investigation, they became the unabashed keepers of the truth. They quite often realized the importance of the situation and answered truthfully, without thought of standing or recourse. With their father standing in the way, any information they might inadvertently have would need to be obtained another way.

By morning, Stan had suggested that John Gervase take his children and stay somewhere else. The fact that Nancy Buckner was now missing pointed toward Gervase's involvement in the case. Mr. Buckner had already expressed his rage toward the man, and it was only a matter of time before other residents began placing blame squarely on his shoulders. The Gervase family wasn't safe staying in their residence any longer, and Stan had seen to it that they had other, more secure accommodations for the time being.

Bit had turned up information regarding Oscar Riviera's known associates, along with their criminal vocations. The culprit who had been most likely to provide Lisa Gervase with four fake IDs had been easy to spot. His name was Henry Flanagan. Brook had been pleased with Sylvie's ability to get Jake Hudson to talk, and that was why she'd been assigned to follow up the lead to search out Flanagan and have a probing conversation that didn't include the state police. Flanagan would be more willing to talk with a private investigator than he would law enforcement. Sylvie being a private investigator had a great deal more latitude when dealing with the public.

"Excuse me," Brook said quietly after she'd walked into the main office. There was a woman at the desk with her back turned toward the door, two students in chairs waiting rather impatiently, and numerous offices surrounding the area. Some of the doors were opened and some shut. There was soft music drifting from the speaker overhead. "I'm here to see Principal Samuel Bissett."

"Yes, yes," the woman replied as she immediately began to walk toward the opening of the counter to the left. "Principal Bissett is expecting you. Please, follow me."

Brook could sense the weight of the stares from the two students, but she was focused on their low conversation with one another. They were calling this woman by her surname, which just so happened to be Bissett.

Either this woman was the principal's sister, or she was his wife.

"My name is Vera. We have been beside ourselves with grief over Lisa," Vera practically whispered as she finally came to stand in front of Brook. "She used to teach here many, many years ago. Right after college, actually. Of course, she'd married John shortly thereafter. We also heard about Nancy this morning. Are you going to arrest John? I mean, isn't it obvious that he's the one behind all this?"

"Actually, Mr. Gervase has an alibi for Mrs. Buckner's abduction," Brook replied, not seeing the harm in releasing that piece of information. Stan was going to give a press statement including that specific detail to ensure the man's safety. It wouldn't do to have the local residents taking matters into their own hands. "How well did you know Lisa?"

"We were actually very close when we were in high school. We also attended the same local college, but that's pretty much when we began to drift apart. She isolated herself once she married into money," Vera shared reluctantly, coming to a stop outside one of the few offices that had the door shut. "I didn't hold onto any hard feelings or anything like that."

"Did anyone harbor hard feelings about the change that Lisa underwent during those early years?" Brook asked, hoping that Vera could provide more insight into the victim's life. She'd

CHAPTER SEVENTEEN 155

included in her profile that the unsub had roots in the area and had known the victim personally. Since she was a firm believer that everything came back to the first victim, Brook was certain that the unsub had witnessed Lisa Gervase rearrange her life to fit into the higher social circles. "Maybe an old boyfriend?"

"Lisa dated Rich Knight during our senior year of high school, but he went into the service after graduation. He hasn't been back to town in years. At least, that I know of." Vera fiddled with the wide belt around her waist as if she wanted to add something more, but then had thought better of it. "I'll let you speak with Sam—I mean, Principal Bissett—while I gather the students who Lisa tutored into one of the empty classrooms."

"Actually, I'd rather you didn't do that," Brook said, though she was too late to do so before Vera had opened the principal's office door. "I'd like to speak with the students one on one, if possible. It's my understanding that I already have their parents' permission to interview them."

By this time, the office door was wide open.

Vera didn't look too convinced to go along with the change in venue, but Principal Bissett had obviously overheard their conversation. He nodded his permission as he walked across the floor of his office.

"That's fine, Vera. Call Jasper Hewitt up to the office first. Ms. Sloane can use my office to talk to each of them." Principal Bissett motioned for Brook to enter his office as he gripped the doorknob. "My wife was only following my directives regarding the assembly hall."

Brook waited for Principal Bissett to close the door and walk back to his desk before she took a seat in one of the two guest chairs. She took her time placing her leather bag on the floor to study him. He was rather young for a principal, and she pegged him to be in his late thirties. He wouldn't have been in Vera and Lisa's friend group back in high school. Still, that didn't mean he hadn't been privy to what was going on around town.

"How did you and your wife meet, Principal Bissett?" Brook asked as she crossed her legs and made herself comfortable.

"I started out as a teacher's assistant to one of the professors at our local college." Principal Bissett picked up a pen off his desk as if it held special meaning. "I met Vera on campus one day, and the rest was history. She's helping out in the main office this week because Tracy had surgery on her hip. Vera is actually our librarian here at the high school."

"Was Vera still close with Lisa when the two of you met in college?" Brook asked, wanting to get a better feel for the victim's early days. "Vera mentioned that the two of them used be quite close."

"No."

Brook waited for Principal Bissett to expand on his response, but he seemed to be waiting for another question. If he expected their short conversation to be an interview, she would be more than happy to oblige. She certainly hadn't expected him to be an obstacle.

"When did Lisa start tutoring the students?"

"A few years ago."

"Did she come to the school for the sessions?"

"Only on Wednesdays. There is an after-school program that Mrs. Gervase participated in, but she mostly met the students at their residences or the public library."

"Why didn't you like her?"

Principal Bissett had parted his lips in anticipation of answering another basic question, but Brook had purposefully thrown him off to see if she could elicit the truth from him.

"I'm a principal, Ms. Sloane. It's my job to make sure that my students have every learning tool that I can manage to find at their disposal. Graduation is less than three weeks away. It hasn't been easy to find someone else as gifted in math as Mrs. Gervase to help certain students study for their final exams."

"You didn't answer my question, sir."

"I didn't know Mrs. Gervase well enough to form an opinion. Her children are still in the lower school, she usually tutored off school grounds, and we ran in different circles." Principal Bissett cleared his throat and set his pen down on the desk. "I'm not particularly fond of John Gervase, if you must know the truth. Not that I would wish this type of devastation and tragedy on anyone."

CHAPTER SEVENTEEN

A knock came at the door, and Principal Bissett called for whoever it was to enter the office.

Theo made an appearance, and Brook could sense that he'd had an interesting run-in with Julie Wilson.

Doubting that she would get any more information out of Principal Bissett, Brook stood and held out her hand.

"I appreciate your time and the use of your office. This is my colleague, Theo Neville. He'll also be questioning the students with me."

While the two men greeted one another, Brook walked around the desk and began to wheel the chair so that it was positioned in a tight circle with the two stationary chairs. She noticed a photograph of Principal Bissett and his wife in a professional setting. Vera's hair was shorter in the picture by at least five inches, indicating that the photo session had been conducted quite a while ago.

Brook was finally able to position the chairs to her liking, preferring that the students feel comfortable, and she'd already mapped out how to initiate a rapport with them. On a scale from one to ten, she'd consider her relationship with her brother close to a zero when it came to utilizing her past during interviews. This was one of those exceptions, because as macabre as it was...teens loved drama.

"We'd like to speak with Addy Wright before beginning our interviews with the students." Brook noticed the way Principal Bissett paused at her request. "Is that a problem?"

"No, no. I'll send for her right away." Principal Bissett glanced at his smart watch. "It sounds as if this is going to be a rather long day. I'll see to it that Vera brings the two of you some coffee. Good luck with your interviews."

CHAPTER EIGHTEEN

Brooklyn Sloane
May 2022
Friday — 11:33am

"Two more interviews to go," Theo said after he closed the door to Principal Bissett's office. "So far, they all respected the victim, none of them thought she was acting strange lately, and most of them actually liked her husband."

"That's because John Gervase wanted to be liked by them," Brook replied as she tucked away the electronic tablet that she'd been using to type in notes of significant details. As Theo had already pointed out, nothing enlightening had come of this day so far. She sure as hell hoped that Sylvie was having better luck with Henry Flanagan. "And before you say that type of need is part of the profile that I drafted, I'd like to point out that Gervase doesn't feel inferior. He's most certainly a narcissist."

"I wasn't going to say a word," Theo replied with a smile. It faded as the bell rang. "Besides, I don't think the husband had anything to do with his wife's murder, either. And seeing as it's lunchtime and the principal was gracious enough to provide us meals, I think I'll use our small break to go speak with the guidance counselor. I'd like to confirm that Julie Wilson was here this morning to assist the grief counselor that's been sent here for the students recently."

Brook stood and picked up her leather bag. She'd rather not have to lug it around the school, but she also had someone who she wanted to seek out before talking to the last two students and heading back to the station. It wouldn't do to leave her personal belongings behind.

"Why don't I meet you in the cafeteria? I'd like to go and talk to Oscar Riviera."

"Nothing like catching him off guard," Theo agreed as he turned the handle. "Here. Give me your bag. I'll look more professional to the guidance counselor if I have a designer saddle bag. This way, you can blend in with the students as you're walking the halls. You could pass as young enough."

"You've been hanging out with Bit too long," Brook muttered as she handed him the leather strap. Mostly because she remembered what it was like to be crammed in the hallways with students who could care less who or what they ran into on their way to the cafeteria. "I will say that my friends and I didn't look like these kids back when we were in high school."

"Tell me about it." Theo opened the office door and stepped to the side so that she could walk out first. "Did you see Ben Greenland's arms? I work out, and I'm pretty sure that I have half the muscle mass that he does at age eighteen."

"He is the football team's star linebacker," Brook reminded him. "They take that kind of thing seriously around here. Still, they all look to be early twenties instead of eighteen or younger."

Brook could see Principal Bissett behind the counter talking to a young woman about the upcoming graduation ceremony. The man's wife was nowhere to be seen, and Brook assumed that she'd gone back to the library for the time being.

"Ms. Sloane and Mr. Neville," the principal greeted, holding up a hand to halt his conversation with the female student. "The staff in the cafeteria know that you are heading to the lunchroom. They'll see that you're taken care of."

"Thank you," Theo called out as Brook led the way through the door and out into the jammed-packed hallway. "I'll meet you in the cafeteria."

CHAPTER EIGHTEEN

Brook hadn't taken three steps in the opposite direction when she remembered that she'd left her cell phone in the side pocket of her leather bag, along with her wallet. She hadn't bothered to bring her purse today, seeing as it had been easier to carry one item. She turned around, but Theo had already been swallowed by the throngs of students rushing about.

She hated being without her phone, but she didn't plan on being more than fifteen or twenty minutes. The length of time depended on how responsive Oscar Riviera was to their conversation. Afterward, she'd grab a bite to eat and prepare to interview the two students left on their list. The one who she was most interested in speaking with was Reed Feltner. Devin had mentioned that everyone in school had heard about the young man's run-in with John Gervase, and she wanted to hear the details firsthand.

"Really?" Brook muttered as she was jostled by the impact of a backpack hitting her shoulder. She sighed and continued walking in the opposite direction of the cafeteria. Oscar Riviera had to be around the school somewhere, and the easiest way would be to simply ask the students. She waited until she spotted a group of teenagers near the front entrance. They seemed to be waiting on someone, and she recalled being a senior and able to leave school grounds. It was almost the highest honor, and she recalled the joy and freedom in those days that she had never gotten back. "Excuse me. You haven't seen the custodian around here, have you?"

"Mr. Riviera was in the stairwell when I came down from last period," a young girl replied as she narrowed her eyes in contemplation. "You're here investigating Mrs. Gervase's murder."

"...also the sister of a serial killer."

One of the young men elbowed the other when he realized that Brook had overheard his friend.

She ignored their insolence, knowing exactly what she'd done when she'd spoken to the victim's clients. Her mission to have them become comfortable with her had worked in spades. It was unfortunate that she'd had to subject herself to the fallout, but she hadn't technically revealed anything that hadn't already been covered in the news.

"I am," Brook replied, ensuring that her blazer was still securely fastened. Theo had left his firearm with Sylvie. For all intents and purposes, weapons were prohibited on school grounds. She'd already spoken with the sheriff, and he had been informed that she wasn't comfortable going without protection for most of the day. While it was a state law, he'd only cautioned her that she should keep her weapon concealed at all times. "Did you know her?"

It was safe to say that the majority of the students in this school had known the victim, either through their parents, friends, church, or a whole list of other ways in which a small community like this knew one another. Still, her question offered up an open-ended reply from anyone who was willing to talk.

"Yeah," the young girl replied. "She went to my church. Pastor Wilson held a moment of silence last Sunday for the congregation."

"Pastor Wilson? I'm pretty sure that I saw his wife near the administration office of the school earlier today," Brook said quizzically, confident that her observation would lead her down the path that Theo was currently taking with the guidance counselor. "Does she teach here?"

"Oh, no." Another young girl laughed at the premise. "Mrs. Wilson is on hand because she's best friends with the guidance counselor. The two of them are practically inseparable. She says she's here to give spiritual guidance to those in need after...well, you know. Anyway, no one really takes her up on it. I mean, she tries, don't get me wrong. But she's not the pastor."

The young girl who had laughed before muttered something underneath her breath. Brook caught enough of the words to know that she'd mentioned something along the lines that Mrs. Wilson wanted to fill the role of pastor, though.

Interesting tidbit, but Brook really needed to speak with Oscar Riviera.

"Are all of you attending the memorial tonight? I believe it's being held at the football stadium."

CHAPTER EIGHTEEN

"Yeah, we're all going. Some of our friends were being tutored by Mrs. Gervase. We'll be there to support them."

"Well, enjoy your lunch," Brook replied before glancing over her shoulder to make sure she had enough room.

While the hallway had cleared out somewhat, there were still quite a few students milling about. She followed the black and white signs that pointed to the staircase, which took her down another hall that seemed devoid of anyone. As she walked by some of the classrooms, she could see that some of them were still filled with students. They must have the later lunch schedule.

Brook finally found a wooden door with a plaque that held the design of a stair graphic. She opened it as quietly as possible, listening for any sound that someone was in the stairwell. Sure enough, Oscar Riviera was mopping a small landing that separated the stairs as they switched directions. He had earbuds in and was listening to music as he worked, giving Brook time to study him from her place by the door.

He was maybe five feet, nine inches tall. His black hair was buzzed on the sides and short on top, exposing a tattoo that had faded in color on the side of his neck. It hadn't been inked by a professional. His cell phone was in the left back pocket of his grey uniform, indicating to her that he was left-handed.

"Excuse me," Brook called out, hoping that he'd hear her over the music. To his credit, he turned immediately and gave her a smile. "Are you Oscar Riviera?"

His grin faltered, but he nodded as he took out one of the buds.

Again, he'd used his left hand to do so.

"Yes, I'm Oscar." It wasn't long before recognition hit. His reaction told her that he kept an ear close to the ground. She wouldn't have appreciated had he pretended not to know who she was given that her and Theo's presence were most likely the hottest topic among the students. "Is there something that I can help you with?"

"I think you already know the answer to that question," Brook replied evenly. She shifted so that her back wasn't against the door. She used the wall for support and crossed her arms to signify that she was making herself comfortable for the upcoming conversation. "I'm not here for you. I simply want to know about the arrangement between Lisa Gervase and Henry Flanagan."

Oscar struggled to swallow as he stalled for time. He stuck his mop back into the grey bucket before taking out his other earbud. She tensed when he glanced up at the staircase, but she honestly didn't think that he would be so foolish as to run. She wasn't the police, she hadn't accused him of anything, and such a poor decision could end up with him behind bars. She quickly deescalated the potential problem.

"I don't care about your past, Oscar. I know that you're doing your best to stay clean, and I don't believe you had anything to do with Lisa Gervase's murder. But she met with Henry Flanagan a few nights before she was abducted, and I need to know if there was something more going on with her besides wanting to leave her husband for Jake Hudson."

Oscar had been listening intently to her small speech, but he only reacted to the last few words.

Jake had been right.

Oscar had no idea that Jake had been having an affair with Lisa Gervase.

"What are you talking about? Jake wasn't having an affair with Lisa, and he has nothing to do with Flanagan. Lisa came to me countless times, wanting the name of someone who could get her fake IDs. I told her that I wanted nothing to do with that life anymore."

"I know that, Oscar," Brook replied quietly, keeping her tone low so that her voice didn't echo around the stairwell. "It's the reason that I haven't involved the police. I don't intend to, either. Trust me, I know how hard it is to turn your life around after making some really poor choices. I actually already have someone meeting with Flanagan right this moment. Your name won't be brought up. He'll believe that we spotted him through security footage taken in the tavern parking lot here in town. I give you my word that he won't know that we linked him to you. All I need to know is if Lisa mentioned anything...anything at all...that would give you the indication that she feared someone else besides her husband."

Oscar rubbed his forehead before he sat down on the top step of the first section of stairs. He rested his elbows on his knees as he settled in to talk to her.

"Lisa wasn't scared of her husband," Oscar countered with an expression of confusion. "Not in the way you believe, anyway. He was never physically abusive toward her. Lisa was all about her kids. He'd warned her time and again that if she tried to divorce him, he would go for full custody. Considering he golfs with the judge every weekend, it was a safe bet that he'd win, too."

"Did you know that she asked Flanagan for four fake IDs instead of three?"

"No. Are you—" Oscar broke off when it sounded as if someone was about to come through the door. Their laughter slipped through the thick barrier, but they eventually moved on. "You're serious about Jake having an affair with Lisa, aren't you? You don't think that he—"

"Mr. Riviera, we're not discounting anyone right now. We are still in the preliminary stages of our investigation." Brook had already been prepared for this path to be a dead end. While the victim's decision to run away with her lover and children had been the catalyst to set things in motion, the fallout was just muddling the actual investigation. The most important undertaking now was figuring out who had knowledge about Lisa's decision to leave town with her lover. "Did you tell anyone that Lisa needed fake IDs?"

Oscar slowly shook his head as he mulled over her question. "No."

"You hesitated," Brook pointed out as she controlled her reaction. Something had come to the forefront of his mind, and it could be the one thread that unraveled the search for their unsub. "Why?"

"I didn't tell anyone," Oscar insisted, becoming antsy enough that he stood and reached for the handle of the mop. "I swear."

Brook was losing him, but she managed to keep herself from pushing him too hard. She tried a different tactic, but still maintained confidence that she would get the answer that she sought.

"Oscar, I know what it means to you to turn your life around," Brook replied softly and with understanding. "I don't want to do anything to cause a hiccup in your plans. Whatever you say to me stays between us. Haven't I already proven that? I could have easily had Sheriff Kennard or Detective Turner bring you into the station for questioning. I purposefully chose to keep this conversation between us. You liked Lisa Gervase. Otherwise, you wouldn't have risked your freedom to help her, and she wouldn't have trusted you enough to ask. All I am asking is if you think it's possible someone discovered that she came to you."

"It's possible," Oscar replied reluctantly, pulling the handle of the broom close to his chest. "Someone could have overheard us once."

"Who?" Brook asked, this time around taking a step forward. She rested her hand on the metal railing as she pressed him just a little bit harder. "Who do you think might have overheard Lisa ask for those fake IDs?"

"Julie Wilson, the pastor's wife."

Oscar had no idea that Brook was already aware of who had been in the vicinity when the victim asked for his help, but such verification meant that some of the players in this so-called game of the unsub were being truthful. It wasn't a method that she preferred, but sometimes tripping up those involved eventually revealed the identity of the guilty party.

Technically, Brook had just reached another dead end.

It was a good thing that she was able to backtrack and take another path.

CHAPTER NINETEEN

Bit Nowacki
May 2022
Friday — 2:11pm

THE LOCAL POLICE STATION had been relatively quiet for most of the day, but a shift change was due soon. Two of the deputies had returned early from their patrols, causing Sheriff Kennard to almost have a heart attack at the sight of them. The man carried extra weight around the middle, and it was doubtful that anyone in town was really scared that he could catch them if a foot chase ensued over something petty. According to his lecture, which had him spitting saliva over his temporary desk out in the main area, one of the deputies was supposed to have waited for directives before vacating the Buckner property.

The sheriff had been so mad that he'd stormed out of the station about five minutes ago.

"...not like her abductor is going to show up at the station and volunteer to be put into handcuffs."

"Hey, I feel for Pete Buckner. I really do. I don't know what I would do if it was my wife, but this is way above our pay grade."

"I don't get Kennard's beef. He was the one to turn things over to the state police, and then the governor called in these civilian clowns. Let them earn their bloated, state-sponsored paycheck."

Bit tossed a peanut M&M into the air, catching it on the way down as he leaned back in his chair.

He'd learned long ago that people tended to dismiss him due to his looks and support role. He was on the thin side with shoulder length hair that had a tendency to look greasy. No matter what kind of shampoo he used, there was no getting the blond strands to look like his sister's hair.

He didn't care about his appearance, though.

Well, maybe his long nose, but he wasn't so vain as to let that bother him. Bottom line was that people forgot that he was in their vicinity and talked openly about a variety of topics. No one ever viewed him as a threat, because he was just the IT guy. Just because he had earbuds in most of the time didn't mean that he was listening to music.

Truthfully, no one had ever really valued his talent, either.

Not until Brook had come along, and he'd almost fucked that up, as well.

He didn't regret a single day that he'd turned his back on his old life. Had he not taken Brook up on her offer to join S&E Investigations, Inc., there was no doubt that his ass would have been either behind bars or dead. He still tended to cross the line, but it was for the greater good.

Bit had purposefully left the door to the office open by less than a half-inch to hear what was being said out in the bullpen. It gave him something to do while waiting for some of his software programs to find information that would help the team out in the field. The shade on the interior window had been pulled shut, so the two deputies and the dispatcher had no idea what he was doing inside the office.

After all, Bit was just the IT guy.

The same could be said for him about them, because the deputies had fallen awfully quiet for some reason. Gail could be heard answering the phones, though. Someone had cut down a tree, and it hadn't been on their property. Bit had never lived anywhere but the city. He didn't envy the deputy who had to

CHAPTER NINETEEN

take that particular call. Gail had been pretty specific that the caller shouldn't have taken a pickaxe to the man's car, not that it sounded as if the dispatcher was making much of an impression on the neighbor.

Bit popped another peanut M&M into the air right as the door flew open.

"You're going to choke on those one of these days."

Bit barely caught the chair from flipping backward.

Of course, the blue M&M missed its target and rolled onto the floor toward the most beautiful woman he'd ever set eyes on. Not that he would ever say a thing to Sylvie Deering that would in any way hinder their working relationship.

Besides, she was way out of his league.

She was in the big show.

The fact that he got to work with her at least five days a week, sometimes more during an active investigation, was more than enough for him.

"You can throw that in the garbage," Bit muttered as Sylvie leaned down to pick up the blue M&M that she'd stopped with the toe of her pointed pink shoe. She was dressed in a pair of white jeans, a pink blouse that didn't hide the black leather holster at her waist, and matching shoes. Her blonde hair had been pulled back into a bun. She didn't like it when her long strands got in the way of her concentration. "Did you find out anything from Flanagan?"

"Were you listening in on their conversation?" Sylvie asked, ignoring his question about the case. She tossed the piece of candy into the garbage as she balanced the cup carrier in her hand. "I take it they got in trouble for leaving the Buckner residence before their shift ended? I ran into the sheriff in the parking lot, and he was steaming mad. Here. I was able to load up on new tea blends at the local teashop, as well as buy us two sweet teas. This one was labeled Dandelion Blend, and the owner said it contains quite a lot of caffeine. I figured why not, especially considering that I ran into a dead end with Flanagan."

Bit did his best not to grimace when Sylvie handed him the large drink.

The bitter battery acid was the last thing he wanted to drink after having enjoyed a bag of M&Ms. He nodded toward the door behind Sylvie. Considering how easy it was for him to hear the deputies' conversation, it stood to reason that they could do the same. He waited until the door was completely shut before responding to her question.

"They were basically complaining about this case being above their pay grade." Bit had spun his chair around to talk to her as she set down her purse and her share of the tea haul on the small desk near the whiteboard. She had already tossed the biodegradable cup holder into a small garbage can that had been shoved into the corner. "John Gervase and his children were taken to a safe location. Detective Turner has been at the Buckner residence most of the day, and I've been doing some research on those properties near the crime scene."

"I like the sound of that. What exactly are you researching, and what have you found?" Sylvie asked as she took a seat with a sigh of relief. She held the straw steady as she took a sip, taking time to savor her favorite beverage. "It's getting hot out there."

"At least the station has central air," Bit offered up as he quickly checked the information on his monitors. Once he was sure that nothing new had come to light, he focused his attention back on Sylvie. "And nothing so far. Mrs. Buckner was taken around eight-thirty last night. The firehouse hosts bingo every Thursday from six to eight. She usually helps clean up afterward."

"Volunteer firehouse?"

"Yes," Bit replied as he tossed the bag of remaining M&Ms onto the table behind him. "I didn't even know that was a thing. I mean, that takes dedication to work a full-time job and then offer up your free time to go running into a blazing fire."

"What time is the memorial tonight?"

"Seven o'clock. The sheriff mentioned that he didn't want the kids to be out too late with everything going on." Music began playing, causing Sylvie to do a double take. He grinned when he reached for his cell phone, which he'd purposefully programmed to play a Bruce Springsteen song. The artist was known as "The Boss", and Bit had chosen a song that best represented Brook's role as their team leader. "What? You have to admit it's ingenious."

Sylvie smirked behind her straw as Bit answered the phone.

"Boss? How is it going at the high school?" Bit straightened in his chair when Brook began to rattle off several things that she needed him to research. "Feltner? Sure. I can have something for you before you get back to the station. Anything else? You're talking about the principal, right? Samuel Bissett? Wife's name? Got it. See you soon."

"What's up?" Sylvie asked as she used the toe of her pink slip-on shoe that reminded Bit of a ballerina to wheel her chair next to his. She read the notes that he'd jotted down on a piece of paper. "Reed Feltner. Teacher? Student? Father?"

"Student." Bit had already begun to type the boy's name into several programs. "Boss wants a prelim on his family. I could hear in her voice that she doesn't think there's much to it, but Feltner got into a verbal altercation with John Gervase over some business."

"Business? What kind of business could this Feltner have with a real estate agent? You did say that Feltner was a student, right?"

"Reed Feltner was standing up for his father, who just so happens to own a hunting cabin that has plumbing problems." Bit could hear Sylvie hum her understanding, because they had all agreed in yesterday's debriefing that the unsub would have had to have privacy to torture his victim. A place where people couldn't hear her scream. Bit did his best not to think about the missing woman, because she could be undergoing the same fate as the first victim. "As for Principal Samuel Bissett, it seems he has a bit of an inferiority complex."

"Since you're looking into the cabin, would you also print a list of any structure similar to that one within a fifteen-mile radius of town? Considering the unsub calls at the same time, he's clearly restricted on time. He wouldn't be able to keep the victim too far outside of town." Sylvie wanted to start cross-referencing names. It wasn't like they could search every isolated cabin or house on the outskirts of Stillwater, but Bit trusted that she could find a connection if there was one. "And I know this is a really odd request, but is there a way for you to find the blueprints for the ice cream factory?"

Sylvie's request had his fingers hovering over his keyboard.

It took a minute for what she was suggesting to penetrate the fog of his sugar haze that he'd been working on for the past half hour.

"If the ice cream factory is where the unsub is taking his victims, I'm never going to be able to eat ice cream again."

Chapter Twenty

Brooklyn Sloane
May 2022
Friday — 9:41pm

THUNDER RUMBLED OVERHEAD AS the slow-moving stormfront began to roll into town with the sound of a thousand crashing cymbals. The heavy rain pouring down from the dark grey clouds above was relentless, not giving the narrow streets enough time to void themselves of all the standing water on their dark surfaces into the drainage grates. As for the lightning streaking across the sky, it was as if Zeus himself was warning the inhabitants below to take heed and remain indoors.

"The memorial was rescheduled for next week," Brook said as she walked into the office with two cups of coffee. She handed one off to Theo before she took a seat in one of the rolling chairs next to Bit. Sylvie was in her seat near the whiteboard. "I don't like how the unsub seems to have escalated events since our team's arrival into town. He isn't running for cover. He's playing his own game according to his own rules."

While Brook hated the bitter taste associated with the coffee here at the station, it was better than nothing. There was no way that she was taking the chance of crossing the street right now to the diner, which was almost completely empty of patrons. Those who had braved the torrential downpour to venture out for dinner were huddled by the door in hopes for a brief respite to make a run for their vehicles without getting completely drenched.

"We've been here two days," Theo reminded her before taking a tentative sip of the hot sludge. "We've uncovered quite a lot. We're making progress."

"Not enough to prevent Nancy Buckner's abduction." Brook should have anticipated such an obvious next step in the unsub's actions. She should have seen it coming from a mile away. A serial killer in the making who had become emboldened with his first kill wouldn't have been able to restrain himself from seeking another high so quickly. Killing was like a drug to him. He'd gotten his first sweet taste of blood, and he liked it. "Well, it looks as if we're stuck here for a couple of more hours. Let's start from the beginning and see what we have so far. If we strip the noise, we might be able to spot something that we missed. Sylvie?"

"Our first victim was afraid that if she left her husband, he would seek sole custody of their minor children. At some point, Lisa Gervase became involved with Jake Hudson. I believe that affair gave her the incentive to run—hoard the money that she made from tutoring, buy fake IDs, and attempt to start a new life somewhere else. She sought out someone to help her—Oscar Riviera. He provided her with a point of contact, and she then made arrangements with his source. Things were set in motion. The unsub somehow discovered that Lisa Gervase didn't live up to her public image."

"The unsub then reacted without too much forethought," Theo mused, staring at the victim's picture that Sylvie had taped to the whiteboard. "Such behavior tells us that the unsub is from the area, has close ties with the community, and was able to improvise a plan to abduct, torture, and kill the victim."

"Detective Turner sent out a patrol unit to check around the area where the Feltners have their cabin, and there was no sign that anyone had been on the property in quite some time," Bit shared with a bit of disappointment. "I already collected a

CHAPTER TWENTY

comprehensive list of properties within a fifteen-mile radius of town in all directions. Sylvie has the addresses and names of the titled owners."

"Thirty-six cabins, seventeen houses, and four private farms that own quite a few acres," Sylvie stated as she dunked a teabag into some hot water that she'd heated up in the station's microwave. "I also had Bit pull the blueprints for the ice cream factory. If the unsub had to make a choice in the spur of the moment, he might have gone to a location where he is most comfortable with. Considering that at least three quarters of the town if not more are employed there, I figured that it couldn't hurt to look into that possibility. I'll see if there is any room or an isolated area in or around the factory where one could...well, torture another human being without the sound traveling too far."

Brook was pleased with Sylvie's initiative. This was the first time that they'd all been in the field together, and it was good to know that they could work as a unit in such active circumstances.

Unfortunately, they were no closer to locating the unsub than when they'd first stepped into town.

"Suspects?" Brook asked as she carefully stood so as not to spill her coffee. She took a sip before setting it down and walking over to the whiteboard. Picking up the black dry erase marker, she put a line through John Gervase's name. "We know the husband had an alibi for the hour in which Lisa Gervase was taken outside of the dry cleaners. No one saw anyone hanging around town who didn't belong. Therefore, we should be looking at locals."

"Reed Feltner's father was out of town, and Reed was at football practice," Theo offered after having done some more leg work following their interview with the students at the high school. "Also, Oscar Riviera was meeting with his parole officer. They're also out."

"Can't we cross Jake Hudson off the list?" Bit asked as he tucked a loose blond strand back up underneath his grey knit hat. "He's younger than the profile suggests, not married, and doesn't seem to have an inferiority complex."

Bit's observation had Sylvie smiling at his accurate deduction.

He shifted awkwardly in his chair at the attention his words had garnered from everyone.

"What? I'm getting better at reading people. Plus, I was talking to him this morning while I ate breakfast. Trust me. He doesn't have an inferiority complex. If anything, his grief had me realizing that he really loved the victim. He also came clean with his aunt. It was obviously surprising to her. She was stunned."

Brook winced, because the more people who knew about Jake Hudson's affair with the victim, the harder it would be for her husband and children. Brook was just relieved that she had been able to keep hidden the fact that Lily had been the first one to share that piece of information.

"Jake Hudson doesn't have an alibi, though," Brook pointed out, still not willing to cross him off the list. "I'd rather err on the side of caution. Principal Bissett wasn't fond of John Gervase, but I also got the sense that he didn't care for the victim, either. Theo, I might have you swing by their residence this weekend to have another conversation with them. See if Bissett has an alibi for both abductions."

"The Bissetts don't have any properties other than their residence in town," Bit shared as he leaned farther back in his seat. "Aren't you going out to the Solano residence tomorrow?"

"I'm heading over there first thing in the morning. We've established that Lisa Gervase's body was left at the location where she and Hudson had been secretly conducting their tryst. I spoke with Stan earlier today, and he's attempting to figure out if Nancy Buckner was having an affair with someone. If he can come up with a name, we might be able to discover where the unsub will—"

"Dump her body?" The question had come from Deputy Bud Wright. Brook hadn't been startled by the interruption the way it had done to Sylvie. Her chair was on the opposite side of the room, and Brook was basically blocking the young woman's view. She had even sloshed some hot tea over her hand. "Do you think he's already killed her?"

Brook had left the door open after having brewed up the rest of the horrible coffee that had to have come from an expired

CHAPTER TWENTY

can of generic garbage. She was pretty sure she'd even spotted rust on the edges, but caffeine was caffeine. She had seen the young deputy at his desk, finishing up some paperwork from an earlier call.

"No," Brook replied softly, not missing the way that Theo was rubbing his chin. Bud Wright was still idealistic, and it was evident that he loved his hometown. He couldn't fathom anyone in the area capable of doing what had been done to Lisa Gervase. "I believe that she's still alive. He actively prolongs their torture."

It came across as callous, but Nancy Buckner was no doubt wishing for a quick death as the rest of them stood in the safety of the station. Brook had seen the looks of disgust that they'd received as they drove back through town before the storms had rolled into the area.

Most everyone assumed that they weren't doing enough to locate Nancy Buckner, but that was far from the truth. Brook had seen firsthand on many investigations with the Bureau how dividing up aspects of a case could get them farther than simply concentrating on one particular task.

Stan leading the search for the second victim was ongoing, and she doubted that he'd even had a chance to eat in the last twenty-four hours. Same could be said for those additional officers that he had out canvassing the town, talking with the residents, and basically attempting to overturn every rock along the side of the road while looking for clues.

"Prepare for the worst, and hope for the best." Sylvie had been the one to offer that advice as she'd taken the napkins that Bit had handed her and wiped off her fingers. "General Elliott imparted that wisdom to me a while ago. Bud, how well did you know Nancy Buckner?"

While the deputy explained that he and his wife attended church with the Buckners every Sunday, Brook couldn't help but wonder when Graham had given such advice to Sylvie. Brook hadn't heard a word from him since their last phone call, and the days that had passed had done little to ease her frustration.

Anger would be a more apt word, but she had tried to see things through his eyes.

Unfortunately, he seemed to be okay with sporting blinders.

"...doesn't seem like the type of woman to have an affair." Bud's point of view on the topic had caught Brook's interest. What if he was onto something? "Plus, how would she even have the time? She's basically a taxi for her three children. One is in cheer, one is involved in football, and the other is in the chess club. Nancy also has her tailoring business. Odds and ends, mostly. If clothes need hemmed quickly, she is always the go-to person. My sister is a tad on the short side and would always take her clothes to Nancy so that they could be properly tailored."

"Bit, can you—"

"Already on it, Boss." Bit had already spun his chair around to face his numerous monitors. "Look at that. We're starting to think alike."

"What? What did I say?" Bud asked as he straightened his shoulders. "Was I able to help in some way?"

"Well, Lisa Gervase was abducted in front of the dry cleaners, and you're telling us that Nancy Buckner had a tailoring business on the side," Theo commented as he rolled his chair over so that he could see what Bit was searching for in the various databases available to them...and most likely, some that weren't on the up and up. "It could simply be a coincidence, but it is a possible connection that is worth checking out."

Bud nodded vigorously, his need to help in any way coming through earnestly until he stopped mid-turn in his bid to go back to work. He observed Theo and Bit for a moment before turning his attention toward Brook.

"Ma'am? I know Sid Thibodeaux. He's owned that dry cleaning outlet for the past forty years, if not more." Bud's previous enthusiasm for helping had faded quickly when he comprehended the severity of making connections from one resident to another. "He even walks with a cane. I can't imagine that—"

"Deputy Wright, we aren't here to randomly accuse the townsfolk in Stillwater of murder." Brook wasn't usually the one who took time to reassure her colleagues when they became uncomfortable with the way an investigation unwound in any given timeframe. Something about the young man's struggle to comprehend the atrocity that had taken place in his hometown had her stepping outside of her comfort zone. "In order to stop an unhinged mind such as we are dealing with right now, we need to find the smallest lead in order to find others. No one in this station is accusing Mr. Thibodeaux of torturing and killing anyone. That doesn't mean he doesn't have an employee, a relative, or even a customer who got it in his head that these women needed to be targeted. We've done our best to treat your fellow neighbors with respect, and we plan to continue to do so for the remainder of the investigation."

Bud slowly nodded, though she wasn't so sure that her words had been effective. The last thing she wanted was for him to keep information to himself for fear of them jumping to conclusions. She'd done her best to explain how their process worked when they were out in the field. Hell, it was the same as when they took on cold cases and were able to piece together a timeline from decades prior.

"Are you going back out on patrol?" Sylvie asked as she crossed the office, seemingly understanding Brook's concern. "It's a downpour out there, but I could use a break. Do you mind if I ride along with you?"

Brook understood Sylvie's motivation for such an offer, but her unique skills as an analyst was crucial if they stood a chance to find a connection between the victims. Still, it was equally important for Bud Wright and the other deputies to understand that they weren't being disloyal in any way toward one another. In fact, they could very well be saving the lives of their loved ones by coming forward with information that to them was otherwise meaningless.

"Where is the sheriff?" Theo asked once Sylvie and Bud were out of earshot. "He might have prejudgments about certain residents, but he's been upfront so far. He can offer us more insight into Mr. Thibodeaux. The ice cream factory employs a lot of people in a fifty-mile radius. There's a small chance our unsub doesn't live in Stillwater. What if he utilizes the services of the dry cleaners? Working an eight-hour shift or even a double shift can make an outsider feel like he belongs in the area to those working with him."

Theo made an excellent point, and Brook was going to have use the rest of the evening to go back over her profile.

Had she gotten it wrong?

Had she steered the team in the wrong direction?

"While you pay a visit to the Bissetts tomorrow, I think I'll take a drive over to the ice cream factory after speaking with the Solanos. I think it's time we meet the Boyles and see what is up with the largest employer in town."

Brook walked over to where she'd set down her leather bag. Once she'd pulled out her electronic tablet, she retraced her steps to Sylvie's chair. On the way, she'd taken the coffee mug from Theo that he'd been holding out to her without ever taking his gaze off Bit's monitor.

Even though Stan was handling the abduction part of the investigation, they were all working on the same case. That meant everyone had a deadline, because Nancy Buckner was running out of time.

CHAPTER TWENTY-ONE

Unsub
May 2022
Sunday — 3:19pm

THE HUMIDITY LEFT BEHIND from the latest round of thunderstorms blanketed the area with an oppressive layer of dampness. There was even a musky odor hanging in the air that contained a smothering sensation when one attempted to breathe.

It was the perfect time to pay Nancy a visit.

He'd only been able to call on her once since he'd brought her out to the cabin. Life had gotten in the way of his enjoyment, but he couldn't allow anyone to notice the changes in his routine. Plus, he'd enjoyed watching from afar as Brooklyn Sloane, her team, and the police chased their tails. He'd known deep down that he would be good at this game, and their incompetence continued to prove that he would win round after round.

Just to be sure that he was still ahead of them, he'd circled the town three times before taking the backroad that led all the way back to his uncle's cabin. He wasn't worried that his name would be associated with any of the surrounding properties. Technically, his connection to his uncle was through marriage.

His aunt had died many years ago, not that she'd been around much when he'd been younger.

He often wondered if she had any scars on her body.

"Oh, Nancy," he called out as he opened the door. The foul smell of body excrements hit him hard, but it wasn't like he'd given her any other option. He set the items that he'd brought from the house down on a rotted table that he'd pushed against the far wall. "I can see that I have some cleaning up to do before we get started with our lesson. We have around two hours together, so we don't want to waste much time. Why don't I catch you up on what has been going on in town?"

He ignored her pleas as he collected the bucket that he'd stored in the corner. It had collected rain from the leak above, which he'd known it would do when he'd positioned the bucket underneath the small hole in the ceiling. Otherwise, he would have had to go out back to the pond, which he didn't want to do since he was on a time limit.

It took him around ten minutes to clean up what had run off from the table to the floor, as well as the table itself. He'd learned from his past mistakes with Lisa, and he should have tended to some of her needs sooner. Maybe if he'd given her water or food within the first few days, she would have last longer than two weeks.

"I brought you some water and a protein bar."

As he took the two items over to the table, he got the sense from her stillness that Nancy believed that she could somehow be saved. He needed to put an end to those hopes and wishes that she still clung to in the forefront of her mind.

"I'm going to remove your gag now, but you should know that no one can hear you. As a matter of fact, you'll be glad to know that I won't be putting your gag back in until I leave for home. I don't like whining. The only screams that I want to hear from you are those indicating that my lessons are making an impression upon you."

His words had the desired effect, because Nancy's eyes widened in fear. They even filled with tears as he managed to pull down the handkerchief that he'd used to keep another one inside her mouth. He removed the cloth that he'd shoved

CHAPTER TWENTY-ONE

onto her tongue, not surprised to find it dry. She had to be dehydrated, which had been part of his problem with Lisa.

"Isn't that better?"

Nancy had begun to cough, but her restraints held her in place. He'd even made sure that she couldn't move her hips by using a cargo strap. Once she'd recovered, he poured some water in between her cracked lips. It was as if she couldn't get enough, but he vaguely recalled going four days without food or water when he'd been eight or nine years old.

"W-why are you d-doing this?"

He and Nancy had known each other all their lives. Wasn't that true of most of the residents in Stillwater? But knowing someone didn't really mean that you had knowledge of every single part of their lives. Otherwise, someone might have...

No.

He shook his head to dispel such thoughts of betrayal to the woman who had raised him.

"I'm doing this to teach you a lesson. No matter what life deals you, it is your responsibility to be a dutiful wife, a loyal friend, and to give back to our community. You failed to fulfill those duties, Nancy. Miserably."

It was good that Nancy was weak from lack of nourishment. She wouldn't be able to fight so hard against what was to come. He set the bottle of water aside before walking over to pick up the container of thermite.

His heart rate began to accelerate, and his palms began to sweat.

There was enough time for him to savor her screams, so he purposefully slowed down his movements.

There was no need to rush such a beautiful process.

"P-please. I h-haven't done a-anything wrong."

Nancy's voice hitched as he brought over the thermite and began to coat her ring finger with the dark, grey powder. He'd so wanted to do this on Friday, but obligations with his wife had to come first. He'd taken the combustible powder and suspended it in a quick-drying plaster base. It allowed him to mold the compound around objects perfectly. Once dry, it could be ignited with ease. He'd pictured this moment repeated while enduring the time spent waiting. It had taken all his restraint, but he'd finally been able to carve a couple of hours out for himself.

"Noooooo."

Adrenaline and arousal began to mix in his bloodstream.

Fear was beginning to invade every pore in Nancy's body. She was trying to pull frantically away from the composition of metal powder that would automatically turn her skin to ash once torched by a flame. There was no stopping her fate, and she would soon find out why she should have made different choices in her life.

The paste had dried quicker than he'd initially thought it would take. He was still experimenting with his plaster to thermite ratio. Making sure to clean his own hands extremely well, he turned the towel over in his hands repeatedly. It wouldn't do to burn himself accidentally.

His fingers were practically trembling in anticipation as he reached for the culinary blowtorch. The device made it so easy to do what was necessary...and what he desired to do most in the world.

He pulled over a chair so that he could get a better viewing angle in order for the violent flame to kiss her wedding ring. It was much like watching the tip of a sparkler. The energetic reaction was white hot.

Her piercing screams were music to his ears.

Chapter Twenty-Two

Brooklyn Sloane
May 2022
Thursday — 4:03pm

"He's on line two."

Brook had been waiting days for this phone call.

Seven agonizing days, to be precise.

This case was a damned good reminder of why she preferred cold cases rather than she did active ones, but there had been no turning back once the governor of West Virginia had officially requested their assistance.

She placed the blame for their predicament solely at Graham Elliott's polished leather dress shoes.

They were mere hours short of a week since Nancy Buckner had been abducted. Brook had no doubt that the woman had suffered horrifically during that time, but neither the state police nor the team of S&E had been able to find an adequate lead in the case.

Nothing had been found to identify the unsub, and no leads had been discovered to pinpoint Nancy Buckner's current location.

The only good news they'd received from the state forensics lab had been about the DNA discovered on Lisa Gervase's body. Unfortunately, there were no matches in the system. Whoever had been responsible for the woman's death, and most likely the subsequent death of Nancy Buckner, had never before committed a crime serious enough to serve time in jail.

Prisoners in state facilities were required to give DNA samples, regardless of the seriousness of their offenses. DNA samples were taken as a security precaution. Unfortunately, those with minor offenses who served time in county jails weren't subject to the same requirements.

The military DNA database was only subject to search with a court order, so there were specific rules prohibiting government agencies from violating the privacy of service members. Chances were good that this type of unsub would never have served voluntarily in any military service. The individual who they were dealing with was weak both mentally and most likely physically in comparison to other men.

As for the link between the victims and the dry cleaner, nothing had proved fruitful on that front.

The owners of the ice cream factory had been nothing but cooperative in providing a list of their employees, schedules, and any of the delivery services that they had utilized over the last year. Theo's visit to the Bissett residence hadn't unveiled anything new, and Brook had spent most of Sunday speaking with the Solanos. The two little girls had been allowed to answer questions under the supervision of their mothers, but nothing had come of those conversations, either.

Monday had been spent trying to figure out who Nancy Buckner could have been having an affair with, but everyone in town seemed to be in agreement that she would never be unfaithful to her husband. Stan had created search units that had combed through nearly every building in town, along with fields and woods that surrounded the immediate area.

Tuesday, Brook and Theo had driven to numerous properties that were located on the east end of town that housed cabins, shacks, and large-sized pole barns. Yesterday, Brook had hit the hardware store to buy a pair of work boots that had been

CHAPTER TWENTY-TWO

more proper for the rough terrain before conducting a search of properties that were south of town. Nothing had come of their exploration, and today had been spent combing through maps in order to split up the west and north, which contained denser woodlands and less open farming fields.

"Follow the script."

Brook stared at the hostage negotiator that Stan's supervisor thought would be an added benefit, though the only thing his appearance had done was stir up the media. The more time that had passed in Nancy Buckner's abduction, the larger the media presence had grown in town.

Right this minute, at least seven different news outlets were parked across the street.

"Ms. Sloane?"

"I heard you."

It wasn't that Ned Bracken didn't have the best intentions. She was sure that he was very good at his job, but the unsub didn't want someone to talk to in a sense that he wanted something in return. The only thing that the unsub desired at the moment was praise for his performance. He wanted her to say that she'd met her match, that he was better than her brother, and that he was smarter than the police.

He needed her to stroke his ego.

Stan was still at the Buckner residence, the sheriff was helping to organize the search parties, and Theo was out speaking with Nancy Buckner's friends. He was still under the impression that someone had to know something about an affair, regardless of how well Lisa Gervase had done in covering up her own affair with Jake Hudson.

Sylvie was back at her desk in the corner, still attempting to make a connection between the two victims. Right now, all her attention was on Brook.

"Bit?" Brook wanted to make sure that everything was in place before she accepted the call. His brief nod had her pressing the button that would have the unsub on speaker phone. "Sloane."

"You aren't very good at this game, Ms. Sloane."

"Aren't I?"

Bracken rubbed his forehead before practically jabbing his finger into the piece of paper that contained nothing but generalized sentences meant to calm an individual down. The unsub didn't seem in any way, shape, or form to be upset. If anything, he was gloating, and Brook fought the urge to take him down a peg.

"If you were, you would have found Nancy by now."

The unsub was talkative today.

There was also something in his whisper that sounded familiar, but Brook couldn't place what was recognizable in the tone. Still, Brook was more concerned that the unsub was in such good spirits.

"What is it that you want from me?" Brook had to clear her throat before she read from the script. She damn well already knew what the unsub wanted from her, and that was a competition. One that she was sorely losing at the moment. "Actually, never mind that last question. I could give two shits what you want from me."

Bracken muttered a few choice words underneath his breath as he pushed the paper with such force that it flew off the table. He pulled his cell phone from his pocket and began to contact someone, most likely his supervisor. Well, the sergeant or lieutenant could damn well take it up with the governor.

"You want to know how good I am?" Brook glanced at Bit, who was making a motion with his hand that she keep talking and prolonging the call. "I know that you're in your mid to late thirties. You're married. You grew up in Stillwater, and your mother most likely was the one who instilled in you this hatred toward other women who didn't live up to her unrealistic expectations. Did she burn you? Is that how she punished you? How am I doing so far?"

Silence filled the other end of the line, but she could still hear him breathing. His respiration was labored, and she'd succeeded in stunning him with her ability to profile his life. Bit slowly began to stand from his chair, still motioning with his hand that she keep the call going.

They were close to pinpointing the unsub's location.

CHAPTER TWENTY-TWO

Sylvie suddenly stood up from the desk in the corner, quickly closing the distance between them with her phone in hand. She held it up for Brook to see that Theo had sent her a text message. By this point, Brook had pushed her own chair back to get to her feet and was using her palms to lean forward on the table.

"You don't—"

"We both know that Nancy is dead," Brook stated matter-of-factly, not caring that Bracken had enough of listening to her go off script. He'd basically stormed out of the office, past one of the state troopers that had been standing in the doorway. "Did you not take into account that she was fifteen years older than Lisa? That had to really upset you, didn't it? There's one thing that I can't figure out, though."

Brook purposefully paused, knowing that they needed mere seconds to pinpoint the unsub's location.

"You know nothing!"

Satisfaction shot through Brook when the unsub's anger got the best of him. Technically, Nancy Buckner's supposed death should have soured the unsub's disposition. Brook figured he was making himself feel better by calling to rub it in her face, but she'd turned the tables on him.

"I know that Nancy Buckner didn't cheat on her husband. As a matter of fact, Nancy remained faithful to Pete during their entire marriage. But you somehow figured out that Nancy and her best friend—Tina Reed—had a falling out. They put up appearances for the sake of their families, but Victor Reed got drunk one night and made a pass at Nancy. She didn't want her husband to know, Tina didn't want word spreading around town, so the two came to an agreement to keep it to themselves. It still strained their friendship. I'm curious, though. How did you find out about their deal?"

Bit was scrambling to write down an address, which he quickly handed to the state trooper.

Brook had immediately muted her end of the line so that the trooper could radio other units.

"Husband. Friend. Betrayal is all the same."

If Brook could keep the unsub on the phone for just a little longer, there was a good chance that the officers responding to the appropriate code over the radio could take him into custody.

"*Is* betrayal the same? Does wanting to protect a friend and another's reputation really justify what you did to Nancy Buckner?" Brook didn't think that she'd be able to keep the unsub on the line for much longer, so she followed up with her original question. "How did you know? How did you know about Victor making a pass at his wife's best friend?"

The line went dead, but Brook was already reaching for the sticky note that Bit was holding out to her. He'd written the same address on it as he had for the officer. Sylvie was already one step ahead with the keys of the SUV in her hand.

"Bit, let me know if that signal starts to move."

"Will do, Boss," Bit called out as Brook and Sylvie rushed out of the office and toward the glass door exit. "Go get him!"

Brook didn't even bother to look for Bracken. He was probably packing up his things and heading back to his barracks. She would deal with the fallout of that situation at a later date.

Sylvie didn't have to plug the address into the GPS. The officer's lights and siren could still be seen and heard driving west of town. Plus, Brook had recognized the address. It was that of the high school. It didn't take long for Sylvie to turn over the engine and pull out of the station's parking lot. While she drove, Brook pulled out her cell phone from her back pocket.

"We have a location." Brook rattled off the address as she attempted to fasten her seatbelt. Sylvie was driving like a bat out of hell, not that Brook would complain. She was somehow managing to close the distance between them and one of the news vans up ahead. Unfortunately, two of them had the same idea to follow in pursuit. "That was fantastic work, Theo. It was exactly what I needed to keep the unsub on the phone long enough for Bit to ping the unsub's burner phone. We'll meet you there."

The officer made a righthand turn.

Brook held onto the door handle as Sylvie somehow managed to pass one of the vans before cutting in front and making the righthand turn in record time.

CHAPTER TWENTY-TWO

"I don't want to know where you learned to drive like this," Brook muttered as she doublechecked the metal clip of the seat belt. "I'd like to live long enough to learn the unsub's name."

"I grew up around race cars. Some of my dad's clients sponsored a few drivers."

"Of course, you did." There was always some new detail that popped up about a team member during a case, and this one was no different. "Watch the—"

Brook closed her eyes as Sylvie began to pass the second news van on a side road that was barely wide enough for two vehicles. It would be fitting that Brook had chosen last week to walk into a church. She certainly wasn't the praying type, but she found herself muttering words that were damn similar.

"Vans don't have the wheelbase to make them stable while turning corners. Their center of gravity is too high. SUVs aren't much better, but it all depends on acceleration and deceleration at the appropriate times."

"I knew that," Brook muttered as she adjusted herself in the seat so that her seatbelt wasn't digging into her left hip. She had somehow managed to get ahold of Bit as the officer made another right. "Is the unsub still in the area?"

"Hasn't moved, Boss. He's somewhere in between the middle school and the high school."

"We're pulling up now." Brook had relaxed somewhat now that the school had come into view. It was quite large, but that was due to the surrounding towns bussing students into the local school district. "You said in between, right? Sylvie, cut through here. The unsub has to be near the softball field. Bit, can you—"

"Nancy Buckner and Tina Reed played softball together from freshman year through their senior year," Bit revealed, having already been on the same page. He'd been a fast learner, and he'd quickly gotten into sync with how an investigation worked between team members. "He's still there, Boss."

Brook had been surveying the landscape, and no other vehicles could be seen with the exception of the patrol car to the left of them and the two news vans behind them. She glanced over her shoulder. Make that three.

"Sylvie, keep them back when we get out of the car," Brook directed, already knowing that they were going to find Nancy Buckner's body. By the time that Sylvie had brought the car to a stop, Brook had already unfastened her seatbelt and had her hand on the door handle. "Bit, call up the school's security footage. The unsub isn't here."

"Without a warrant?"

Fuck.

"No. I'll speak to Stan and get back to you."

"How could he have driven away so fast?" Sylvie asked as she turned off the ignition. She was out of the car and scanning the area, as well. "We were here in under three minutes."

"Long enough to toss the burner and drive away. He most likely left it near the body." Brook waved to the officer who had weaved through a connecting parking lot. "Sylvie, can you keep things under control here?"

"Yes. Plus, it looks like the backup is arriving."

Sure enough, the sound of sirens pierced through the area after the officer who they had followed shut his own off upon pulling to a stop next to their SUV. Brook had already begun to make her way down the sidewalk that led to a large diamond baseball field. She shielded her eyes against the sun, examining every visible inch of the field.

It didn't take her long to spot the body of Nancy Buckner.

Brook slowed her steps as she continued to make her way to home base. By the time that she was thirty feet from the body, she'd already figured out which direction the unsub had taken to transport what was left of the woman. The second victim wasn't nude like Lisa Gervase, though she no longer had skin on her left hand.

Had he undressed the first victim based on what her betrayal had been?

If so, why burn Nancy Buckner's left hand? Was it due to the best friend's husband hitting on her?

"Don't walk any farther," Brook warned the officer, putting out her hand to ensure that he followed her instructions. She'd heard him approaching from behind, but forensics would want first crack at the baseball field. The dirt would have the

CHAPTER TWENTY-TWO 193

impressions left behind by the soles of the unsub's shoes. "Did you get ahold of Detective Turner?"

"He's pulling into the parking lot now, ma'am."

Brook had almost forgotten that she'd had Bit on the phone. She placed it to her ear, hoping that she was wrong about the conclusion that she'd come to regarding the school's security cameras. In all likelihood, the baseball field was too far away from the school buildings. As for the middle school, there was a line of trees that prevented a good enough view from that angle.

The unsub would have already scoped out the area, which could potentially mean that they would be able to go back by at least three or four weeks to see if someone had scouted the area that didn't belong. Of course, that was highly unlikely given that the unsub could very well have children. The unsub would have already known the layout of the grounds. She hadn't brought up family in their phone call today, but she'd been more concerned about keeping him on the line.

She'd also taken a guess about the death of the second victim.

"Please stay here and make sure that no one gets anywhere close," Brook instructed the officer. She wanted to canvas the area farther out, hoping that the unsub made a mistake under duress. She'd certainly made him angry enough. "Thank you."

As much as Brook wanted to get closer to the body, she would wait for the forensics team. She understood how important it was to secure evidence, and she'd seen individuals arrested on something as simple as the imprint of a shoe's sole.

Would they get that lucky in this investigation?

Only time would tell.

"How bad?" Stan asked as he walked closer. Brook could see the chaos behind him. Sylvie was doing the best she could to keep the press at bay, and she should be able to join Brook soon given the amount of officers arriving on the scene. "Did he leave her displayed like the first victim?"

"Not exactly." Brook began to see a few more cars pulling into the school parking lot. One of them was Principal Bissett. She was curious as to how he found out so quickly that a body had been dumped on school grounds. "Nancy Buckner's body is still dressed in the clothes that she disappeared in. He didn't get to savor her pain like he was able to with the first victim. She died quicker than he'd anticipated. Probably from shock, just as with Lisa Gervase, only Nancy Buckner was older. She just couldn't take the strain."

"I've already called in forensics," Stan replied, running a hand over his face. "I was at the Buckner's place. I made sure I left an officer with—"

"I don't think Mr. Buckner took your advice," Brook stated softly, feeling for Stan. Mr. Buckner was ignoring the officers attempting to keep him back. It was of no use, but Stan was going to have to convince the man not to get too close for the sake of the investigation. "No offense, Stan, but you look like shit. After today, go home and get some sleep. Forensics will take the scene, and I'll help oversee what I can if your sergeant or lieutenant doesn't try to have us kicked out of town after my phone call with the unsub."

"You're not going anywhere, if I have anything to say about it." Stan took time to walk up to the officer nearest the scene. He stood still for a moment, and she thought she saw him make a cross the way Catholics did when saying a prayer, but she couldn't be sure from the way his back was toward her. He eventually turned back around and continued walking until he came to a stop beside her. "What do you need?"

"A warrant for the footage of the high school's security system. All of it. All the way back to the beginning of last month."

"You'll have it in under the hour."

Stan didn't bother to say anything else as he began to retrace his steps toward where Mr. Buckner had made it past two of the officers. She could hear Stan explaining to the grieving man that seeing his wife in such a manner would only make things worse. It wasn't until Stan began to explain how important it was for forensics to be able to process the scene for DNA evidence left behind by the killer that had Mr. Buckner falling to his knees and sobbing.

"They're vultures," Sylvie murmured after she'd left Sheriff Kennard and a deputy to deal with the press. All seven news crews had arrived, and every camera was directed toward Mr. Buckner. "Theo is canvassing the back roads right now. It's a

CHAPTER TWENTY-TWO

long shot, but he's going to record with his phone every vehicle that he passes on the backroads north of here."

Brook nodded, appreciating Theo's effort. The unsub had clearly driven close enough to carry the victim's body without too much effort. They hadn't passed any vehicles, so the unsub had to have utilized one of the back exits.

"I want to walk around the other side of the baseball diamond. Do we have any gloves in the car?"

Sylvie pulled two latex gloves out of her back pocket. She held one of them out to Brook.

"I also have a plastic baggie in my other pocket, just in case we find something." Sylvie held up her hand before Brook could launch into a lecture. "I know, I know. Don't get too close to the scene, and don't touch anything that appears to be evidence left behind by the unsub. I'll head back to the parking lot. One of the officers has to have numbered markers in the trunk of his car that we can use as markers."

Brook was fine with a moment alone.

When she'd been with the Bureau, she hadn't been requested to walk a lot of crime scenes. Still, she'd drafted her most accurate profiles by doing a walkthrough. Those that were outdoors made it somewhat difficult to get a feel for what the unsub might have been thinking during the act. Add on that their unsub hadn't killed the victim at this location, it made it even harder to discern his motives and technics.

She was already aware of the reason for this specific locality, but she'd been giving it some thought since they'd arrived at the high school. It couldn't have been easy to carry a dead body to and from the baseball diamond.

Even a small adult woman usually weighed more than a hundred pounds.

Brook might have to reevaluate her summation of the unsub's physical build.

Brook didn't wait for Sylvie to return. She'd eventually catch up, but Brook wanted to see if she'd come to the right conclusion. If she were the unsub, she would have used something to transport the body from a vehicle to the baseball diamond.

She began to slowly and methodically walk around the entire field, even going behind the batter's cage. As she got closer to the tree line, she surveyed the ground before taking any steps that could potentially damage any evidence. When she spotted what she'd been looking for, she immediately took pictures with her cell phone before calling Theo.

"Where are you?"

"East of the high school. Why?"

Brook glanced down at the flattened grass where the tire of a wheelbarrow made an impression that was distinctive and proved without a doubt that the unsub hadn't cut through the parking lot. A wheelbarrow cut the estimate of the unsub's strength once again. He'd had to use an equalizer.

It appeared that he'd also known about the security cameras.

"I know how the unsub transported Nancy Buckner's body to the baseball diamond. I want you to secure the scene before anyone else figures it out." Brook glanced across the field to where the media was currently setting up cameras to give live reports from the scene. Sure enough, Sarah Evanston was off to the side, keeping a close eye on Sylvie as she made her way across the grass on the west side of the field. "There should be some type of backroad that leads from the high school to the middle school. Find it. I'll meet you there."

CHAPTER TWENTY-THREE

Brooklyn Sloane
May 2022
Friday — 5:26am

THE LOWER LEVEL OF the B&B had the distinct, delicious smell of bacon hovering in the air. There were times that a specific fragrance or the faintest noise brought Brook back to her childhood. She even strained to hear the sound of a metal meat fork scraping a cast iron frying pan, but she couldn't hear anything through the thick door that separated the kitchen from the dining room. Grabbing a coffee mug from the tray next to the large carafe, she poured herself some Dark French Roast that rivaled the grounds back at the offices of S&E Investigations, Inc.

She loathed starting the day with thoughts of Jacob swirling around in her head.

"Good morning."

Brook didn't bother turning around at the interruption.

Sarah Evanston was a pain in the ass, and her cameraman wasn't much better.

After Brook had realized how the unsub had transported Nancy Buckner's body from his vehicle to the baseball diamond, she'd retraced her steps to the parking lot. Sylvie had joined her, and they had both stopped to speak with Stan. He'd finally gotten Mr. Buckner's son, who must have arrived shortly after his father, to take the man home. The detective had promised that he'd call them the moment they were permitted to drive to the state morgue to identify Nancy Buckner's body.

Once Brook had caught Stan up-to-date on what she'd discovered, he'd promised to request additional forensics technicians. Once Brook had been given reassurances that both scenes would be properly processed, she and Sylvie had to maneuver out of the parking lot. Considering that Sarah Evanston seemed to be glued to their hips, she'd pushed for her cameraman to follow them.

"No comment."

"I guess that I should have given you time to drink your coffee."

Brook had been debating on waiting for Audrey to bring out breakfast, but it wasn't worth the hassle. She didn't even bother to put a dollop of creamer into her coffee. Instead, she decided that she'd take her mug back upstairs while waiting for Sylvie and Bit to finish getting ready. All three of them were driving to the station so that they could have the SUV close by in case it was needed.

Theo would be using the other vehicle to conduct field interviews of the staff at the middle school.

It was a long shot, but Lisa Gervase's daughter attended fourth grade. Speaking to the girl's teacher had been low on the priority list, but that was where they were in the investigation.

"Look, I know that you don't like me. I'm just trying to do my job."

"Your job isn't to one-up the other reporters. It is to report the news," Brook stated matter-of-factly, finally turning around to face the reporter. Once again, the woman's hair and makeup had been styled and applied to perfection. "It should be about warning the women of this town that their lives are in danger. Now, if you'll excuse me, I need to go see if I can stop another woman from being abducted, tortured, and then killed."

"Did you ever find out who called me at the station?"

CHAPTER TWENTY-THREE

Brook hadn't been able to take three steps toward the staircase when Sarah had decided to inquire about the message that had been left on her voicemail.

"One of my teammates was able to recover the deleted message." Brook figured she could at least answer the reporter's question. "I haven't had a chance to hear it yet, but my colleague had the sheriff and deputies listen to it earlier this week. They didn't recognize the voice. Obstructing evidence collection in an ongoing murder investigation is a felony. I wouldn't be surprised if you were questioned in this matter once the state investigators have time to come back around to you. I'd be arranging for some bail money if I were you."

Brook had been given a printout of what had been said, and there had definitely been a leak of some sort in one of the state police departments. Whether that leak was inside Stan's own squad, the forensics lab, or even the morgue was anyone's guess.

"If you receive another tip, please let me know right away."

Brook had done her best to remain civil with Sarah. The woman wasn't easy to like when she was clearly only looking out for her own self interests. If Brook thought it would garner the right response, she would have used such a means to goad the unsub into making a mistake.

Such methods had been used before.

Hell, she'd done exactly that with her brother not too long ago, not that he'd taken the bait.

Unfortunately, this particular unsub was very unstable and subject to unpredictable violent actions. There was no telling what his next move would be, and Brook wasn't about to take a chance with someone else's life when they were no closer to apprehending a suspect than when they had first set foot in town.

This time, Brook had made it to the staircase and had even been able to climb three of them before Sarah decided to try and get an official comment one more time. What the reporter didn't know was that she'd caught Brook's attention enough that she'd decided to hear the woman out.

"I might know who knew about Nancy Buckner's affair."

"What makes you think that Nancy Buckner had an affair in the first place?"

"It's obvious, isn't it?" Sarah seemed so sure of herself for coming to such a conclusion.

Stan hadn't given an official press briefing yet on yesterday's events. He was scheduled to speak at seven o'clock this morning in front of the local police station, which was why Sarah had been up so early. It was also the reason that she was hoping for some inside information to be able to drop on her viewers before any other station could get the best of her.

"You might have been able to keep the press from getting too close to the crime scene yesterday, but we were still close enough to zoom in on the body from the roof of the gym. Nancy Bucker was missing her left hand, just like Lisa Gervase. That signifies that they were both unfaithful to their husbands, right?"

Brook purposefully didn't reply.

Instead, she leisurely lifted her coffee mug and took a sip of the steaming hot beverage. The rich flavor hit the back of her throat and spread warmth throughout her body.

Sarah would have to do better than a theory that every single news station had been glued to since the news had broken regarding Lisa Gervase's affair with Jake Hudson. The only ones that Brook felt for were her children. Brook knew from experience that dire consequences of decisions made by parents determined not only the course of their own lives, but also those of their children. Aiden and Madison would never be able to outrun the damage caused by the events prior to and the subsequent tragedy of their mother's death.

"I overheard someone at the diner saying that if anyone knew about an affair, that person would be Pastor Wilson."

Brook made sure that she gave no reaction to the rumor.

She tilted her head as if to digest the news, and then she followed it up with an observation.

"Really?" Brook could feel the vibration of her cell phone that she'd tucked into the side pocket of her blazer. She ignored the call to focus on the conversation at hand. "Pastor Wilson's church is nondenominational. There is no confessional. Are

CHAPTER TWENTY-THREE

you saying that Pastor Wilson and Nancy Buckner had a close physical relationship?"

Before Sarah could respond, Audrey had come through the swinging door with a tray of scrambled eggs. She didn't seem startled by Sarah's presence so close to the door, and she even managed to get around the woman without her having to move.

"Nancy attended one of the pastor's weekly group meetings," Sarah revealed, crossing her arms in satisfaction.

She had no idea that Brook had already been made aware of the connection, and it had fallen flat last night around eight-thirty. Brook had stopped by the church to have a conversation with the good ol' pastor himself. He seemed to be at the heart of almost everyone's lives in town. He'd confirmed that Nancy had spoken to him in confidence regarding her friendship with Tina.

The weekly group meeting that Sarah had mentioned was nothing more than a bible study group, and the reason that her friendship with the woman had even come up in a private conversation had been because Tina hadn't attended the group for weeks. Pastor Wilson had pulled Nancy aside and had wanted to know if everything was alright between them. Whoever had seen the two of them talking clearly had no idea what the topic had been about, thus spinning the rumor mill even more.

"She was very close with the pastor, from what my sources are telling me."

Sarah had all but admitted that her sources were from random patrons at the diner who were as much in the dark about the victims' lives as everyone else.

"I knew Nancy," Audrey said softly as she placed the metal tray overtop a can of methanol gel chafing fuel that she'd taken the time to light while listening in on her guests' conversation. She wiped her hands on her apron as she met Brook's stare. "She wasn't the type of woman to have an affair. She loved her husband very much. She loved her family even more. None of that should have mattered, though. She didn't deserve a death like that."

Brook still fully believed that the unsub had grown up in Stillwater. He hadn't taken Nancy Buckner because of an affair, but rather what he had deemed a sin for damaging her friendship with Tina. It was Tina who the unsub felt for in this situation, which meant the focus of the investigation needed to be on her.

"Sarah, I do have a statement for you," Brook said, making a quick decision on how the rest of her morning would be spent. She quickly said what was on her mind, hoping that it would leave enough of an impression on the unsub to force his hand. She wanted another chance to speak with him on the phone. "The families left behind don't care in the least about any of the poor decisions their loved ones made during their short lives. They are simply left with a void that will never be filled, while only the good memories of their loved ones will carry on in their hearts."

Brook had no idea if Sarah would be able to recall the statement word-for-word since she hadn't written anything down, but the meaning behind Brook's sentiment would ring loud and clear. She didn't remain in place to hear Sarah's other questions. There was a lot to do today, plus her phone had started to vibrate again.

Brook answered with irritation.

"Graham, I don't have time to—"

"There is no time to explain, but I need you to tell Kate to come with me."

Graham's ominous tone spoke volumes.

Whatever his reason was to get Brook and the team out of the city seemed to have come to fruition.

"I'm asking that you trust me, if only just this once."

CHAPTER TWENTY-FOUR

Kate Lin
May 2022
Friday — 5:34am

"CAN YOU AT LEAST tell me where we are going?"

Kate Lin stood side by side with General Graham Elliott in front of the elevator bank of her apartment building. She hadn't even known that he'd been aware of where she'd lived, yet she awoke to have him knocking on her door before her morning alarm had even gone off. He'd been very polite, even having Brook on his cell phone to let Kate know that it would be in her best interest to do as he said and follow his directives. After she'd disconnected the call, he'd asked that she change out of her pajamas, pack a small travel bag with a week's worth of clothes, and take anything else that she would need while being away for a while.

"There is a black town car waiting for you downstairs. The driver will be taking you to my vacation house in the Hamptons. You'll have the run of the place while you are there." General Elliott had always come across to her as a serious man. He might have been retired from the military, but he was still deep in the life. She'd heard the team talk about his work with the government, and they hadn't even seemed to know what kind of contracts that he'd taken on once he'd retired from the Marines. "I'll call and let you know when you can come back to the city."

The elevator doors slowly slid open.

General Elliott stepped forward and held out a hand to keep the door from closing. She assumed that was his way of saying that he'd like her to enter the elevator first. She did so reluctantly, but Brook had seemed genuine in her bid to have Kate do exactly as General Elliott suggested.

Once he was by her side and he'd pressed the button for the lobby, she decided to ask another question that he might or might not answer. She honestly couldn't tell from his demeanor.

"Can you at least tell me if this is about the case in Stillwater? Is the team safe?"

Kate had only been at S&E Investigations, Inc. for a couple of months. The opportunity to work with one of the best profilers in the Bureau's history had been mind-blowing. She had never thought that she would receive a call for an interview, let alone such a generous offer. Her father hadn't been too thrilled to find out that his only daughter would be working for the sister of a serial killer, but he'd understood Kate's position on the matter.

Brook Sloane understood serial killers in a way that others could only dream of, and the value in which the opportunity to work with her could contribute to Kate's future success as a federal agent was monumental. Either that, or her association with S&E Investigations was about to get her killed.

"This has nothing to do with S&E Investigations or the case."

It was as if he'd read Kate's thoughts, and she had a feeling that was all he would say on the matter.

General Elliott reminded her a lot of Brook.

The two of them were both professionals, didn't care for small talk, and expected the most out of the people who they surrounded themselves with. Kate respected their stances, because they got the job done, whatever that job might be for that particular moment. Still, it was a lot to just uproot her own life for an entire week based on the simple word of one of the firm's owners.

CHAPTER TWENTY-FOUR 205

Technically, Brook had also agreed with this...peculiar...request.

"And yes," General Elliott surprised her by following up his previous response. "The team is safe where they are."

His answer was cryptic, but she didn't get the chance to ask any more questions. The elevator doors opened, and she had no choice but to step out so that another passenger could enter. She'd seen him before and recalled that he was an intern at the nearest hospital who worked third shift. He barely glanced their way as he waited for them to step out and allow him access.

"This way," General Elliott murmured, resting his hand on her lower back.

He guided her through the small foyer.

She didn't live in one of those fancy apartment buildings with a doorman. It didn't take them long to exit the building. The sun had yet to rise, and the city lights were still responsible for illuminating the sidewalks. A man waited by a town car, holding the back door open for her. He was maybe six feet tall, bald, but came across as friendly, if his smile was anything to go by.

"This is Gus. He'll be driving you to your destination. Should you need anything while you're there, he'll be giving you his cell phone number. Call if you have an emergency. Otherwise, be ready to come back to the city at a moment's notice. Do not leave the house under any circumstances. Agreed?"

Kate had worked so hard to get things ready for the team on their next case. She'd read every file associated with the murders of the mayor's parents. She'd even pulled and read real estate transactions from around the area, believing that the death of the couple could be related to the rising cost of land around the time that they were killed inside their barn. She was in the middle of using Bit's new ninety-eight inch, 4K, LED display touch monitor to set up the murder board. Bit had someone who he trusted to come in this past Monday and hook it up in the large conference room. They both figured that if Brook could witness the software in action, she wouldn't baulk at using it. Such a software application would then allow the murder board to appear on everyone's electronic tablets with full read/write privileges.

"Is there any way that I can convince you to let me grab something from the office?" If Kate were going to be cooped up for the next week or so, she'd rather be able to continue working on the case. All she really needed was the tablet that she'd left in the charging station on her desk. "I won't take more than three minutes. Please. I know that I wasn't Ms. Sloane's first choice for this position, and this is the first time that she's given me such a huge role in an investigation. I need to get this right."

Kate had no idea what emergency had prompted such a severe reaction as to all but force her to leave the city before sunrise, but she was fully aware of how important it was to prove that she could contribute to the various investigations that came across their desks.

She got the distinct impression that General Elliott was about to deny her request.

"Three minutes. That's all I'm asking for."

General Elliott lifted his left arm to look at his watch.

"Fine. Three minutes. No more."

General Elliott gave more specific instructions to the driver regarding which route to take to the Hamptons while Kate settled herself into the backseat of the town car. Relief had washed through her that she would still be able to get things completed on her end before the team finished their case in Stillwater.

"Kate?" General Elliott had motioned to the driver that he would shut the door. Gus walked around the back of the car while General Elliott leaned down to impart one more warning. She was already on edge, but the seriousness in which he was making his request had the hairs on the back of her neck standing on end. "It's important that you remain in the house at the Hamptons until Gus comes to collect you. Do I have your word?"

CHAPTER TWENTY-FIVE

Brooklyn Sloane
May 2022
Friday — 8:17am

"WHAT IS HE DOING here?" Sylvie asked quietly as she brushed past Brook in the doorway of the sheriff's office. "I thought Deputy Rogers had been suspended, pending review?"

Brook had overheard the sheriff talking with the mayor on the phone. At least the conversation hadn't been with the governor. The murder of Lisa Gervase had sent this town into a downward spiral. Now that there had been a second murder involving another beloved resident, decisions were being made in a blind panic.

Granted, Deputy Lionel Rogers had technically not done anything wrong. He'd had a relationship with a reporter. That wasn't a crime, and they had subsequently proven that he had not been Sarah Evanston's source. Given the tenuous grounds, it had only been a matter of time before the deputy had been reinstated, but that had to be one of the shortest suspensions Brook had witnessed in her career.

"The mayor wants the sheriff to add more patrols to the area. He's approved overtime, too." Brook took a sip of her coffee.

She grimaced at the bitter taste, wishing that she'd brought the entire carafe with her from the inn. "Since we supplied evidence that Deputy Rogers wasn't the one to feed Sarah the information, the mayor sees no reason to be down an officer. Speaking of which, is there any progress on that front?"

"No," Sylvie replied as they both walked farther into the office. Brook closed the door for some peace and quiet so they could go over the day's schedule. "Bit said it was all but impossible to trace where a message of that type came from, especially considering the twenty-odd lines that the station's phone system has set up to their staff and contingency circuits. With that said, he mentioned that the warrant included a tap. He set something up on her line to specifically trace every call that is transferred from the main switchboard to her direct line."

"Do I want to know what he's doing out there?" Brook asked as she sat down in the chair next to his empty one. She exchanged her coffee for her tablet. She lightly touched the display before removing the stylus from its magnetic strip. "I warned Stan that Bit wasn't available for anything other than this case."

"The warrant came through for the school's security footage, but some signals were crossed with the state forensics lab. Bit wasn't being given access to the recordings." Sylvie claimed the chair in front of the desk in the corner, as usual. She pushed at her black-rimmed glasses, causing them to sit a bit more comfortable on the bridge of her nose. "Stan is taking care of the mix-up. Once it's all sorted out, we can go over your changes to today's schedule."

Brook attempted to concentrate on the things that she wanted to get done today, but her thoughts kept returning to this morning's phone call. Graham wouldn't have whisked Kate out of D.C. if there hadn't been an immediate threat. She could only assume that he'd learned something during a threat briefing when he'd been in Africa regarding some risk to their homeland.

Nuclear?

Biochemical?

The possible threats were endless, and her hand itched to call him back. If he'd simply explained the situation to begin

CHAPTER TWENTY-FIVE

with, she wouldn't have so nonchalantly ignored his request to leave town. The classification of the threat had to be high and immediate. She would have made sure that everyone had been a safe distance from the city if he'd made that distinction clear.

On the other hand, Brook understood that if everyone involved took action to save the lives of their loved ones, there would be immediate panic among the masses. Where there were whispers, there was always someone in charge able to hold them accountable.

Graham had asked for her trust, and she'd finally given it to him.

He was probably wondering why she hadn't done so to begin with, and she would have responded that he hadn't made his plea sound as urgent as he had this morning. There were times that he was as hard to read as she assumed she was during any given conversation. Her best course of action right now was to proceed ahead with the investigation and pray that he had things handled in D.C.

Around ten minutes later, Bit finally came into the office with two energy drinks in his right hand.

"Stan the Man isn't half bad once you get to know him," Bit said as he set the cans down next to his keyboard before cracking one of them open. "Smells like an ashtray, though."

"What can you tell me about Tina Reed?"

Brook's question had caught his attention. Bit glanced over his shoulder at Sylvie, because she was the one with practically an eidetic memory. While she didn't classify herself as having one, she came damn close.

"Tina Reed. Forty-eight years of age, mother of one daughter who resides in Kentucky, wife of Victor." Sylvie motioned toward one of the front windows. "She owns the boutique next to the teashop down a few blocks from here. Victor is one of the managing shift supervisors at the ice cream factory. As you already know, she was best friends with Nancy Buckner."

"Well, until Victor tied one too many on and hit on Nancy." Bit paused long enough to take a sip of his energy drink before casting Brook with a questioning gaze. "Shouldn't Theo be here for this meeting?"

"Theo is at the middle school interviewing Madison Gervase's teacher."

Brook had pulled up the shared files, finally locating the one with Tina Reed's name on the label. Once Brook had opened it, she perused the bullet points that Sylvie had already rattled off from the top of her head. Brook also took time to read the woman's statement that had been given to Stan the day after Nancy Buckner had disappeared. Theo had incorporated his notes from his interview with the woman, and he'd been thorough, as usual.

"I'm going to take a walk around town," Brook advised, deciding to try another tactic to gain insight into the lives of the townsfolk. She turned off her tablet and set it down on the table. "Sylvie, keep trying to find that needle in our haystack. Bit, let me know if you can find anything on the security footage from both the high school and the middle school. Make sure you go back at least three weeks to see if anyone unusual was scouting the area."

Brook fastened her blazer as she stood, not wanting to make anyone outside of the station uncomfortable by the sight of her firearm. She picked up her purse that she had hung from the back of the chair and slid the strap over her shoulder.

There were still a couple of items that she needed to address.

"Sylvie, would you please call Tina Reed and set up an interview with her for one o'clock this afternoon?"

Brook decided not to finish her coffee. She'd stop in at the diner across the street.

The unsub had to get through an entire day acting as if everything was normal in his life. He would have to go through the motions with his wife and colleagues, all the while fighting back the urge to call her about her statement to the press.

"Bit, see if Sarah Evanston said anything about me when she went on the air this morning. I'll take a look at it when I get back. Oh, and Kate isn't in the office today. She's working remotely for the rest of the week."

"What?" Bit asked as he whipped around to face her. She'd tacked on the last part about Kate as she'd neared the door to

CHAPTER TWENTY-FIVE

the office. "What do you mean? I just spoke to her last night. She seemed fine. Is she sick?"

"She's not sick. General Elliott needed her assistance with something outside of the office."

Brook had carefully chosen her words.

She had no idea what was going on, and she might never know. Graham dealt with volatile situations that would have the majority of people living in fear twenty-four-seven. She didn't like to admit that she should have extended him the courtesy of listening to him earlier last week, but she couldn't rewind time. She'd wished for that many times in her life, but nothing could change her reality.

"I'll bring back lunch."

Brook closed the door behind her before either of them could ask her anymore questions about Kate. They would likely reach out to the young woman, but Brook was confident that she was as much in the dark as to why Graham escorted her out of the city as Brook was at the moment.

"Going somewhere?"

The question had come from Stan, who was currently sitting at a deputy's desk.

"Taking a walk," Brook offered up, noticing that Gail was on the phone and the deputies had already gone on patrol—even Deputy Rogers. Sheriff Kennard wasn't anywhere to be found, either. "I'll be back with lunch."

"You're speaking my language. Hey, just so you know, but forensics found something else at Lisa Gervase's crime scene. This is going to sound odd, but there was a dollop of sap on her heel."

"Dollop?"

"Something my grandmother used to say," Stan defended with a shrug. "Anyway, they said the sap came from a maple tree. There are no maple trees where she was found on that dirt road. Only rows of pine trees on either side." Stan nodded toward the monitor in front of him. "We canvassed the areas east and north of town relatively well, so I'm going to start marking off places in the west and south where these trees are found."

"Theo and Sylvie have a map hanging in the office," Brook said as she began to walk toward the exit. "They already made a grid, so cross off any properties that you're able to eliminate. We're talking hundreds of cabins and homes, but we'll eventually figure out the location where the unsub is torturing his victims. Call me on my cell if you need anything."

Brook stepped outside and immediately regretted not having thought through her idea. The doors to several media vans began to slide open in unison as the camera techs grabbed their equipment.

Even the reporters were scrambling for their microphones.

"I'm just stretching my legs," she called out, making sure that her voice carried across the street. "No comment, as usual."

Nothing she said was going to get them to back off, and she could just imagine her picture being splashed across the news that she was window shopping while women were being murdered in a small town. They would spin the story however they wanted to in order to garner more viewers. There was nothing she could do about it. As a matter of fact, now would be the perfect time to do something rather mundane so that they got the idea that following her would be nothing more than a waste of time.

She crossed the road after looking in each direction, much to the amazement of the press.

"Detective Turner said today that your profile was updated to include..."

"...anything new on the case?"

"Are you any closer to..."

Brook ignored all the questions being thrown in her face, even holding up a hand to make sure that one of the microphones didn't hit her in the head. She never once faltered in her stride or else she wouldn't have been able to step up on the curb. Without addressing any of them, she continued on until she was able to reach the diner.

The door opened before she could grab the handle.

"Leave her alone," Samuel Bissett said as he turned his back to the glass. "Are you okay?"

"Yes, thank you."

CHAPTER TWENTY-FIVE 213

Brook could sense that the attention of the diners eating their breakfasts were solely on her. She couldn't fathom why the principal of the school where a body had been found last night wasn't in his office. This was one of the reasons that she'd wanted to take a walk around town, though she never would have guessed that she'd be running into one of the prime suspects so quickly.

After all, Principal Bissett was of the right age, had been born and raised in the area, was married, and according to what Bit had discovered right before the unsub called into the station yesterday...expecting their first child. "I'm surprised to find you here, Principal Bissett."

"I'm heading over to the school now. Seeing as the superintendent believed it was in the best interest of the students and their families to have a day off, I thought I should enjoy a breakfast with my wife. It's times like these that we are forced to appreciate those who mean the most in our lives." Principal Bissett slid his hands inside the pockets of his slacks before lowering his voice. "Wouldn't you agree?"

After Brook had entered the diner and turned around to face Principal Bissett, she had a relatively clear view of the police station now that the members of the press were disbanding back to their vans. Unfortunately, they'd also caught sight of the same vehicle that she had as it pulled up next to the curb. Theo's drive out to the middle school hadn't yielded an interview with Madison Gervase's teacher.

"If school has been cancelled, why not spend the entire day with your wife?" Brook asked nonchalantly as she slowly began to make her way to the counter. She would place a lunch order for the group back at the station and pick it up around noon. "These murders have unsettled everyone, and I'm sure your wife will feel more secure with you by her side."

"Vera will be joining me, of course." Principal Bissett pulled out his wallet when a young cashier came up behind the register with a smile. "While Mrs. Buckner wasn't part of the school system, most of the students knew her from homecoming, prom, and the like. The dry cleaners can only handle so much business, and she would take the overflow of students needing dresses, suits, or tuxedos tailored for such events."

"Excuse me," Vera said with a slight nod of acknowledgement toward Brook. "Sam, I'm going to spend the day over at Tina Reed's residence. I just ran into Meg Jackson, and she said that Tina isn't doing so well with the news about Nancy. Meg said that she'll drop me off at home later this afternoon. I have that appointment we discussed earlier at four o'clock today."

The cashier had already taken Principal Bissett's credit card and was ringing up his ticket. She was apparently good at multitasking, because she asked Brook if she'd like a table or would rather place a to-go order. Brook quickly asked for the correct number of lunches, choosing the lunch special for all of them. Since the media's attention was across the street, Brook would use their distraction to slip out and walk down the street to some of the other shops.

Someone had to be minding the boutique today if Tina Reed was at home.

"...don't know her all that well, Vera. Are you sure that she's going to want a houseful of people?"

"I'm friends with Meg, and that's all that matters. There is a killer out there, Sam. The town needs to come together, and I want to be a part of that healing process."

Vera had rested a hand over her abdomen. Brook wasn't going to ask how Bit had come by the knowledge that the Bissetts were having a baby, but she sensed that neither one of them had told anyone the news. They were on the older side of starting a family, and Brook wasn't so sure that had been by design. It had been Sylvie who had somehow discovered that the couple had experienced fertility problems over the years.

"You're all set," the cashier said with a smile. "You can pay when you pick up your order at noon. Is there anything else that I can help you with?"

"I'll actually take a large coffee to go," Brook replied, noticing that Vera had set her hand on her husband's arm to pull him aside.

CHAPTER TWENTY-FIVE

Brook faced the counter so it appeared that she was giving the couple some privacy. Their voices had lowered as they each gave their points of view as to what they should be doing today.

"...said yourself that there is a killer targeting women from Stillwater. I don't feel comfortable not having you by my side."

"I promise that I'll be careful, and I won't go anywhere without Meg."

"Fine, but call me throughout the day."

"You won't forget about our appointment like last time?"

"I didn't forget last time," Principal Bissett corrected her before leaning down to kiss her cheek. "I got held up at work when the superintendent made a surprise visit to the high school."

"Here you go," the cashier said as she slid the large coffee across the counter. "I'll just add it to your lunch tab."

"I appreciate that." Brook had no reason to stay and listen in on the rest of the conversation. She'd heard enough to have Sylvie and Bit check out a few things of interest. Seeing as the couple was still standing near the door, Brook began to politely ask that they step aside so that she could exit the diner. "Excuse—"

Fire sirens suddenly pierced through the glass of the diner.

Considering that such sounds were prominent in the city, Brook didn't think much of them at first. Everyone else in the diner had either turned toward the windows to see which directions the trucks were heading or stood up from their tables for a better look.

Brook kept moving, managing to make it past the Bissetts and open the door.

Two gentlemen rushed past the opening.

"...drive other there. Should we call him?"

"Hey!" Principal Bissett must have recognized the men. He didn't even seem to care that he'd stepped in front of Brook, once again blocking her exit. "Whose house caught on fire?"

"You didn't hear?" One of the men turned around to walk backward. He was swinging his keys in his right hand. "The Gervase house just went up in smoke!"

CHAPTER TWENTY-SIX

Brooklyn Sloane
May 2022
Friday — 11:02am

GREY SMOKE BILLOWED FROM the right side of the house where the garage had all but collapsed in on itself. The volunteer fire department had managed to save most of the massive three-story home. One of the fire personnel had already called in the county's arson investigator, claiming that he'd caught the scent of accelerant.

Brook wasn't sure how anyone could smell anything other than the heavy stench of burning wood and burnt rubber. It wasn't the pleasant fragrance that signified residents using their fireplaces during the autumn season, either. This strong odor included burning tires and maybe even some other chemicals that were usually stored in a garage.

"Turner is getting us permission to walk through the house." Theo came to a stop beside Brook as she stared at the chaos in front of them. He was wearing one of his favorite white dress shirts, but he would likely have to throw it out after today. No amount of dry cleaning would ever be able to get the smell of smoke out of the fabric after they'd walked through the house. "He thinks it's been long enough."

The fire squad had put out the large blaze within an hour of the call being placed.

While residual smoke was still rising up out of the garage, doors and windows to the house had been opened so that there wouldn't be too much smoke damage to the rest of the interior. Stan had managed to get ahold of John Gervase, directing him to remain where he was and not to drive back to town. The structure would be secured by officers before they left the scene.

"It doesn't make sense," Theo murmured, crossing his arms as he made himself comfortable. While Stan might be doing his best to get permission for them to enter the premises, such a request could still take time. "This type of act doesn't fit the profile."

"No, it doesn't," Brook said in agreement. She casually turned to make it seem like she was engaging in conversation with Theo, when what she was really doing was viewing the bystanders across the street. The fire had drawn quite the gathering, including the pastor and his wife. Vera was standing next to a couple of women, while Patty and Ron Lincoln were huddled together with their daughter. As for the media, they were garnering every piece of footage they could in order to air it online for the twelve o'clock news. "I considered that someone in town might be blaming John Gervase for the murders, but then I looked around. Who do you see missing?"

Theo shifted his stance so that he was facing her sideways, giving him the ability to see the other side of the street. His gaze scanned the spectators, eventually coming to land on a group of teenagers. Brook recognized some of the girls that she'd run into at the high school, along with some of the first victim's former students.

Brook then refocused her attention back on Patty, who quickly looked away when she'd been caught staring at them. She brought her daughter a little closer against her right leg.

"Devin." Theo rubbed the side of his jaw. "Shit. That kid still thinks his uncle is guilty."

CHAPTER TWENTY-SIX

"You should go and talk to the parents." Brook glanced over to where Stan was vying for her attention. "While I think this was nothing more than a distraction, I still want to take a look inside the house. You've been here on a couple of occasions before Mr. Gervase left town with his children, but I want a chance to do a walkthrough."

"I'll join you in a few minutes," Theo said before he began to cross the street.

"Everything okay?" Stan asked when she fell into step with him on the way up the small path.

Clouds were moving in overhead, and more rain was supposed to arrive in the area by this evening. Right now, the temperature held a bit of humidity, but the heat that she was sensing wasn't from the sun.

"We believe that there is a chance that Devin Lincoln might have set the fire," Brook shared quietly as they finally entered the house through the front door. The smoke was heavier inside, regardless that the windows and doors had been open for a while. "We're not sure, of course. And I don't want to make reckless allegations, but there would be no need to try and burn this house down other than gratification. It's personal."

"I'll let the arson investigator know your theory and to also tread carefully." Stan let Brook take the lead. He'd already been in the residence many times, and he'd seen all there was to see. She wasn't looking for anything in particular, but that didn't mean something wouldn't show itself. "This family has been through enough."

Brook took note of the modern décor, unlike that of most other homes in the area. The stark difference in the lives of the sisters was evident based on their styles, but the victim hadn't been interested in money. She'd done everything she could to get her children out of this house, regardless that they would have been on the run for the rest of their lives.

Brook reminded herself that in cases involving a serial killer, the most valuable leads always came from the first victim. Stan remained silent as she took in family photos, trinkets, and even the son's drawings that had been displayed on a cute bulletin board alongside the pantry door. The front of the stainless-steel refrigerator was free of any clutter, just like the rest of the house.

A place for everything, and everything in its place.

Brook pulled out her phone to call Sylvie and Bit, wanting them to add more items in the search engines of their databases. Once they'd put her on speakerphone, she began to rattle off her requests.

"We've been attempting to connect the victims, and I still want the two of you to search for links, but widen it to men who had trouble back in high school. Include all the fathers of her students, clients of Mr. Gervase, and even the men in the congregation of her church. She spent a lot of her time at the church in between the choir practice and her helping out in the weekly group sessions." Brook paused in the entrance of John Gervase's home office. "Try to do so without alerting Principal Bissett, please."

"Pastor Wilson has yet to provide us with a full list of his congregation," Sylvie said after a moment. "He did give us a list of regulars, but he claimed that he would need time to divulge any of the other names."

"It's a tricky area, if you know what I mean," Stan murmured as he stepped around Brook to cross the large area rug of the private office. He didn't stop until he was on the other side of the desk. "As for Gervase's list of clients, I've already given that list to Bit. Doesn't mean that there aren't others who contacted Mr. Gervase, and who didn't utilize his services."

"Stan makes a good point. Who is the rival real estate agent in the area?"

"Linda Harrison," Sylvie replied automatically. "She doesn't reside in town, though. She does live in the county, but most of the properties that she sells are from the neighboring towns. I can reach out to her office, see if she would be willing to give us her list of clients."

"Do that," Brook agreed, slowly taking in the framed photos and various degrees and awards that had been hung up on the wall. "Oh, and Bit?"

"Yeah, Boss?"

CHAPTER TWENTY-SIX 221

"I know this might be a tough assignment with the HIPAA laws in place, but see if you can figure out if any of those men went to the hospital for burns when they were young. I know you're about to have a lot of names to sort through, but maybe you can find if there are any articles from back then involving burn victims or fires."

Brook disconnected the phone as she continued to peruse the contents of Mr. Gervase's office.

Something wasn't right, and she couldn't quite place her finger on it.

"I mentioned that the unsub might have been a burn victim in this morning's press release," Stan mentioned as he went through the desk drawers once more. "I'm hoping that it will cause someone to come forward with information."

"I'm not so sure that the unsub was saved from a house fire," Brook responded as she came to stand in front of the desk. They had gone back and forth on what fire meant to their unsub. "The unsub burns his victims. The unsub didn't come up with that on his own. I believe that was how he was punished as a child."

"Like being forced to place his hand over an open flame?" Stan proposed with a grimace of disgust. "I haven't interviewed one person who had burn marks on them that were noticeable."

"Me, either." Brook took one last look around before she decided to look through the rest of the house. "Just because we didn't see any burns, doesn't mean that they weren't there. Maybe the unsub had been abused on a regular basis. Cigarette burns are popular with abusers."

"I'm going to keep going through Gervase's desk. The search warrant is still good, and you never know if we missed something during the initial search."

"I'll go upstairs to look through the bedrooms, then."

Brook quietly made her way back through the house until she reached the bottom of the staircase. She was closer to the garage, and it was harder to breathe without the urge to cough. As she began to climb the stairs one by one, she continued to mull over the events of the past week.

Technically, the past two weeks, given that the unsub had reached out to her when she'd still been in D.C.

She needed to rely on her training and years of experience, because the answer could very well be in this house. She reiterated to herself once more the one avenue of approach that had never failed her.

It always comes back to the first victim.

Chapter Twenty-Seven

Sylvie Deering
May 2022
Friday — 8:58pm

THE POLICE STATION WAS relatively quiet given the day's events.

Every now and then clicking sounds could be heard from Bit's keyboard, Theo's chair squeaked every time that he shifted his weight, and a broken tile would pop if Brook walked over it while studying the murder board. Gail had gone home, two deputies were out on patrol, and the sheriff had gone to pay Pete Buckner another visit.

Not a lot had transpired after the fiery start to their morning.

It all came down to searching for a needle in a dozen haystacks.

"Little T, I just sent you the list of clients who purchased or sold property from Linda Harrison over the last thirty years. She's older, and she has been in the business for quite some time."

Sylvie both loved and hated Bit's nickname for her, but anything was better than Tinkerbell.

She'd always been made fun of for her petite stature. Having blonde hair and blue eyes hadn't helped people's perception of her, either. Bit had first given Theo the moniker of Big T, but that was due to the size of Theo's build and stature. It wasn't that Theo was bulky. Quite the opposite, actually. He kept himself lean, and he worked out on a consistent basis. His shoulders were broad. When he wore t-shirts, his muscular frame was quite noticeable. Upon learning that Sylvie loved to drink tea, Bit had decided that he would call her Little T.

"Thanks," she murmured, still engrossed with a vast spreadsheet on the display of her laptop.

She'd finally finished sorting through all the properties that surrounded the town. For how small of an area, there were hundreds and hundreds of cabins, sheds, outbuildings, equipment structures, and the like that could serve the unsub's purposes. If he'd used a friend's place or an abandoned shack that in no way tied back to him, she was simply wasting time.

Something had been nagging her, though.

She just needed to figure out what it was before calling it a night, or she would never be able to sleep.

Not that any of them were getting more than four or five hours, at best.

"I need some more tea," Sylvie replied as she stretched her arms high above her head. "Does anyone want anything while I'm up?"

Theo and Bit both turned down her offer.

"I think I'm going to drive back over to the Gervase residence," Brook said, finally turning away from the murder board. She'd literally been staring at it for an hour, not that anyone was surprised by her methods. "I shouldn't be too long."

"Want me to go with you?" Stan asked as he appeared in the doorway with a Styrofoam container in one hand and a fry in the other.

"Please tell me that isn't from our lunch at the diner today," Sylvie asked as she placed a hand over her stomach. Nausea had immediately kicked in at his smile. "That's disgusting."

"I didn't have time to eat it earlier." Stan shrugged, as if food poisoning wasn't a thing. "Brook? What is it that you need to see back at the Gervase house?"

"I don't know yet."

CHAPTER TWENTY-SEVEN

Stan looked at the rest of them, as if they had an idea of what went on in Brook's head. The way she went about solving a case was exceptional, as they'd learned earlier this year. She had an unprecedented way of piecing together bits and pieces of a case so that it fit and led her directly to the identity of their unsub.

"And go home, Stan," Brook directed as she shook her head after glancing in his direction. "Your suit is wrinkled, you have bags underneath your eyes, and you're eating food that has been sitting out for almost nine hours. We'll see you in the morning."

"No can do." Stan shoved another fry into his mouth. "We still haven't found Devin Lincoln. I have two patrol units canvassing the area and looking for his ass."

"We know that he set the fire," Theo reminded him, having been the one to track down Devin by phone. The two of them spoke at length after Devin had confessed to pouring gasoline in the garage and throwing a match inside. Unfortunately, nothing Theo could say to the young boy had gotten him to return home. He'd also been smart enough to turn his cell phone off so that they couldn't trace him. "I know that he'll do the right thing."

"We'll call if anything comes up," Sylvie promised Stan as she closed the distance to the door.

Stan had backed up a couple of paces so that she could exit the office and make her way to where a small counter served as the station's kitchen. There was a portable microwave, a coffee machine, and even a mini fridge tucked underneath. It wasn't anything fancy, but it served the needs of those who worked here.

It didn't take her long to heat up some water in the microwave. She preferred their kitchen back at the offices of S&E Investigations, though. They had a stovetop that allowed her to use a kettle and steep tea leaves. Having only a microwave, she'd had no choice but to purchase teabags when she'd stopped into the teashop the other day.

"I don't feel right about heading home without that kid being located," Stan said as he shifted to the side once more so that he wasn't in her way. The food in his container was a little ripe, and she had to turn her head as she passed by him. "Granted, he shouldn't have tried to burn down his uncle's house, but I get why the boy is acting out."

"I don't think you'll have to worry about Devin Lincoln tonight," Theo said as he abruptly stood from his chair. He walked around the table that served as Bit's desk to stand near the window that faced the main thoroughfare of town. Since Sylvie hadn't made it to her preferred corner, she followed behind him until they were both staring out into the dark. The sun had set maybe fifteen minutes prior. "I'll take him back home."

Sylvie could hear Stan's footsteps behind her.

"I'll be damned," Stan muttered as he finally witnessed what Theo and Sylvie had spotted across the way. A slight shadow could be seen from the streetlamp above, but it was clear that Devin was near the alleyway next to the diner due to a streak of lightning illuminating the dark sky above. Stan practically threw the fry in his hand into the Styrofoam container in disgust. "Theo, you know that I need to—"

"Tomorrow morning," Theo replied quietly, having grown fond of the teenager. "Please. Devin has been through enough already. He knows that he's in trouble, and now he's going to have face his parents. Let me take him home, and you can do what you need to do first thing in the morning."

Stan seemed undecided, and Sylvie noticed that Brook had remained quiet on the subject. She wouldn't interfere unless absolutely necessary, and she might decide not to in this instance. Devin's involvement had been a distraction that they hadn't needed in a chaotic day. Had Bit not confirmed that the superintendent had prevented Principal Bissett from attending a doctor's appointment with his wife, their day could have gone a lot differently in the grand scheme of things.

"Well, shit." Stan retraced his steps and tossed the rest of his food into a garbage can. He then pointed a finger at Theo to stress his directives. "Straight home. I'll radio for the patrol car to keep an eye on the Lincoln house. The last thing I need right now is that kid to go on the run after it came to light that I could have brought him into the station earlier. He committed arson."

CHAPTER TWENTY-SEVEN

"I doubt John Gervase will press charges," Theo said as he brushed past Sylvie so that he could exit the office. "Still, I appreciate the leeway. I'll make sure that he gets home and that the patrol car is stationed outside before I leave for the night. I'd like to be there when you take him into the station in the morning."

Stan finally nodded his agreement before running both hands down his face.

"Go. I'll stay inside for another five minutes so that I don't spook him."

Sylvie shared a knowing look with Brook, who was busy gathering her purse and the keys for one of the SUVs from a chair that she'd dropped them into earlier. Sylvie reached into her tote bag for the small, compacted umbrella that she'd stuffed inside before they left the inn this morning.

"Here," Sylvie replied, handing Brook the one thing that would save her from getting drenched. "You're going to need it. Let's hope that Theo can get Devin into the other SUV before the skies open up."

"I won't be long," Brook said, sliding the strap of her purse over her shoulder. "Call me if anything comes up."

Sylvie noticed how Stan turned to monitor Brook's departure.

It wasn't surprising that the man was attracted to her. She had long black hair, blue eyes that were like looking into crystals, and a heart-shaped face. Never once had she talked about her personal life, but the team had all decided over drinks one Thursday evening that she basically didn't have one.

Brook worked, therefore she existed.

Bottom line was that she was a workaholic, and she would never consider getting involved with someone while her brother remained at large. Granted, he'd only killed women up to this point, but it was evident from his past behavior that Brook brought out the worst in him.

It was one of the reasons that the team always dedicated a few hours every Sunday when Brook wasn't in the office. Bit had been the one to discover that she never came into work on Sunday afternoons.

Ever.

For all they knew, that was her time to unwind at her condo. Sylvie didn't think so, though.

She couldn't come up with a valid theory, but it worked for the team to sort through all the information on Jacob Walsh that she'd put together over the years. Brook deserved to live her life, and they would do whatever they could to help in that area.

Now that Theo and Brook had left the station, some of the previous sounds had dissipated, leaving only the faint clicking of Bit's keyboard as he worked. Stan had gone out into the bullpen, but she figured he'd be heading home soon enough. Right now, she had a hot cup of tea in her hand, and she could finally settle in and find out what had been bothering her about the list of names associated with the properties located to the north of town.

Forty-five minutes or so later, Sylvie had long past finished her tea and was on her third pass of the list that Bit had managed to put together involving all the names of those on the titles listed with the local courthouse. Some went back for generations, and that was where she'd finally discovered the needle hiding in their haystack.

"Bit." Sylvie scrambled to her feet, grabbing her laptop off the desk and almost tripping over the charging cord as she made her way over to him. "Call Brook. I found him!"

CHAPTER TWENTY-EIGHT

Brooklyn Sloane
May 2022
Friday — 9:27pm

BROOK SLOWLY PULLED THE vehicle to a stop in front of the Gervase residence. Even with the windows rolled up, the acrid scent of smoke was overwhelming. As she shifted the gear into park, she surveyed her surroundings. Situational awareness had been stressed upon continually during her training with the Bureau.

The properties out this way were on larger lots, so the next house was at least two hundred and fifty feet away, if not more. Across the street was another home, but the longer driveway was relatively the same distance back from the street. The sidewalks were empty this time of night, and the bystanders had long since departed the area.

Once she turned off the engine, the irregular taps of the large raindrops somehow became even louder as they made impact with the roof of the SUV. She couldn't even hear her own breathing. Technically, her return to the Gervase residence could have waited until morning. This visit was more to put her mind at ease than anything else.

They'd clearly missed something in the evidence, and her instinct was screaming that it was something she'd come across while inside the home earlier today. The fire might have been a mere distraction, but she was certain the answers were somewhere amidst the ashes.

Had she been wrong about her initial impression of John Gervase?

Had she constructed the profile incorrectly, thus missing out on what was right in front of them? There was no denying that she'd been distracted lately. She had fully believed that she could handle all the changes, take on all the responsibility, and still be able to hunt her brother.

She'd spent the last six months believing that he was still in D.C. Still watching her from afar and planning on when to strike out at her for attempting to live her life. Granted, her new way of living was far from perfect, but even the slightest attempt toward normalcy should have drawn him in.

"Shit," Brook murmured underneath her breath. She didn't bother to reach for the umbrella that was on the floor of the passenger seat. Such an attempt to cover herself would be useless with the way the rain was coming down at a slant and blowing around everywhere. All she would accomplish with that task was the destruction of the umbrella. She did grab her cell phone from her purse, though. Shifting behind the steering wheel, she managed to slide the phone into the back pocket of her jeans. "This better be worth it."

Without any more hesitation, Brook palmed the keys, grabbed the handle, and shoved the door open with her shoulder. As quickly as possible, she ran from the SUV that she'd parked in the driveway to the front door. When Stan had reached out to John Gervase about the fire, he'd asked that they lock up the house after the fire station had secured the garage as best as possible. The neighbor across the street had a key, which Stan had borrowed and given to Brook before she'd left the station.

By the time that she'd opened the door and stepped inside, she was soaked through to the skin. She reached behind her and pulled out the hair tie that she'd used earlier to gather her hair back. It didn't take her long to resecure the wet strands,

CHAPTER TWENTY-EIGHT

though she'd miss a few as they some were still plastered to her right cheek.

Brook flipped the switch to the left of the front door.

Light flooded the large foyer.

Thankfully, electricity had been restored to the main house.

She stood still for a moment, adjusting to the bright illumination. Once she had her bearings, she began to slowly and methodically walk the main level of the house. While this wasn't the crime scene, she still catalogued every nuance as if it would help her establish a connection.

Every vase, candle, and knickknack had its place in the residence. From the entryway and into the formal dining room, one wouldn't be able to guess that children had resided in the house. Not one picture was crooked, and every artificial flower had been strategically placed inside their decorative containers.

Lisa Gervase had wanted to please her husband, and she'd clearly spent a lot of time ensuring that their home represented their lifestyle.

Upon entering the living room, there were signs of an actual family.

Photographs were displayed everywhere, from the fireplace mantel to the walls. Smiling faces of children on sunny days in the inground pool that was in their backyard smiled back at the onlooker. Some of the pictures had John Gervase's family in them, while others included Lisa Gervase's side of the family.

Brook positioned herself in the middle of the living room so that she could turn in a full circle. The large foyer couldn't be seen from the center of the living room. Neither could the formal dining room.

The victim had practically led a double life, and no one had been the wiser.

Such a detail didn't shock Brook in the least. She knew all too well what it was like to have parents be the role models of such a feat.

Brook stayed in place a while longer, studying the photographs on the mantel. One of them reminded her of a specific one hanging on John Gervase's office wall. It was then that she noticed it, but she needed to confirm her suspicions. Not wasting time, she made her way out of the living room and down a hall off the kitchen to where the private office had a large view of the backyard and its accompanying inground pool.

Her gaze quickly sought out the photo in question.

Smiling faces stared back at her after having enjoyed a day in the pool. John Gervase, Aiden Gervase, and Devin Lincoln all wore swimming trunks. Lisa Gervase, Patty Lincoln, and their two daughters had on bathing suits and bright smiles from a fun-filled sunny day.

Ron Lincoln, on the other hand, was the only one with a long-sleeved swim shirt.

Right in front of her was the answer that they had all been searching for—the identity of the unsub.

The material of his swim shirt had still been wet when the picture had been taken. While it was difficult to distinguish, one could still faintly make out the multiple nickel-sized scars on the skin of his chest.

He'd been repeatedly burned at some point in his life.

He was of the right age.

He was married.

He had children.

And Lisa Gervase had ultimately trusted him to keep her secret of needing money to leave town with another man.

Brook figured that the victim had told her brother-in-law a great deal more than he'd let on, which had been the trigger that had set him off on his killing spree. And now he'd gotten a taste of what it was like to be the administrator of such depraved torture.

He wasn't about to stop now.

The fire had begun to make more sense to Brook now that she'd figured everything out. Had Devin been attempting to burn down the house to protect his father? Or was all his pent-up anger simply just that? Theo had been walking across the street as Brook had backed out of the parking lot. Would he be able to get the truth from the young man?

Pulling her phone out of her back pocket, she quickly dialed Stan. She'd all but told him to go on home, but he shouldn't

CHAPTER TWENTY-EIGHT 233

be leaving town. They had a lot of work cut out for them. It would be up to Bit and Sylvie to connect the dots in order for Stan to make an official arrest. They had to have more than just a photograph that simply proved Ron Lincoln been the subject of abuse.

"Stan? It's Brook. I'm still at—"

The house went dark.

Brook's vision went completely black.

Reacting instantly, she spun around so that her back was to the wall. The rain against the house was deafening until Stan's voice could be faintly heard coming from her phone.

"Listen to me carefully," Brook cautioned as softly as she could while drawing her firearm from its holster. She removed the safety before continuing. "Ron Lincoln is the unsub. The power just went out at the Gervase's residence. Radio for backup."

She disconnected the line before Stan could respond.

Brook trusted that he would follow protocol.

In the meantime, she needed to figure out how to take advantage of the situation. Ron Lincoln no doubt felt that he had the upper hand, but she never walked into a house let alone a room without having mentally canvassed every aspect of the space. She had memorized the floorplan earlier today when she'd canvassed the home, more out of mental exercise than a belief that a threat was present.

The dark would not be a hindrance to her the way Lincoln would assume it would be, and that could work toward her advantage. There were three entrances on the lower level. The front door, the door that led from the garage into the kitchen, and then the patio door.

As Brook slid her phone into the pocket of her blazer, she recalled the diagonal manner in which the silver deadbolt had been positioned on the patio door. That entrance had been locked, but there was a good chance that she wouldn't be able to hear the lock disengage if Lincoln used a key to gain entry. The rain was too heavy against the windows to make out much of anything like footsteps in the hall.

Again, such a factor could be to her benefit.

Brook's vision finally adjusted enough that she could just make out the outline of furniture. Without knowing what entrance that Lincoln would come through, she needed a better position. She needed to be on the offensive side of this equation.

It hit her then that was why there had been missing framed photographs from the Lincoln's residence. Brook had assumed that Patty had removed the ones with her sister in order to give those pictures to the media, but it had been Ron who hadn't wanted the police to figure out that he'd been burned not unlike the victims.

Brook could only assume that Ron Lincoln had come to the Gervase residence to remove any pictures remaining due to Stan's press conference this morning. He'd mentioned her profile, along with the fact that the unsub might have been burned by a parental figure during his childhood.

Devin must have realized it first, and his first instinct had been to protect his father. In all likelihood, the teenager had been in denial. He wouldn't have wanted the police to believe that his father was guilty, so he'd attempted to burn the Gervase residence down to the ground.

Had the young man come to his senses?

Was that the reason he'd sought out Theo tonight?

All the details and evidence could be sorted through later.

Right now, she needed to gain the upper hand.

Various images of each room flashed through her mind. She recalled the position of each chair, table, rug, and numerous pieces of furniture. There were certain delicate vases that wobbled with too much movement, and the second to the bottom step of the staircase creaked under one's weight. The formal living room offered her no concealment, but there was space between the large grandfather clock and the wall in the foyer that gave her a clear shot no matter which entrance Lincoln decided to enter the house.

Brook quietly and efficiently counted her steps until she was in the doorway of the office. Pausing only long enough to make certain that she couldn't hear the rustle of fabric or labored breathing, she managed to sidestep the antique table with the

CHAPTER TWENTY-EIGHT

vase positioned in the middle. It didn't take her long to reach the spot that would give her adequate leverage. The grandfather clock was tall, effectively blending her in with the shadows.

All she had to do now was wait...

Chapter Twenty-Nine

Theo Neville
May 2022
Friday — 9:39pm

"Ron Lincoln is our unsub."

Theo didn't waste time as he pointed toward a chair in the corner of the office.

"Devin, you sit in that chair, and you don't move." Theo wiped his good eye, wanting to clear the water from his lashes. The sky had opened up before he could escort Devin back to the station. "Bit, go ahead and call Brook so that she can—"

"We can't get a hold of her," Sylvie said as she held her cell phone to her ear. "I have Stan on the line. He claims that she was on the phone with him when the power cut out over at the Gervase residence. What was that, Stan? Yeah, we'll contact the sheriff and meet you there."

Bit didn't hesitate to reach for the phone.

Sylvie disconnected the line before meeting Theo's gaze.

"You have the keys. You're driving."

"Please, don't hurt him," Devin said as he stood from the chair that he'd just claimed. His hair was soaking wet with drops of rain clinging to the ends of his red strands. "He's sick. He needs help. I thought—"

"Did your dad go back to the house?" Theo asked, wanting clarification on the dangers that they could be walking in on. "Devin?"

"He said he needed to get some things," Devin replied as he set his hands on his head in disbelief that the situation had gotten to this point. "He promised me that he would get help. He said—"

"We've got to go," Sylvie muttered in disgust, brushing past Theo as she headed for the door. "Bit, don't let him leave this station."

Theo followed close behind as Bit began to explain everything that had happened in the last half hour to the sheriff. The rain hadn't let up, and by the time that Theo and Sylvie had reached the SUV, their clothes were soaked through to the skin.

Since the keys were in his pocket, all Theo had to do was press the ignition button.

The engine purred to life.

"I figured out it was Ron Lincoln after I went through the list of property owners a third time," Sylvie explained as she finally secured her seatbelt. "An uncle of his by marriage owns some property west of town. Surnames were different, but I recalled spotting the name from Lincoln's background check. I should have caught the connection sooner."

"Devin said that he heard his father and mother arguing early this morning," Theo explained as he turned out of the parking lot. Thankfully, the weather had chased away the media a couple of hours ago. He stepped on the gas pedal knowing that time was of the essence. "They had both heard Stan mention that the unsub might have burns on his body associated with childhood abuse, and Patty Lincoln started to become suspicious of her husband. Devin said his father got her to believe that he was innocent by reminding her of a story his mother had shared with her about a fire breaking out in their house when he'd been a child. She bought it again—hook, line, and sinker."

CHAPTER TWENTY-NINE

"We never want to believe that someone we love is capable of doing horrific things," Sylvie murmured, holding onto the side handle as Theo took a turn a little too fast.

"Devin went searching and found not only the framed pictures that his father had taken from the house, but also greasy ashes in the back of the minivan. He confronted his father, who then promised to seek help if the boy kept his secret. Devin agreed to burn down his aunt and uncle's house, but it didn't go quite as planned." Theo made another hard turn, not surprised to see lights and sirens up ahead. Stan must have already been en route to the Gervase residence. "Once he had time to think about it, he had a change of heart."

"You mean he got scared," Sylvie amended as she got ready to unfasten her seatbelt. Theo caught sight of her hand moving toward the metal clip. "I feel for the kid. I really do. He's going to be fucked up for the rest of his life."

Neither one of them spoke about the correlation between Devin Lincoln and Brook. No one ever seemed to consider that each killer who was apprehended by the police left behind family members who spent the rest of their lives wondering what had happened, how they'd missed the signs, and if there had been anything they could have done to ultimately stop the tragedies.

"You take the right side of the house, and I'll take the left," Theo directed as he slammed on the brakes to bring the SUV to a stop right behind Stan's unmarked cruiser. Sylvie had already opened her door. Thunder and lightning weren't going to make their jobs any easier tonight. "Be prepared for anything."

Theo hadn't even bothered with his seatbelt. It didn't take him long to run parallel to Sylvie. His clothes had already been soaked, so the rain made no difference to him.

Stan was already at the front door, his firearm drawn as he placed his left hand on the doorknob. Theo spotted the man's flashlight, which aided him in being able to make out movements.

Theo did his best to push aside the flashes of memory from when he'd been ambushed by another unsub late last year. It had all but been impossible to put what had happened behind him since he'd been left with a constant reminder. Losing his right eye affected every single aspect of his life. He wouldn't let it define him, and he'd worked hard to ensure that it wouldn't influence his actions in the field.

The next few moments would reflect his success in dealing with his own limitations.

Chapter Thirty

Brooklyn Sloane
May 2022
Friday — 9:40pm

THE FIRST TELLTALE SOUND finally came from the kitchen, which was what Brook had counted on by taking a position in the foyer. While it was still quite dark, the difference in shade levels from the double patio doors made it possible for her to make out any shifts in movement. She evened out her breathing so that her inhalations and exhalations weren't audible.

Stan and the others should be here momentarily.

Once their sirens could be heard, she didn't doubt that Ron Lincoln would make a run for it. The most likely avenue of retreat would be through the double patio doors, around the pool, and into what she considered a conservation area with thick vegetation. It was heavily wooded in any regard.

Lincoln's only option was to leave everything behind, but he wouldn't find that task much of a hardship. While he'd done his best to be able to hide in plain sight, that would no longer be an option.

Not wanting to miss her opportunity, she shifted her gaze slightly to the left to obtain better night vision. Sure enough, a dark figure finally made itself known as he ever so slowly made his way toward the office. He no doubt believed that was her location, but he would soon discover that she'd moved somewhere else in the house.

Patience was key, because the large foyer allowed her to only see so far around the corner of the wall.

It was her hope that he would believe she'd made her way to the front door, only to seek cover in the formal living room. She couldn't very well discharge her firearm without being completely confident that he had a weapon of some sort, but that shouldn't be hard to detect once he was directly between her and the patio doors on the far side of the kitchen.

Brook tensed when she finally heard the sirens cut through the heavy rain against the side of the house.

Shit.

As much as she was relieved that the calvary had arrived, Lincoln would now need to make a decision. She counted on him to run. In anticipation, she leaned down slightly so that she could use the sole of her shoe to push off the wall should a chase ensue.

She then thought better of it when another idea came to her.

There was no way for any of the officers or her team to make it around the back of the house to cut him off without her somehow delaying him. The moment that she heard the soles of his shoes turn on the hardwood floor, she called out to him while remaining in the shadows.

"Does this make me the winner?"

Brook ever so slowly held out her arms and raised her weapon when he came to a stop right in front of the patio doors. He'd come here hoping to remove any shred of evidence about his burns, but he'd found her here instead. He wouldn't have had a weapon on him, but it appeared that he'd improvised. A glint of light bounced off the blade of a knife, courtesy of headlights being shined across the front of the house. The brief flash outside was just enough to provide her with a clear enough outline.

Lincoln spun around in response to her question as she'd hoped, buying her the time that she needed.

CHAPTER THIRTY

He attempted to search her out in the darkness.

"You haven't won yet!" Lincoln shouted in rage, his words echoing throughout the home.

"Haven't I?" Brook kept her weapon trained on him as she finally stepped forward.

There was at least fifty to sixty feet between them. The large foyer, the open kitchen, and beyond to where the patio door was located between them gave her the leeway to take a few steps in his direction.

Granted, he most likely had difficulty making her out in the darkness, but the location of her voice would have been enough for him to know her exact position.

"You're here," Brook pointed out. "I have a gun trained at your chest, I'll be able to shoot you before you take a step toward me, and the police are pulling up in front of the residence as we speak. You wanted this, Ron. You wanted to be stopped, which is why you reached out to me in the first place."

It was evident that Lincoln was torn with his decision on whether or not to run. All she needed to do was buy enough time for one of the officers to make it around the back of the house.

"It's over, Ron."

"No!"

"Yes. Your wife, your children, the town...they will all know before sunrise that you killed your sister-in-law and Nancy Buckner. They will know you are nothing but a sick, twisted—"

"Shut up! Shut up! They both deserved what they got, and I had a responsibility to punish them for their sins." Lincoln was breathing hard now, but it was as if his words had calmed the range of emotions within. "I'm not done, either. This isn't —"

The front door slammed opened, causing Brook to step toward the side so that whoever was entering the residence would be able to identify her by the shape of her figure.

Lincoln spun around and flipped the deadbolt, but she was already advancing before he turned the handle. By the time that he'd taken two steps outside in the pouring down rain, she'd broken out into a run that would only be faltered by the need to go around the massive kitchen table and chairs.

Brook had done her best to keep him in her sights, but his silhouette had blended in with the darkness as she was finally able to reach the patio door. Not even the beam of Stan's flashlight had been able to keep up with man's pace. Not knowing his location gave her pause from running straight out into the rain where he could ambush her.

"On your right," Stan murmured to give his position, holding his firearm steady as they both stepped out into the rain. He used the flashlight to scan the pool area. "There. Go!"

He'd been advising her that he was close to her right side so that she didn't react when he fell into step beside her. Lincoln was already by the pool and about to go around to take off toward the back line of the property. If he reached the woods, it would be an all-out manhunt. They hadn't gotten far when Theo's voice rang out loud and clear, telling Lincoln to stop.

As lightning illuminated the backyard, she could clearly see Lincoln making a run for it. Theo rammed right into him without stopping, sending both him and Lincoln into the deep end of the pool. Sylvie had come around the right side of the house as more sirens could be heard approaching the front of the residence.

"Go around," Brook called out, just in case Lincoln was able to get the upper hand and swim to the other side of the pool. "Stan, can you—"

Brook had been going to direct him to a better position so that she could cover the front, but he was handing her his flashlight.

"Take this." Stan then holstered his weapon as he advanced toward the side of the pool where Theo was coming up for air. He all but dragged Lincoln to the surface, leveraging the man's arm so that he couldn't take both of them under the water again. Theo had basically wrapped his right arm around Lincoln's throat, still maintaining a hold of his weapon. Theo had also been able to lock the man's left arm behind his back. "Theo! Bring him here!"

It took Theo a few moments to garner complete control, but he was finally able to push Lincoln forward. Stan had leaned over the edge and grabbed Lincoln by the shirt until he was able to get a better grip on the man's upper arm.

CHAPTER THIRTY

"Turn him," Stan directed, his grip enabling Theo to release his chokehold on Lincoln.

Stan mimicked the action, though.

He also pulled up hard enough that the restriction caused Lincoln to reach up and attempt to loosen the hold. Theo recognized what Stan was doing and helped lift Lincoln's lower body out of the water.

Brook kept the beam steady on Lincoln so that there were no surprises to be had during the arrest. "Knife?"

"At the bottom of the pool," Theo said, not even sounding out of breath. He managed to use the ledge to haul himself out of the water, pausing only long enough to holster his weapon. He adjusted his eyepatch before getting to his feet to witness said arrest. "I'm not going to lie. That felt damn good."

"I guess that I don't have to ask if you're okay then," Sylvie said as she came to stand next to Theo. She took time to holster her weapon. "That was one hell of a flying tackle."

Stan was in the process of reading Ron Lincoln's his rights.

Since Brook held the flashlight steady, it was all but impossible not to notice that Lincoln was staring right at her. He hadn't said a word since they'd fished him out of the pool, and she doubted that he would open his mouth for anyone but his lawyer at this point.

He was smart, she would give him that.

"Nice work," Brook stated as she switched her focus to her teammates. One, it would rub Lincoln the wrong way at her cavalier dismissal. Two, she truly wanted to express her gratitude. "I take it that Devin told you that he was trying to cover for his father? It didn't take me long to figure it out after seeing pictures of the family. Lincoln always wore a swim shirt to cover up his burns."

"Sylvie actually had it figured out by the time I got back to the station," Theo advised with a proud smile. "Get this. One of Lincoln's uncles has a different surname. He's the registered owner of an old cabin on the north side of town."

"I only wish that I'd figured it out sooner," Sylvie replied with regret, crossing her arms in order to preserve some of her body heat. With the rain still coming down and the wind picking up, not even the recent string of warm temperatures was enough to stave off the chill. "If you ask me, tonight was a little too close for comfort."

Brook had kept an eye on Lincoln the entire time that she'd been talking quietly with her team. He was still making direct eye contact with her. There was an internal rage inside of him that would almost certainly eat away at him every single day that he remained behind bars. There had only been two killers over the course of her career that she bothered to keep tabs on, and Ron Lincoln would be added to the list.

In her profile, she'd included a passage that stated had Lincoln started killing earlier in his life, there could have been a chance that he would have gone down in history as one of the most prolific killers to date. Due to circumstances that they may never understand or even come to know, he'd waited to give into his sick and twisted fantasies.

Maybe it had been due to Lincoln's marriage to Patty or even the birth of his firstborn child.

Whatever the reason that had delayed his response to those hidden urges, he hadn't been able to control his emotions the way that Jacob had learned to do at an early age.

Still, the Ron Lincoln's of the world shouldn't be dismissed due to the ease in which they'd caught him.

Two weeks was nothing in the grand scheme of things, especially when other serial killers were never identified or apprehended. Unfortunately, extreme emotions such as those that Lincoln was experiencing right now in this moment made him unpredictable.

They would boil inside of him, and they wouldn't have an outlet.

He would be a risk to anyone who he had unfettered access to in the future, including prison guards and even his own lawyer.

Seeing as the justice system had its flaws, just like everything else in the world, it would be in their best interests to monitor the progress of his case. Technicalities happened, mistakes were made, and the fallout of such things could have a devastating effect.

CHAPTER THIRTY

"We have our work cut out for us over the next couple of days," Brook said quietly as she observed Stan lead Lincoln through the rain toward the front of the house. Other deputies and officers had arrived on scene, and their flashlights provided enough light for them to guide the way. "Our job now is to make sure this conviction sticks. Let's do that to the best of our abilities."

Chapter Thirty-One

Brooklyn Sloane
May 2022
Tuesday — 7:02am

THE LOWER LEVEL OF the inn had a mixture of savory fragrances that hovered in the air. The team had stayed to enjoy breakfast before their flight back home, and Stan had joined them for a farewell meal. They'd spent the time discussing some loose ends that would need to be wrapped up over the course of the next couple of weeks, but there wasn't anything that couldn't be handled remotely from their main offices in D.C.

The cabin where Lincoln had taken, tortured, and ultimately killed his victims had been located and processed by a state forensics team. They had discovered the culinary blow torch and the thermite, along with half-melted wedding rings of the victims that Lincoln had kept in a tin can. Every piece of evidence had been catalogued, including the minivan that he'd used to transport the bodies to the drop sites. Additional statements had been collected, press briefings had been held, and charges had been officially filed by the state prosecutor's office.

As expected, Ron Lincoln and his lawyers would attempt to submit an insanity plea.

Theo had spent most of the prior evening with Patty Lincoln and her children, who had all decided as a family that they would not be attending the trial. It would be months before such proceedings occurred, anyway. There was no rulebook when it came to handling such a situation. Not even time would heal what had been broken in that family. The harsh reality was that they had no choice but to live with the broken pieces, because they would never be whole.

"There is one thing that I can't figure out," Stan said in a contemplative tone as they walked down the porch steps. The SUVs had already been packed full of their equipment and luggage. "Pastor Wilson and his wife. There's something off about them."

Brook came to a stop once they reached the sidewalk.

She held her sunglasses in her left hand as she readjusted the strap of her purse on her right shoulder. She'd thought long and hard about the Wilsons, because Stan had been right to trust his gut.

It had just taken Brook a couple of weeks to make the connection.

"You'll want to tell Detective Klein to check out Julie Wilson. She's one of the people involved in his drug syndicate out this way."

Stan had been staring at the church while he'd taken a pack of cigarettes out of the interior pocket of his suit jacket. He'd just lifted a cigarette to his mouth when her words had registered with him.

"Shit," he murmured, finally placing the filter in between his lips. He didn't say another word until he'd tucked the pack of cigarettes back into his pocket. "You are fucking kidding me."

"For what it's worth, I don't think Pastor Wilson knows a thing about his wife's extracurricular activities," Brook surmised as she heard Theo and Bit come out of the B&B behind them. They were in deep discussion about the ending of a movie that had recently released, and whether the main character had lived or died in the last scene. "Detective Klein might even be able to

CHAPTER THIRTY-ONE 251

get the pastor to help bring down the drug ring if he approaches the situation correctly."

"You can't leave here without telling me what tipped you off," Stan said before he pulled out his lighter and lit the end of his cigarette. She resisted the urge to cough as he inhaled and then exhaled a cloud of smoke. "Seriously. What makes you think she's connected to Klein's case?"

"Besides the nervous tension that she displayed when I was questioning her?" Brook turned so that she was facing Stan. Sylvie hadn't been far behind Theo and Bit, but she'd been in deep discussion with Jake Hudson. The young man had a chance to get his life together, but he needed to stop making decisions that would ultimately destroy any chance of a future. "Julie was a little too eager to share that she'd overheard Lisa Gervase ask Oscar Riviera to help her acquire fake IDs. If she'd wanted to help apprehend the unsub, she would have come clean with Sheriff Kennard the second that Lisa Gervase had been reported missing. She kept that information to herself for a reason."

"Fuck me," Stan muttered as he took another drag on his cigarette. He stared across the street with contempt. "I missed it."

Brook shrugged off his self-deprecation. It wasn't useful, and Julie Wilson's reluctance to share vital information could have been justified by her desire to protect her husband's parishioners. Brook all but told him that before following up on other indicators of the woman's alleged illegal acts.

"Julie has been stopping by the high school more often than not, claiming that she's really good friends with the guidance counselor. While that may be true, I think she's been using said friendship to gain access to her street dealers. I overheard one of the deputies talking about busting a couple of seniors a few weeks back for possession of drugs. Don't get me wrong. It could all be unrelated, but..."

"I'll have Nathan look into her." Stan used his left hand to remove the cigarette from in between his lips. He then held out his right hand. "Brook, it's been an honor. Seriously. You are hands down one of the best investigators that I've worked with over the years."

"You're just blowing smoke up my ass because you want an inside link to Bit," Brook said as she purposefully brushed aside his praise. "I lucked out when I hand-selected this team, Stan. Every single one of them contributes something to every case that is more beneficial than most people realize."

By this time, Theo and Bit were standing nearby to give their regards to the detective. Sylvie had finished saying her goodbyes to those inside, and she was now walking down the steps of the porch.

While most of the media had packed up and left town over the weekend, Sarah Evanston had stayed to get one more exclusive with John Gervase. He'd recently returned to town, and he'd been soaking up the attention like a sponge that had been left out in the sun for months on end.

Sarah's cameraman was currently standing next to his van while on the phone explaining to someone that he was still waiting for the reporter to bring her luggage down so that they could finally leave town.

While Stan shook hands with the men, Brook took the last few steps to the passenger side of the SUV.

Sylvie already had the keys in her hand, so she could drive them to the airport while Brook got caught up with her emails. She'd made sure that her electronic tablet was in her purse, since she'd already stored her leather bag in the back with the rest of the luggage.

The moment that Brook had opened the passenger door, dread washed over her at the sight of what had been place on the front seat. As if it were a brick of C4 instead of a leatherbound copy of Harry Potter and the Chamber of Secrets, she ever so slowly set her purse on the floor of the passenger seat. The present left for her was the second book in the series that she'd loved as a child, and one that had helped her escape reality from time to time. Jacob always left her a collector's copy when he passed through the city to check on her, which he'd done last November with the first book from the popular series.

Her brother was in Stillwater, and he'd been here recently.

CHAPTER THIRTY-ONE

They'd left the vehicles alone for maybe eight minutes between the four of them while they had transferred their luggage from their rooms, and not in consecutive minutes, either. Jacob's window of opportunity had been extremely slim, but the time of day that they had chosen to leave town had allowed him to have the advantage of slipping into town sight unseen.

Brook's hearing had faded, but it was gradually coming back to where she was able to recognize the conversation behind her.

"...stay in touch. I mean it," Stan said to the group.

"You do the same," Theo replied good-naturedly. "If you're ever in the city, you should..."

Brook tuned out their conversation.

She cautiously stepped back and swept her gaze around the area. It was so early in the morning that no one was really in view. There was an older couple entering the diner a block down, a deputy's car pulling into the station, and one of the shop owners entering their storefront.

Moving around the SUV with leaden steps, she surveyed the church's parking lot.

Everything in her line of vision had become more vivid, and the sounds of the area had become amplified as her senses heightened with awareness.

"Brook?"

Sylvie had been the one to notice Brook's odd behavior, but she was too busy connecting the dots to address the situation. Sarah Evanston's driver was still complaining to whoever was on the other end of the line. The reporter who applied her makeup flawlessly, styled her hair to perfection, and basically taunted Jacob Matthew Walsh on a live broadcast.

"Jacob is here."

Brook wasn't sure if she'd spoken loud enough for the others to hear, but she somehow managed to turn around while drawing her weapon in one motion. She took off at breakneck speed up the porch stairs and burst through the front door. Audrey and Jake had still been sitting at the dining room table, both startled at the loud sound of wood smacking wood.

She could hear commotion behind her as the others scrambled to keep up.

Time was of the essence.

She was the first to reach Sarah's door.

Calling out the woman's name, Brook hoped like hell that she was wrong in her belief that the woman was already dead. By the time that Brook had quickly tried the doorknob and found it locked, Sarah hadn't responded, and Theo was already motioning Brook aside. With one forceful kick, the jam broke, and the door swung open.

Brook's hearing once again began to fade as she set eyes on Sarah Evanston.

The woman's face had been essentially butchered, courtesy of Jacob Walsh.

His signature was unmistakable, but there was one thing missing—his final stab wound to the abdomen.

Sarah Evanston was still alive.

"Call an ambulance!" Brook called out, rushing over to the woman while managing to grab a throw blanket that had been positioned over an ottoman.

Pressing the material against Sarah's cheeks, Brook scrambled to assess the situation.

Blood was everywhere.

The window was open.

There were even handprints of blood on a thick tree branch near the window from where Brook was positioned on the floor.

"The window, Theo!"

"Go around," Theo called out to the others. "Block off the sides, back, and front!"

Though they were on the second floor, there was a huge maple tree next to the house. Branches large enough to hold the weight of an adult male. Brook had taken the time to study every inch of the B&B the day that they had arrived, as she had gotten accustomed to doing with every place that she stayed overnight.

Habit.

Just like her brother, who would never have entered the premises without have an escape plan. He would have timed

CHAPTER THIRTY-ONE

this attack down to the second, but he couldn't have counted on the cameraman walking up to Sarah's room to bring her a blueberry muffin and a coffee during breakfast.

The reporter had slept in, and she'd needed the extra time to shower, dress, and pack.

The blueberry muffin and coffee had been placed on the bedside table. The fact that they hadn't been disturbed told Brook that Jacob had waited and bided his time to ensure that his plans wouldn't be interrupted again, leading Brook to believe that he'd already been in the room when she'd accepted her breakfast. The closet door was half open, and images of how Jacob had gotten the upper hand flashed through Brook's mind.

Someone should have heard Sarah struggling, screaming in pain as Jacob mutilated her face.

Why hadn't she...

Brook used part of the blanket to wipe away the blood that had splattered all over the woman's neck.

He'd choked her to keep her quiet.

From the bruising that was already forming, she would have been too busy struggling for air as the blade sliced through her skin.

It was amazing that he hadn't crushed her windpipe.

"Sarah, stay with me. I mean it. Don't let him win," Brook warned as she pressed the material harder against the woman's facial wounds. The cream fabric was already rouge in color from having soaked up copious amounts of blood. "Please, don't let my brother win. Fight, Sarah. Fight!"

Chapter Thirty-Two

Brooklyn Sloane
May 2022
Saturday — 2:03am

THE SUDDEN KNOCK THAT hit the front door of Brook's condo had her instinctively reaching for her weapon.

She rarely had guests, and never in the middle of the night.

It wasn't that she thought her brother would randomly knock on her door one night, but the manner in which he had tried to insinuate himself in her last case had her wondering just how far he was willing to push the envelope.

Brook cautiously made her way across the hardwood floor, keeping her firearm at her side as she eventually looked through the peephole.

For a brief moment, she debated not answering.

She wasn't in the mood to deal with Graham tonight, but he'd know that she'd purposefully ignored him if she didn't open the door. He was aware of her insomnia and her nocturnal habits.

She flipped the deadbolt.

"This couldn't wait until morning?" she asked wryly once she had him in her sights.

Graham was still wearing a suit, his tie straight as an arrow, and not a piece of lint could be seen under the artificial light. He'd come straight from some meeting, not that she would ask about his work with the government. Interestingly enough, he had a bottle of scotch in his right hand.

"It could have, but I was in the neighborhood."

Brook glanced down at the bottle of alcohol.

"An apology?"

"No."

Brook held back a small smile.

They were too much alike.

She'd known that when she'd met him, and she'd accepted it when they'd gone into business together. Figuring they might as well bury the hatchet, she turned on her bare feet and left him standing in the doorway.

He'd eventually make his way inside.

She placed her firearm back into its holster on the table before continuing into the kitchen. It didn't take her long to locate two fresh glasses. She preferred her scotch over ice, so she pressed her glass against the lever positioned in the fridge. Since her condo had an open layout, she could see Graham studying the dining room wall. Considering that it was similar to the murder board at the office, there wasn't much he hadn't seen on that front.

Still, he couldn't have been all that surprised to know that this was how she spent the majority of her time.

"Impressive decor," Graham murmured as he set the bottle of scotch down on the dining room table. "Morbid, but impressive."

"What can I say? I'm a one trick pony."

He removed his suit jacket and hung it neatly on the back of the chair that she'd been sitting in when he'd knocked on her door. He continued to survey the wall in front of him as he broke the seal on the bottle of scotch.

"You didn't have to check up on me," Brook replied softly as she walked over to the couch and set the glasses on the coffee table. She'd been listening to some light jazz and didn't see any reason to turn it off. "A phone call would have sufficed."

CHAPTER THIRTY-TWO

"You mean the same phone calls that you've been sending directly to voicemail?"

This time, Brook did crack a small smile.

She sank into one of the cushions of the couch and pulled her feet up underneath her. It was true that she'd been sending his calls to voicemail. She hadn't been ready to talk. If she was being honest, she still wasn't ready to forgive the way he'd gone about getting her out of town.

"I'm fine."

"That's just standard bullshit." Graham had uncorked the bottle before walking toward the coffee table. He then poured both of them some scotch, giving her the one with ice before he took a seat on the other end of the couch. He held up his glass in salute, waiting for her to do the same before he savored a healthy taste of Glenlivet XXV Single Malt. "That's like me shilling out an apology."

"The next time that you want me out of town, just say so."

"And here that's exactly what I thought I did that day in your office," Graham surmised with a smirk. He shifted on the cushion so that he was facing her with his elbow on the back of the couch. "I'll do my best to be more direct."

"I take it since Kate is back in the city and I haven't received a call from another state governor who needs assistance on an active case that everything is back to normal?"

Brook wasn't really in the mood for alcohol tonight, but she held onto her glass.

The chill from the ice was a needed distraction from overthinking his visit.

"Since the threat is over, I don't see the harm in sharing with you that we temporarily misplaced one of the U.S. Navy's Block 5B Tomahawk Land Attack Missiles. Specifically, a BGM-109A(V)2 that our contractor has been developing. Just in case you were wondering, that is the variant that carries the infamous *Dial-A-Nuke* W80 intermediate yield two-stage thermonuclear warhead. The situation was contained, and now it's back to business as usual." Graham hadn't bothered to mince words, and she was appreciative of being told the facts. She must have let the silence drag on a little too long, because he wanted his quid quo pro. "This is where you give a bit of insight on what happened with the investigation in West Virginia."

"You already know what happened. We apprehended our unsub, a reporter was irreparably harmed by my brother for basically calling him out on national television, and we might have to close our doors once business dries up as a result."

Brook rethought her stance on the alcohol.

She took a healthy gulp, relishing the warm sensation in the back of her throat. "It's not like clients are going to purposefully put themselves in harm's way for being associated with the firm. Me, to be more precise."

Graham took a moment to mull over her words, but it wasn't like she hadn't covered all the facts. There was no denying the fallout. S&E Investigations was going to suffer due to what had transpired in West Virginia, and there wasn't a damn thing that she could do about it.

"I spoke with Agent Houser today," Brook shared, figuring Graham might as well know what had transpired after she'd called the federal agent in charge of Jacob's case. "Sarah Evanston will go into witness protection. She's facing numerous surgeries, a lot of counseling, and a brand-new life that she'll be forced to accept. I should have listened to the voicemail that she received at the station. If I had, I would have known then that Jacob was going to make a move. I made a mistake, and it cost the woman everything that she held dear. And don't give me platitudes that I can't be everywhere and do everything at once. It doesn't take away that all of this could have been avoided if I'd taken thirty seconds to listen to what had been retrieved from Sarah's voicemail."

"Fine. I won't. Why don't we focus on the fact that no previous victim has ever survived your brother," Graham murmured contemplatively as he studied her. He was staring at her as if she had all the answers. "What will be the fallout?"

Brook wasn't sure the outcome of the situation, and that was what had her concerned the most.

Jacob wasn't one to make mistakes, but he'd miscalculated the situation. Brook had spent every single minute since she'd set eyes on his gift to her, and she'd theorized what had gone wrong.

CHAPTER THIRTY-TWO

It had everything to do with Sarah Evanston's cameraman making the sudden decision to take her a blueberry muffin and a cup of coffee. Such a diversion had taken up time that Jacob hadn't counted on, and Sarah had fought him, adding precious seconds to his timeline.

"I don't know," Brook replied quietly as she drained what was left of her scotch.

"Yes, you do."

Graham rested his hand over hers, his warmth attempting to invade the cold that was always inside of her. She had rested her left arm on the couch while she'd been staring at the dining room wall. She'd tacked Sarah's photograph right in the middle, because everything would now be centered around her.

"You know him inside and out, Brook. What will be his next move?"

Brook took a deep breath, hoping to settle her conflicting emotions. She wasn't obtuse. Graham had been hinting for a while now that he wasn't pleased with her continuing to keep her barriers in place, but he needed to open his eyes to the carnage that took place when she couldn't contain a situation.

Sarah Evanston was proof that Jacob would always be a part of Brook's life until she somehow figured out a way to eliminate him. In order to do that, she was going to have to somehow convince Agent Russell Houser that Sarah Evanston would eventually make the perfect bait.

"You want to know what Jacob's next move will be?"

Brook was so tempted to give herself permission to hold onto Graham's hand a little longer, but the reality of what she was facing had her pulling away. She stood up from the couch and made her way over to the dining room table. As she poured herself some more of the expensive scotch that he'd brought with him, she stared at the picture of the woman who could potentially be Jacob's downfall.

"Jacob won't be able to stand the thought of a woman like Sarah Evanston breathing the same air as him after he'd made the calculated decision to end her life."

Brook picked up her glass and stared at the woman's photograph. The reporter would never again be able to stare in the mirror and view the flawless features that she'd been given at birth. All she would be able to see was Jacob Walsh's face smiling down at her as he ruined her perfect life.

"My brother is going to hunt her down, Graham. And he won't stop until she's dead."

Chapter Thirty-Three

Jacob Walsh
May 2022
Tuesday — 6:29am

The overcast sky was indicative of the immediate future.

All of Jacob's plans for his baby sister had to be put on hold while he took some time to right a wrong.

He pulled his hat lower on his forehead as he stood across the street from Brook's favorite cafe. She'd kept the same daily schedule for the past six months in hopes that he would reveal himself. He savored her desire to put an end to their cat and mouse game, but he simply enjoyed it too much to allow her to reach the finish line.

He wasn't fooled into the believing that the back and forth between them was a game.

What they had was more than that, and something that only two close siblings could understand.

While he waited for her to exit the cafe with her large caramel macchiato in hand, he went over the events of last week.

Jacob hadn't experienced such rage since his teens. He'd spent years learning to control such emotions, and he'd become somewhat of an expert at it. Truthfully, all he felt now was disdain for those who believed their lives were quintessential.

The way society viewed their existences was sickening, and Sarah Evanston had been the perfect example.

Jacob had made it his job to monitor the news for anything unusual that might involve his sister and the team that she'd assembled, always looking for ways to twist the proverbial knife into her side. He'd spotted the situation in West Virginia the moment it had garnered national attention, and he'd paid attention to the news coverage the entire time that Lisa Gervase had been missing from her home.

There had been something about it that had garnered his interest enough to go on a road trip. It could have simply been a waste of his time, but it had been a chance that he'd been willing to make. His instincts and his patience had paid off, too.

Once he'd gotten himself hired as a truck driver for the service used by the ice cream factory, getting information about the case had been easy. He'd even had a bit of fun doing something out of his usual routine.

Staying in one place too long dulled his senses.

Maybe that was why he hadn't calculated each and every oversight that could have occurred when he'd decided to indulge in his favorite pastime. The fact that he could also bait his sister had been a bonus, only circumstances hadn't been kind to him.

He'd never failed in anything that he set his mind to...ever.

And he wasn't about to start now.

A rush of adrenaline that never failed to flow through his veins at the sight of his baby sister began its gratifying journey. She was wearing a light grey suit today that seemed to have been tailored to her body. Two-inch heels, a white blouse, and her long black hair flowing free down her back. She peered up at the sky as if she could ward off the rain until she made it to her office two blocks down. She'd grown into such an amazing woman with so many internal flaws...she truly was beautiful.

Brook stopped mid-stride to survey her surroundings, and her gaze swept right over him as he'd already known her habits. A man who was slightly taller than Jacob always took the same

CHAPTER THIRTY-THREE

walk to work at the same time. Jacob used him as a shield, which was easy considering how structured these city folks were with their daily routines. Right after the sign lit up next to the traffic light, the small group of people began to cross the road. By that point, Brook had already turned and continued down the sidewalk toward her office building.

Jacob loved the time that he was able to spend with her.

Unfortunately, he had some unfinished business to attend to.

"I'll be back soon, dear sister."

~ The End ~

A deadly sin turns into a violent obsession in the next pulse-pounding thriller by USA Today Bestselling Author Kennedy Layne...

Click HERE

In an abandoned warehouse on the outskirts of a rural town in Northern Illinois, three brutalized bodies were discovered in different stages of decomposition. The crime scene produced no evidence, police had no leads, and the killer vanished back into the murky shadows.

Until eight years later...

When evil that has been dormant within the community begins to stir, former FBI consultant Brooklyn Sloane is brought onto the case. What she and her team discover is far darker and more twisted than they have ever dealt with before, igniting an urgent manhunt to catch a cold-blooded killer.

But this killer is smart, cruel, and has been one step ahead of them the entire time. When Brook begins to unearth the truth, a shocking revelation changes the course of the investigation. She finds herself racing against the clock when the killer is determined to possess another soul, and this time the victim might be a little closer to home.

OTHER BOOKS BY KENNEDY LAYNE

Touch of Evil Series

Thirst for Sin
Longing for Sin

The Widow Taker Trilogy

The Forgotten Widow
The Isolated Widow
The Reclusive Widow

Hex on Me Mysteries

If the Curse Fits
Cursing up the Wrong Tree
The Squeaky Ghost Gets the Curse
The Curse that Bites
Curse Me Under the Mistletoe
Gone Cursing

Paramour Bay Mysteries

Magical Blend
Bewitching Blend
Enchanting Blend
Haunting Blend
Charming Blend
Spellbinding Blend
Cryptic Blend
Broomstick Blend
Spirited Blend
Yuletide Blend
Baffling Blend
Phantom Blend
Batty Blend
Pumpkin Blend

Frosty Blend
Stony Blend
Cocoa Blend
Shamrock Blend
Campfire Blend
Stormy Blend
Sparkling Blend
Hallow Blend
Dandelion Blend

Office Roulette Series

Means
Motive
Opportunity

Keys to Love Series

Unlocking Fear
Unlocking Secrets
Unlocking Lies
Unlocking Shadows
Unlocking Darkness

Surviving Ashes Series

Essential Beginnings
Hidden Flames
Buried Flames
Endless Flames
Rising Flames

CSA Case Files Series

Captured Innocence
Sinful Resurrection
Renewed Faith
Campaign of Desire
Internal Temptation
Radiant Surrender
Redeem My Heart
A Mission of Love

Red Starr Series

Starr's Awakening
Hearths of Fire

Targets Entangled
Igniting Passion
Untold Devotion
Fulfilling Promises
Fated Identity
Red's Salvation

The Safeguard Series

Brutal Obsession
Faithful Addiction
Distant Illusions
Casual Impressions
Honest Intentions
Deadly Premonitions

About the Author

Kennedy Layne is a USA Today bestselling author. She draws inspiration for her romantic thrillers in part from her not-so-secret second life as a wife of a retired Marine Master Sergeant. He doubles as her critique partner, beta reader, and military consultant. Kennedy also has a deep love for cozy mysteries, thrillers, and basically any book that can keep her guessing until the very end. They live in the Midwest with their menagerie of pets. The loyal dogs and mischievous cats appreciate her writing days as much as she does, usually curled up in front of the fireplace.

ABOUT THE AUTHOR

Email:

kennedylayneauthor@gmail.com

Facebook:

facebook.com/kennedy.layne.94

Twitter:

twitter.com/KennedyL_Author

Website:

www.kennedylayne.com

Newsletter:

www.kennedylayne.com/meet-kennedy.html

Printed in the USA
CPSIA information can be obtained
at www.ICGtesting.com
LVHW022320011024
792691LV00038B/956